SPAWN
OF
WAR
AND
DEATHINESS

Also from B Cubed Press

Spawn
Of
War and Deathiness

Edited by
Tom Easton

Cover Design
Bob Brown

Published by

B Cubed Press
Kiona, WA

Copyright

J. J. Steinfeld, "Godot's Eternal Taxi Service," first appeared in a slightly different version, in *Gregor Samsa Was Never in The Beatles: Speculative Fictions New & Selected* (Ekstasis Editions, Victoria, BC, 2019).

James Dorr, "The Sidewalk," first appeared in *Terminal Fright* (Fall 1996).

Bruce Taylor, "Mr. Wetzel and His Wurlitzer," first appeared in the collection *Alleymanderous and Other Magical Realities* (ReAnimus Press, 2017).

Anthony Panegyres, "Reading Coffee," first appeared in *Overland Literary Journal* (Spring 2011).

Tom Easton, "Wallflower," first appeared in *Tomorrow* (November 1996).

Melvin Charles, "Dream Chair," first appeared in *Haunts #21* (Spring 1991).

D. Thomas Minton, "The Schrōdinger War," first appeared in *Lightspeed Magazine* (2013).

Sarah Seddon as Sahara Frost, "The Last Death," first appeared in the anthology *Diabolical Plots: Year Four,* David Steffen, ed. (2018).

Alma Alexander, "The One about the Last Prayer," first appeared in *Val Hall: The Odd Years* (Book View Café Press, March 2020)

Editor's Foreword

Tom Easton

When B Cubed Press opened three anthologies—*Alternative Deathiness, Alternative War*, and *The Protest Diaries*—to submissions, writers sent in a flood of wonderful stories, far more than enough to fill three anthologies. Therefore the publisher decided to use mostly unpublished stories. Then, of course, there remained the problem of what to do with all the wonderful reprint stories. He could just reject them, but... In a stroke of genius—or madness (you pick)—he decided to do *another* anthology, just for the best of the reprints. *The Spawn of War and Deathiness* is the result.

If the titles make you wonder, well, B Cubed Press is openly political in its orientation. When the White House started talking about "alternative facts," it was immediately inevitable that someone would play with that. B Cubed Press's first title was *Alternative Truths*. Then came *Alternative Apocalypses* and *Alternative Theologies*, and more.

Deathiness? Well, first came "truthiness," meaning "not really truth but it sounds good." So "deathiness" means "not really death but it sounds good"? That works, in a world where various sorts of zombies and walking dead abound, at least in fiction.

Spawn? Well, Death and War are two of the classic Four Horsemen of the Apocalypse, who are men only because men made up the myth. There is no real reason why one or more cannot be women (as you will see in the stories to follow). And that makes spawning quite conceivable. Indeed, if you consider history, the Four have been quite prolific.

I have done a few anthologies before. As an editor, I like to organize the contents of a book in line with themes (a fantasy book might have sections on witches, dragons, heroes...). With this book, there was a problem. The parent books identified two major themes, which often overlapped. I needed something else. Eventually, I came up with three Part titles—Transformation, Resolution, and Conclusion—

that yielded clusters of roughly equal size. You are permitted to think that a story or two should be in a different cluster, but the book Is What It Is.

Enjoy!

And come back soon. B Cubed Press will have more for you.

Tom Easton
Dedham, MA
November 2021

Table of Contents

PART I: TRANSFORMATION

Change is the essence of life—and death. It can mean a new choice—or a new pair of boots.

Spawn of War and Deathiness

The Final Choice

Irene Radford

Death sat at the bar wondering what he had forgotten to do. 11:02 P.M. December 31. There was something he had to do before midnight, or the new year would not arrive. Time would stop. Life would be frozen in an endless cold sleep. Souls would have no home.

Change would not continue to shape the universe.

Fates would not be fulfilled.

Death took a sip of his drink and concentrated on his duty.

The potential suicide in the corner vacillated in her decision. Her well-cut red suit looked too bright and cheerful for her mood. She twisted a diamond wedding set around and around her heart finger. Death shouldn't leave until she made up her mind.

Suicides always disrupted the schedule of appointments. He didn't like *last minute* changes.

But there was something else...

He checked his appointment book. The potential suicide wasn't listed anywhere in the last few pages. In two minutes, a man with a heart condition would run out of time. Death grabbed his staff of office and left the bar. If the woman in the corner made her decision in the next two minutes, she'd still need two more to find a means and a place.

The little black appointment book with magnificent gold calligraphy on the cover burned in the pocket of his flannel shirt beneath a down vest. His staff of office, half again as tall as he, shrank to the length of a walking stick. The ebony end that curved back on itself to form a window for a huge black crystal, dissolved into a knob with the winking crystal set into the end. No flowing black cape and skeletal hands for the heart attack victim. This candidate for death needed the reassurance of a familiar personage to make the transition quietly.

Death sidled through crowded Times Square. He appeared to be just another reveler on New Year's Eve.

His candidate jumped up and down, waving to friends and strangers alike. He paused in his excited dance only long enough to chug-a-lug the whiskey in his hip flask.

Death tapped his shoulder.

"Hi! I'm George. Who are you?" The candidate greeted Death.

"Hello, George. You have an appointment."

An over-weight, middle-aged body collapsed on the sidewalk. George turned to look at his former shell. "I guess I have to leave now. Before the New Year."

"Yes, you do."

"Pity. I've never actually been here on New Year's Eve when the ball dropped." He looked wistfully at the great ball of light atop a near-by building. "I guess now I never will. Can't I stay a little longer, just until the ball drops?"

"Sorry, George. 11:07. You are precisely on time. You can't linger, even to see the New Year."

George looked back at his former self, one last time. A Good Samaritan had already begun CPR on the limp body.

"He might revive me."

An ambulance siren wailed in the distance.

"He can't revive you. I have touched you. Your Fate is determined. If you choose to wait, or refuse my escort now, you will wander aimlessly as a lost soul for all time. Your choice."

"Some choice." George looked back on his body with longing in his eyes and posture. Then he nodded in quiet acquiescence. Death took George's elbow and led him out of the crowd.

Two minutes later, Death blinked his eyes and transported back to the bar. Little Miss Indecision was still dithering, still twisting her rings, occasionally tugging at them. They wouldn't come off easily. She'd worn them long enough that her finger and knuckle had grown thicker. Death pulled out the appointment book once more. A little book now with only a few names left. The page with George's name dissolved under his gaze.

"Who's next?" he asked the book.

At year's beginning the book had been a huge tome that had gradually dissipated to this thin reminder. Not many names left. Not much time before one year faded into the next. Choices and change had to continue. Unless...

Death ordered a drink. He took a sip, remembering when alcohol tasted good; made him feel good.

Strange, he wasn't supposed to remember life, only his duties as Death.

Time. 11:26. There was something he had to do. The appointment book heated up again. A child dying of cancer. A child ready for the release of pain. Too bad his parents weren't ready to let him go. They had made all of the child's decisions for him. This last choice had to be his alone.

Death walked into Pediatric Intensive Care at Mercy Hospital dressed as a teenage candy-striper, the staff of office now only a small syringe on a tray with a black crystal plunger. The family of the candidate hovered around the bed. Tears and aching hearts filled the room with an aura of misery.

The candidate smiled at Death. "Hi, I'm Mike. About time you showed up."

"Hi, yourself, Mike," Death replied in his feminine voice.

Mike's body convulsed and gasped for breath.

"No. You can't die. I won't let you," Mike's mother threw herself onto the little boy's body, oblivious of tubes and machines. The woman looked up directly into the eyes of Death. "Take me instead. He's so little. He hasn't had a chance to live yet. Take me!"

Time stopped until a choice was made. Fate required a death.

"Can you do that? Change the appointment?" Mike asked, eyes wide and wondering. Momentarily he was free of the constraints of his body. Only his soul knew what transpired.

"Fate dictates that my appointment is in this room, at this time," Death announced to all those present. "The name of the candidate is not known until the actual moment of death. Anyone here may accept the fated death."

"Take me," the mother said resolutely. "Spare my little boy."

"No, Mom." Mike looked around at his loving family, frozen in time until the choice was made. "Think of Dad and the family. Julie and Tom need a mom. Dad needs his wife. They'll learn to get by without me. Life will be a lot harder on them without you than me. Let me go. I'm tired of hurting. I'm tired of watching you hurt because of me."

Emotions flooded Death. He remembered pain and how love lessened it. Getting involved with his candidates was not a part of the job. But Mike was so strong, so adult, he reminded Death of...

Death refused to remember *life*. Change and a choice of fates belonged to others now, not him.

Mike climbed off the bed, leaving his body behind. "Time to go. Good-bye, Mom. Bye, Dad, Julie, Tom."

Time resumed. The family clung to each other in sorrow.

Death and Mike walked slowly toward a swirling circle of light, leaving life behind.

A car accident diverted Death's attention on his transport back to the bar. Smashed metal, flying glass, the smell of hot gasoline ready to ignite. Agony! Desperate pleas. Death put aside the memory. Those terrible things must have happened to someone else.

He checked the most recent victims. Serious injuries, but no one needed his guidance to the other side yet. He made a note in his appointment book to check back with the five passengers and three drivers once they reached the hospital.

The little black book didn't accept the note. The accident victims would not face a final choice within the remaining minutes of this year. What would happen to the book at one second past midnight? Death did not know.

Or could not remember.

Which?

Death looked at the last page of his book curiously. He saw an appointment listed for 11:59:59. The assignation hadn't been there earlier in the evening. No place, cause, or name followed the time. Strange. What did he have to do in the last second of the Old Year to make certain the New Year came? The thought of all the souls of humanity drifting homeless for eternity made him shudder. Time must continue. People must experience change and make choices. Fates must be fulfilled.

He returned to the bar, drawn there as if by a magnet. His staff glowed brighter as he approached. The appointment book suddenly felt heavy. He checked, but no new appointments had been added past the cryptic one in the last second of the old year.

The bartender took Death's order for another drink. Automatically Death assessed the man's condition: arthritis, right shoulder and knee, weak and clogged arteries, and swollen feet. Six months tops.

A newcomer opened the door of the bar. The noise of the New Year celebration in Times Square filled the shabby drinking establishment with a moment of lively joy. The potential suicide wavered a moment in her decision. The door closed and the noise died. As the old year was dying.

Death hefted his little black book once more. "I need time to look in on the Pope. I have to keep tabs on all the assassination attempts and a few great musicians and artists. There isn't enough time. Something I have to do..."

Death sipped at the drink that was supposed to taste good or make him feel good but did neither. He watched himself in the mirror behind the bar. He looked like any other generic, middle-aged male, not too prosperous, nor too downtrodden, his staff of office hiding as a black umbrella propped against his stool. The persona fit this neighborhood. He was used to the instant changes in his appearance. He didn't like terrorizing people—except some of the truly evil personalities. When Mother Theresa finally passed on, Death had chosen to be another elderly nun so as not to frighten the woman. But that determined lady hadn't been frightened by life. Why should Death in any guise scare her?

11:43:05. A sense of desperate need tickled his senses. The potential suicide in the corner passed her crisis and decided to give Life one more year.

Death followed her onto the street. He had too much to do in the last seventeen minutes of the year.

His long staff appeared in his hand, keeping its proper shape and size—Nine feet of shining ebony, slender top curved into a full circle. Thousands of facets from the crystal reflected tiny pin-pricks of light. His black-hooded cloak folded around him. He became one with the shadows, seeking the source of that last appointment. Only when the candidate, location and circumstances were chosen would his guise take shape.

His hands tingled with the power encased in his trappings. His staff glowed in the reflection of streetlamps. Aware, not fully active. Yet.

Out on the street, Death turned the staff right and left, seeking. A faint glow emanated from the crystal when it faced right. A very dark alley. Streetlights shot out, garbage piled high. A haven for vagrants, criminals, and violence.

The appointment book burned with impatience.

"Just another mugging," Death sighed. "I'd hoped for something spectacular to close out the year."

The crystal glowed brighter, taking on red tones. "Odd. Red indicates a death of great importance, someone who will stop time if his, or her, destiny goes unfulfilled." That had happened with Princess Diana as she clung to life for agonizing moments, but others had stepped in to continue her work. One instance when the victim became more powerful dead than alive.

While the world mourned her passing, people continued to make choices and grow through change.

Death followed the crystal with increasing urgency. For the sake of all lost souls, time had to continue.

The woman who had chosen life over death walked ahead of him, head high, shoulders back. She had chosen life and her posture reflected reawakened joy and confidence. Her high heels tapped a rhythm onto the sidewalk akin to the song of life.

Grunts. Cries for help. Scuffling feet and thumping bodies.

Death hurried.

He rounded the corner into the alley. Three Lives standing. One desperate Life sprawled amid piles of junk and empty boxes, right leg twisted unnaturally beneath her. The skirt of her red power suit hiked up immodestly and torn at the side seam. Blood spilled on the pavement.

11:58:47. In the distance the shouts from Times Square increased. Close up, one of the standing Lives lifted a gun and took aim at the Life who waited. A feral smile grew around broken and rotted teeth. All four Lives were fully conscious. All four knew that Death awaited one of them.

"Should have given us the diamond ring along with the purse right off, yuppie bitch. We'd have let you off with a sore head," the youth with the gun sneered at his victim.

The diamond on the woman's left hand winked in the weak light, almost as brightly as Death's black crystal. A cherished wedding ring. A promise of love. The muggers had broken her leg while she struggled to protect the ring.

There was still time for Death to offer choices.

All four Lives froze in a tableau that screeched of man's violation of his covenant with Life. The black crystal in the staff passed from red to blinding white. The appointment book grew heavier and hotter yet.

11:59:45. Time stopped.

Death looked anxiously from the crystal to the Life who awaited his touch. Time awaited the next candidate. Who? The book didn't tell him.

"Don't kill me!" the woman who had left the bar filled with renewed purpose yelled at the three muggers. "You've got my purse and my jewelry. I can't run away. My leg is broken. Leave me alone."

No one moved. Nothing moved, not even the freezing wind.

Death waited. A curious sensation of warmth engulfed him. He'd been cold so long he'd forgotten what warmth was. Not exactly warmth, an absence of heart-chilling cold. But with the warmth came pain too. Sharp pains filled his leg in empathic sharing with the woman. Curiosity and dread warred with fear for mastery within him. His heart raced and then seemed to stop. This was the last appointment in his book and he would be an active participant instead of an escort after all the choices were made.

Fate had caught up with him at last.

"Help me, please. I don't want to die," the woman called to Death. Her hand reached out in entreaty.

Death heard himself issuing the same plea a year ago. He remembered fear and its copper taste on his tongue.

He shook off the memory and the residual tremors. He had a duty to perform.

"I have an appointment with someone in this alley. One of you must go with me." Death's voice echoed around the alley, like a bronze bell. The three muggers remained frozen in time. Not so much as an eyelash twitched among them.

"Take one of them." The woman pointed to the tableau of criminals frozen in the act of theft and murder. Her hand wavered and almost pointed directly at Death.

Death tried to retreat within the folds of his hood. "They are outside this decision, Ma'am. Only you and I are here." Her name eluded him. Why? This had never happened to him before... before he became Death.

A year ago, he had wanted so desperately to live that he had chosen to become Death rather than accept his fate. And now he was faced with another Life in the same dilemma. One of them must die.

He planted his staff in front of him. The glowing black wood gave him authority and confidence. Someone in the alley had to die. Time would not resume unless Death escorted a candidate to the other side. He still had a choice.

"I'm not volunteering to die," the woman screamed. "I'm not ready to die! I just decided to live. Please let me live!"

"I can't give you that choice," Death lied.

"Do something." The woman grabbed the staff and shook it in desperation.

Death jerked back on the length of wood in panic. "The staff is my badge of office. Only I may touch it." His hood fell back. This time he knew his appearance was the classic personification of Death, a skeletally thin face, pasty white. Deep-set eyes that looked into eternity.

The woman held tight to the staff, shaking it again.

"You. Must. Let. Go." Death grabbed the black staff with both hands, trying to wrest his tool away from her. "You. May. Not. Touch. It."

"If you won't help me, then let me have it to save myself." She clung to the staff as if it were Life itself; a Life she desperately wanted. Now. A few moments ago she'd almost thrown it away. "I can use this as a weapon to save myself!"

Power raced up and down the wood binding her to the staff and to Death. He almost let go. Desperation kept him glued to the wood.

If he let her live, what would happen to him? Someone had to die or time would not resume.

Who would it be?

What choices were left?

The only way to cheat fate and Death is to become Death, *another voice had told him a year ago.*

Death stumbled. The woman twisted the staff and tripped him with it. Death dropped to his knees. His cloak fell away revealing a red woolen suit, the same cut as woman's. Same blouse. Same scarf around the neck. His skeleton took on flesh but remained pasty white.

"Who are you?" The woman rolled to her left, away from the collapsing body of Death. She stood up in one fluid motion with the staff in hand, as if her leg hadn't been broken a moment ago. Her shoulders hunched and she aged a thousand years in a moment.

"There is something I have to do before midnight." Death's voice remained deep and solemn, echoing and reverberating around the alley. Which one would die? His right leg twisted unnaturally beneath him.

The muggers came back to life.

A mighty roar rose from Times Square. "*10.*"

Three shots rang out in rapid succession.

"9."

The muggers turned and bolted from the alley.

"What do you have to do? There isn't much time." Shock made the standing woman's words weak and squeaky. She bent low to catch Death's words, feeling for a pulse, trying to stop the flow of blood from his chest. She didn't have enough hands, or medical knowledge to save him/her.

"*8.*"

Death grabbed her lapel and pulled her closer yet. His claw-like hands seemed incredibly strong for someone who'd just been shot in the belly, the heart, and the lung.

"7."

"Tell me what you have to do. I can help," she cried.

"There is a way for you to survive this encounter."

"6."

"I have survived, you're the one who is dying."

"One of us must die at the stroke of midnight. You have taken the choice away from me. The only way to cheat death is to become Death." He repeated the words spoken to him a year ago. A lifetime ago.

Everyone was fated to die. The choice of when fell to only a few.

"5."

"Become Death? You mean I'll die too. Who are you?"

"4."

"I am your destiny, your fate. Life or Death. You must choose. As I chose a year ago. I loved life too much to give it up. I still do. But I no longer have the right to make that choice." Choice and change belonged to the living. Everyone had to die. Fate determined when and where. No choice.

Except for the last death of the year.

"3."

"If it means living, I'll become Death, I'll become Santa Claus or whoever it takes. Just so I can live. I decided not to kill myself over my husband's infidelity and a mangled career because I realized that life is too beautiful to waste."

"I thought the same thing last year at this time." A fiery car crash, pain beyond enduring, and still he had clung to life rather than let Death take him. "And now I know that all Life is beautiful. If one of us does not die then time will cease, taking all Life with it. Life must be preserved."

"2."

"Then why must I become Death? I'd rather be alive."

"Death, like change, is a part of life. If Death does not walk the streets, then all Life will cease. The choice is yours."

"What is that supposed to mean."

"You'll find out."

"1! Yeah! Whoopee. Yahoo!"

The body of a young man, who had refused to die in a car crash the year before, took on the last vestiges of the woman wearing a red suit. He/she collapsed in the alley. The last page of the old appointment book dissolved.

A skeletally thin, old hag, dressed in tattered red and black draperies, with eyes that burned clear through to eternity stood up and retrieved Death's cloak, without dropping the staff. All memory of her life, her decision to live, her wrestling match with Death, faded. She was Death now, with duties to perform.

From the folds of black cloth fell an enormous book bound in black leather. The gold calligraphy on the front was fresh and new, spelling out one word.

"Appointments."

"Let's see. Victims of an automobile accident. Mercy Hospital," the old hag cackled. "Five passengers. Three drivers. Four of the eight need an escort in two minutes. A musician is shooting a bad batch of drugs in central park in six minutes. The pope can wait a little longer."

She morphed into a young nurse wearing bright turquoise scrub pants and a white tunic with tumbling pink and aqua teddy bears. The staff of office coiled around her neck like a stethoscope, the black crystal blocked the metal bell at one end.

Death popped into the emergency room of Mercy Hospital, ready to escort those who needed her.

A diamond on her left hand winked in the bright hospital lights as she escorted the first death of the new year into the swirl of light.

Spawn of War and Deathiness

A Fresh Start

Rob Butler

"What about a rabbit?"

"A rabbit?"

"Yes. Great fun. Nibbling lettuces. Sitting in the warm sun in green pastures. Lots of sex."

"Is this a male rabbit or a female rabbit?"

"Whichever you like."

Ernest Smith scratched his chin thoughtfully and once again adjusted his position on the rather uncomfortable chair in which he had been told to sit.

"Well, a male rabbit is probably preferable. Certainly as regards the sex. A female rabbit would just be having babies all the time."

"Splendid. Male rabbit it is then."

Ernest jumped. "No, no I wasn't agreeing to it. I was just musing."

The figure on the other side of the desk held its pen poised in obvious disappointment.

"Ah. What a pity. I thought we had it there." It tapped the pen a few times and shuffled its papers. Ernest wondered idly if he should enquire why they still used pen and paper.

"Elephant?"

"Too large."

"Mouse?"

"Too small."

"Perhaps something quite different? Spider?"

Ernest pulled a face. "No, I hate spiders."

"That's not really a logical reaction, Mr. Smith. You are unlikely to continue to hate spiders if you *are* a spider."

Ernest sighed. "I suppose not. Don't really fancy it, though. My wife loathed spiders too. If I ended up back in our house, she might tread on me. Diana does that with spiders. Then I'd be straight back here again, wouldn't I?"

It was not really possible to tell what expression the figure's face might have displayed at this point as its face was merely a swirling greyness. However, there was a definite air that the last thing it wanted was to see Ernest straight back again. It tried to be brusque.

"Well, come, come now. We must decide on something. Time is pressing."

"I thought you said Time didn't exist here."

"Yes, well, strictly speaking that's the case, but I am getting a strong sense of time passing nevertheless."

Ernest shifted in his seat again.

"Are you also a grey swirling mass inside your robes or is it just your face?"

"Let's not change the subject, shall we, Mr. Smith. What do you want to go back as?"

"I really can't understand why I have to go back as something different. Why can't I just have another crack at being a man? I promise I'll be much better next time around."

The figure sighed. "That wouldn't be too difficult, would it? You made your wife's life a misery. You were always off with other women, you never gave her any help around the house, you left her to bring up the children largely on her own, and you frittered away all the money she had inherited from her parents. I imagine she wasn't too displeased when you died."

"I see. So, I'm being punished?"

"We prefer the term 'downgraded.' There has to be some measure of suffering before we allow you another chance at the highest level of life. You need to see things from a different viewpoint, to gain some understanding of what it feels like to be undervalued or just simply ignored and overlooked. Living the harsh and difficult life of some lesser creature will give you that understanding. Do you see now why we are doing all this?"

Ernest nodded.

"Yes, I do. And I've made my decision. I'd like to go back as a woman."

"A woman?"

"Yes. You won't let me go back as a man so I suppose a woman's probably the next best thing. It's sort of a lesser creature really, isn't it? And you said I needed to see things from a different viewpoint so it seems the obvious answer to me."

"You really haven't learnt anything at all from your past lives, have you, Mr. Smith. I don't know how you..."

The figure went very still. It stopped tapping its pen. The grey clouds seemed to eddy for a time in a more agitated fashion. Then it raised one hand and Ernest disappeared. It started to write.

"Authorization for transfers. Mr. Ernest Smith (current subject) and Mrs. Diana Smith (his widow). Reverse time frame to the start of their marriage and replay up to the present point. Ernest to become Diana and vice versa."

Spawn of War and Deathiness

Caretaker in the Garden of Dreams

David Tallerman

Hunching his shoulders against the bitter wind, Gug-Shabeth gazed out over the long field. When he tutted beneath his breath, the Ka birds stirred in alarm from the branches overhead, circled once amidst the twilight sky, and then returned to their perches to glare down at his tumescent head with belligerent crimson eyes.

They didn't fear him. After all, why should they? They could easily dodge any attack his malformed arms might make.

Gug-Shabeth returned his watery stare to the long field. There, other birds had nestled amongst the crop, their leathery wings tucked around them like cloaks, their proboscises probing the strange fruits that grew there.

The scarecrow he'd built was nothing now but a cruciform frame draped with scraps of greying meat.

He was failing in his responsibility. But if they had ever intended him to succeed, ever cared at all, then they would not have made him so carelessly; every thought, every step, would not be such torment. No, the gods had little time for this patch of their creation, if indeed they had time for any of it, in their wantonness and their cruelty.

Still, what he lacked in form did not change his function.

Gug-Shabeth trudged painfully down the mound and onto the field, felt his feet drag down into the ebon soil. The nearest Ka took flight and circled warily, their tiny faces expressing outrage at the interruption of their meal. When he grunted at them, they dispersed resentfully to wait him out in the trees. With all the time in the world, they could afford a little patience.

Gug-Shabeth turned his attention to his crop. Each chi was roughly spherical, its root invisible beneath the earth. Each was translucent, and visible within was layer inside layer, until at the very centre there shone a blue flame that shimmered and flowed. Some shone brightly, others only dimly. Every so often, one would flicker out altogether, and in an instant the shell that housed it would rot and soak into the earth as if it had never been. Many others showed signs of where the Ka birds had fed. The outer leaves were split and raggedy or gouged away altogether.

From those nearby, Gug-Shabeth selected the chi that glowed most palely. He dug into the hard earth until its root was exposed, levered it free and tucked it under one arm. Above, the Ka birds whistled their protest. How dare this shambling thing touch their food? Annoyed as much by the pain in his gnarled fingers, Gug-Shabeth turned his face to the stars and howled in fury, and the birds spun skywards in a whirl of panic and charcoal feathers. He glared after them for a moment and then trudged back across the field, the uprooted chi still cradled beneath his arm.

Laboriously, Gug-Shabeth clambered over the stile that crossed the fence and dropped heavily to the ground on the other side. The path was barely visible as a stain stretching into the darkness. Arriving at the foot of the hill, he crossed the bridge there, ignoring the cloying lap and sugary scent of the waters running beneath his feet. Beyond, the path rose again, but he bent his weight into the incline and gritted his mangled teeth and made no sound of complaint, for who was there to listen, or to care?

Finally he came to the peak of the rise, and beyond stood his home and the garden that grew about it, nebulous as ever under the perpetual twilight.

Gug-Shabeth set the chi on a rock and stared at it intently, until he was sure its flame still burnt, however slightly. Satisfied, he turned his attention to the meat-garden. Though it had been here when he'd first arrived, it was he who had nurtured the garden and had built his home beside it. While it was his, to use as he saw fit, he harvested its produce only when he had to.

Milky orbs gazed back at him from beneath frayed, pink leaves; bleached femur branches dwindled to thin tibia and patella; finger-bone twigs grew in weedy clusters; and everywhere hung bunches of moist red orbs, their thick sap dripping to clot in the tissue-grass.

Gug-Shabeth set about his task. He took windfall where he could, or picked from the lowest branches and from the ground foliage. Still, his muscles ached terribly, particularly his hopelessly crooked back.

Yet once he began to work there was nimbleness in his fingers, and he partly forgot the pain. The more he crafted, the more his discomforts subsided, the faster his knotted fingers spun in the damp air; for once Gug-Shabeth had been a fine craftsman, and though he didn't remember those times, yet some part of him awoke sometimes and worked marvels.

Soon, where he laboured in the clearing at the heart of the garden, there was another body before him. If its dimensions were strange, it was better made at least than he himself.

Gug-Shabeth stood back with a rumble of satisfaction.

He returned to the stump, checked the chi one last time and saw it was still lit, though barely. He carried it back to the clearing with both hands. When he reached the still body, he knelt over it and dug his nails deep into the skin of the chi, prising it in two with a sigh of exertion. Softly hissing, it split like an eggshell, and the glimmer of flame dripped out and into the open mouth of Gug-Shabeth's creation.

For a long while afterwards there was nothing but the sigh of wind in the bleeding willow and the croak of distant insects. Then the thing opened its eyes and stared up at Gug-Shabeth and screamed.

It lay screaming for what seemed an age. But eventually the noise became hoarse and was strangled off with a gurgling cough. Gug-Shabeth sat patiently on his haunches and waited. At last the thing sat up, glanced fearfully about, and said in a voice hardly above a whisper, "This isn't right. I'm not supposed to be here."

Gug-Shabeth, whose sharp teeth were crammed haphazardly into his mouth and whose tongue was a useless stump, could not speak to answer. Instead, he stood up and started towards the gate of the garden, and motioned for the thing to follow. After a while it fell in behind him.

"There was an accident," it said, "I remember an accident. And then... darkness, for a long, long time."

Gug-Shabeth grunted sympathetically and started up the path beyond the gate. The thing he'd made followed nervously behind him, speaking in snatches, not seeming to care that he didn't answer it.

"Am I dreaming?" it asked. "Is this a nightmare?"

He led the way down the incline and over the bridge, up the hill beyond and between the trees and over the ancient stile, and all the while the thing mumbled to itself and asked questions that he had no means of answering. When they stepped onto the packed black earth of the long field, it said, "Am I dead? Am I in hell?"

Gug-Shabeth shook his head and pointed towards the crucifix at the centre of the field. The chi-thing gazed back at him with anxious eyes, then crossed over to the dilapidated frame and inspected it warily. Gug-Shabeth came up behind it, caught hold of one foot and lifted it into position upon the lower bar. He strapped the foot in place with the thong of leather hung there and turned his attention to the other.

"What are you doing?" the thing asked nervously.

It made as if to struggle, then seemed to think better of it and glared at him instead. As his creation, it couldn't resist him, any more than Gug-Shabeth could defy his own function. He eased its arms into place across the wide crossbar and bound those too.

The creature flailed a little, testing its bonds. Finding it could move no more than its head, it began to wail softly.

Gug-Shabeth wasn't without pity. But he understood necessity, and knew too that his little construction housed a chi that would soon have faded and passed. He had merely borrowed it a while from the order of things. Its suffering would be short and worthwhile.

As he walked away, back towards his home amidst the meat-garden, he could hear the thing screaming behind him, as the first of the Ka birds settled on it. A living chi fascinated them, so much so that they would abandon the easy, plentiful pickings growing around them. Yet it would take them a long while to search out their prize from its prison of flesh. He had hidden it carefully and deep.

For that while, his crop would be safe.

Soon enough he would have to build another, another construct of meat with one fading chi nestled within as sacrifice to keep its kin safe–soon, but not yet.

And for a time at least, Gug-Shabeth could rest his weary bones and be at peace.

Spawn of War and Deathiness

The Soul Man

Mike Murphy

The gun tasted horrible. *What did you expect it to taste like?* John Clifton asked himself. *Chocolate?* Heather and Joey were at the park. There would never be a better time. As soon as the Feds found out about his insider trading, it was prison for sure. He couldn't face that! His family... hell, the entire world would be better off without a screw-up like him around.

John put the awful-tasting gun back into his mouth, sighed a heavy sigh, and, shaking, pulled the trigger.

<<>>

"You're next," he heard.

"Huh? Where... Where am I?" He took a quick look around. Everything was white. *Gleaming* white. While Clifton was still in the clothes he was wearing when he killed himself, the tall, blond man before him was dressed in a sparkling white robe.

The man sighed sadly. "Why do they always send them *straight* to me?" he asked. "You'd think there'd be an orientation first."

"Who are you?"

"The Attendant."

"What... What is this place?"

The Attendant was amused. "My, but you're full of questions, aren't you?"

"Where am I?" John asked adamantly.

"The recycling center."

"Recycling? For what?"

"*Souls,*" the Attendant said matter-of-factly. "It's my job to turn your soul around and send it back to Earth."

"But I don't want to go back," John informed him.

"Too bad," the other man said. "There are only so many souls to go around. We need to re-use what we can." He paused, looking down at something in his left hand that resembled an iPad. "You're one of the lucky ones."

"How so?"

"When you were born, you got a *brand-new* soul. Lots of people get used ones."

"Why don't I have a say in this?" wondered Clifton.

"Because it's *His* plan," the Attendant said.

"Who?"

"The *big* Him," the blond-haired man explained. "A long time ago, He worked out a grand plan for everything in the universe."

"And my reincarnation is a part of that?"

"It is now."

"What about free will?"

"That *again*?" the Attendant asked. "I can't tell you how many new arrivals bring that up."

"Well?" John prompted him. "Do I have free will or don't I?"

"You *do*."

"Aha!"

"But the Boss has *bigger* free will," the Attendant explained. "It's kind of like the federal government's rules trumping any state's."

"That's not fair!" complained Clifton.

"You can't go changing the grand plan any time you like! Do you know how much time He spent putting all that together?"

"A long time?"

"Eons!" the Attendant exclaimed. "Every time somebody exercises his–*ugh!*–free will, the whole plan has to be tweaked to work again." He sighed and added, "It's kind of like a GPS."

"*What?*"

"The Big Guy has mapped everything out, just like a GPS maps out your route. If you fail to take a turn it tells you to take, it has to recalculate your directions... because you exercised your free will." He touched Clifton on the shoulder. "C'mon," he said. "Time's wasting."

"Do you know how I died?" John asked the Attendant.

The robed man pressed a few buttons on his tablet. "Suicide," he said. "If it wasn't for your relatively new soul, you might have gone somewhere... else."

"You *don't* see the problem?"

"Enlighten me... but quickly."

"I killed myself!" John explained. "What makes you think I want to come back to life as something else?"

"You have no choice," the Attendant informed him, pressing a few more tablet buttons.

"I'll just kill myself again," Clifton said.

"Please don't! That will cause all kinds of trouble." He lowered the tablet to his side and called out, "One soul going down!"

<<>>

The rumble of distant thunder could be heard in the barnyard. The cows mooed. A chicken clucked. Sensing the time was here, she jumped from her nest. Her eggs were cracking!

Clifton poked his way out with his egg tooth. The air was cold on his soaked body. *A chicken*, John thought. *He sent me back to Earth as a chicken!*

He looked around and spotted a puddle. As a man, he would have stepped over it but, as a chick, it was just right. He snuck away from his family, waddled into the puddle, and drowned himself.

<<>>

"You again?" the Attendant asked, shocked.

"I warned you," Clifton said. "I don't want to be alive anymore–as *anything*."

"Oh, this is gonna mess up the plan! He won't be happy!"

"Then let me stay here. If you send me back down –"

The Attendant suddenly realized what went wrong. "I made it too easy for you," he said. "I need to... I've got it!" Again, he called out, "One soul going down!"

<<>>

The newborn puppies yipped in their basket, their eyes still closed, trying to sniff out a route to their mother's milk. *What the... I can't see!* John thought. *That son of a...*

He heard the puppies yipping and realized he was one of them. *My eyes won't open until... Well played, sir. Well played. Once I can see, just you wait!*

<<>>

Weeks passed. His eyes opened, and he was given a name: Roscoe. He could hear a woman–his "owner"–whistling and calling for him as he bounded along the grass, but he wasn't stopping. The road was nearby and busy at this time of day. He made it just as a truck was rounding the corner. The driver never saw him. The last thing John heard was the woman's weeping.

<<>>

"This is getting annoying!" the Attendant said.

"I'm not crazy about it either," Clifton assured him.

"You're making a lot of extra work for me... and for Him."

"So let me *stay*."

"Not on my watch!" the man with the blond hair said adamantly. "One soul going down!"

<<>>

The overhead lights were blinding. John felt someone spank him.

"Congratulations, Mr. and Mrs. Ramsey," the doctor said. "It's a boy!"

<<>>

It had been a tough day for the Ramseys. The doctor thought the little guy had colic. "Honey," Mrs. Ramsey asked, exhausted, "where's the baby?"

"He's right..." Mr. Ramsey started before realizing their son wasn't there.

His wife jumped from their bed. Before long, she was at the top of the stairs, screaming hysterically.

She had found the baby.

<<>>

"You broke their hearts!"

"I *told* you I'd –"

"I've had it with you, Mr. Clifton," the robed man said. "*He's* had it with you too."

"So I can stay?" John asked eagerly.

"I suppose that's the easiest way to keep you out of my hair for eternity."

"Great!"

"Your soul's getting worn out anyway." He started typing on his tablet. "I still have to find..." He stopped talking, his eyes lighting up. "Perfect." He turned the tablet around so John could see the picture on the screen.

"That's my *wife*."

"Widow, actually," the Attendant clarified.

"If you take her..."

"Yes?"

"My son... He'll be an orphan."

"Since you killed yourself," the Attendant told him, "I didn't think you'd mind."

"Didn't think I'd..." Clifton began, shocked and angry. "What kind of a dad do you take me for?"

"A dead one."

"Heather and Joey were the only bright spots in my life," John told the Attendant. "I didn't commit suicide because of *them*." He reached out and grabbed the robed man's shoulder. "*Please* don't," he pleaded.

"But we need a soul."

"How about *me*?" Clifton asked.

"Again?"

"No tricks this time," John told him.

"Promise?"

"Cross my heart and hope to... well, you get the idea. You let Heather live, and *I'll* go back down to Earth."

"Your soul can only stand one more trip," the Attendant warned him.

"One more is all I need," Clifton said.

"If you kill yourself again –"

"I won't," John responded quickly.

"Your soul won't have the strength to make it back up here," the robed man finished. "You'll be plain d-e-a-d."

"I understand."

The Attendant did some more typing on his tablet. "There's a lemur in Madagascar who's about to give birth," he said.

"Madagascar?"

"You have something against Madagascar?"

"No, but I was thinking..."

"*What?*" the Attendant asked, frustrated to his last nerve.

"That I could be somewhere... near my family," Clifton continued.

"With all the trouble you've caused me," the blond-haired man said, "you... you want a *favor?*"

"Please?"

He turned to his tablet again. "*Anything* to be rid of you!" After a bit of typing, he said, "There's a mouse living in your garage. She's about to have babies."

"We have mice in the garage?" a surprised Clifton asked.

"Remember: *No* tricks."

"None."

"One soul going down... again!" the exasperated Attendant called out.

<<>>

Joey looked down at the welcome mat. "*Ick!*" he said. "Mom!" he called.

"What is it, dear?" Heather asked from behind the screen door.

"Look what Kitty did!" Joey answered, disgusted.

"Oh, that's too bad."

"Is it... dead?" the boy asked.

"Yes."

"Kitty *killed* him?"

"It looks that way."

"But... why?"

"Cats do that sometimes," she explained to her son. "They're hunters. Kitty thought she was protecting us."

"From *that?*" he asked, pointing.

"I know it doesn't make sense now, Joey, but one day, it will," she assured him. "Do me a favor?"

"What?"

"Get me the dustpan and brush from the kitchen."

"OK," Joey said after a sniff.

Once he was inside the house, Heather mumbled to herself, "How sweet. He's so empathetic." She opened the screen door, stepped out onto the stoop, and looked down at the mat. "It's just a little mouse," she said.

After the Atrocity

Ian Creasey

It's twenty minutes since the duplicator's last glitch, so I ask one of the guards outside to fetch me lunch, hoping that for once I might be able to eat it uninterrupted by urgent repair work. "Yes, Miss Ruiz," he says as he salutes. I don't have a rank or a uniform—just a lab coat—but they still salute me. At first I found it endearing; now it just reminds me how much I miss Caltech, where nobody ever salutes anyone.

While I wait for my meal, I watch the crawlers assemble the body of Abu Hameed. This copy—the ninth—is nearly finished. Each copy has appeared quicker than the last: I've improved the duplicator's speed, at the price of needing more operator oversight.

The workbench is electroplated with gold, a non-reactive metal that shines under the lab's fluorescent lights. Abu Hameed's naked body lies directly on the bench, but it's not uncomfortable for him because he isn't alive yet. And no-one cares about his comfort anyway, not since he killed ten thousand people in the Atrocity.

His ribs stand out from his chest, and his wild beard needs a trim. His eyes are closed, but nevertheless he looks like he might leap off the bench at any moment. I shiver. To calm myself, I move the high-grade cutter torch to my desk, within easy reach. I feel safer knowing I can fire a lethal bolt into his heart.

Lunch arrives. The smell of a burger and fries is a welcome antidote to the duplicator's acrid tang. The tray has a selection of sauce sachets: this is what passes for menu variety at the base. I'm just about to choose a mustard when the door opens.

"Sophie Bryant to see you, Miss," the guard announces.

A tall black woman walks in, wearing a jacket and skirt more colorful than any of the base's military uniforms.

"You're the lawyer?" I ask. "I'm Violeta Ruiz."

She nods, and extends her hand for me to shake. "Pleased to meet you. I do have my own office, you know. Why did you insist on someone coming here? This is a classified lab. I was the only lawyer who could get clearance."

I point at the nearly-complete copy of Abu Hameed on the workbench. "I want advice from someone who knows what's going on and isn't just rubber-stamping something they haven't seen."

I pause to take a few bites of food, wondering how best to phrase my doubts. I vividly remember waking up on the same gold bench as Abu Hameed's latest copy. The duplicator is so important that it needs to run twenty-four hours a day, with an operator on constant standby to resolve glitches and improve speed. I'd copied myself to create an additional operator. The military would never have entrusted their most important prisoner to the duplicator without seeing that proof of concept.

The experience of being copied has given me a sharper sense of empathy. And the more copies of Abu Hameed that I make, the more sinister it feels. I don't know where they all go, but I presume they aren't forming a choir.

"I'm worried about what's happening to these copies," I say. "Whatever it is, I'm facilitating it. I don't want to be party to anything illegal."

"There's no need to worry." Bryant gestures to Abu Hameed and says, "I'm his lawyer. It's my job to make sure he's treated appropriately."

"He has a lawyer?" I ask, surprised. I've never seen Bryant when the collection team comes to take finished copies away.

"Of course he does. This is the United States of America—we have a constitution and a legal system. Detainees get lawyers," she says proudly. I half expect her to show me her diploma.

The lunches come in large portions for soldiers' appetites. I've eaten as much as my calorie app recommends, so I drop the rest of the food into the duplicator's intake hopper. I always find it ironic that the anti-American terrorist is made out of all-American burgers.

"That's why I'm here," Bryant adds. "I was cleared to enter this lab because I already know there are copies of him."

"So you must know what's happening to them," I say.

She doesn't reply, and I remember that the detainee's official designation is only Prisoner 75832. "I know who he is," I tell her. "He's the most famous terrorist on the planet! There's no need to be coy about it. They're interrogating him, right?"

"Obviously," says Bryant.

"It must be hard going, if they need so many copies."

"He's a hard guy," she says, her face an impassive mask.

She's not going to volunteer anything, so I'm forced to come straight out with the question that's been nagging at me. "Is he being tortured?"

"Of course not!" she snaps. "Torture is illegal. There are interrogation protocols, and I make sure everything's done by the book."

"Sounds like a lot of work," I say. "When this copy's finished, there'll be nine altogether—plus the original. Do you attend every interrogation?"

"They're all recorded," Bryant says, her voice rising in anger. "I can watch any session I like. Don't accuse me of not doing my job!"

"All right, all right," I say. "Keep your voice down." The original Violeta is asleep in the back room. She has a heck of a temper, and I don't want her blaming me for waking her up. We argue quite enough already.

"Keep my voice down?" Bryant points to the motionless Abu Hameed. "What, am I interrupting his beauty sleep? My God, get your priorities straight! Whose side are you on? There are terrorist plots we need to uncover. There could be a ticking bomb, a bioweapon, a nuclear meltdown…Don't you worry about him!"

"Someone's got to," I say, barely restraining myself from adding *even if his lawyer doesn't*. I suppose the job falls to me, since I'm the only other person in the world who knows what it's like to be a copy.

"Does he get visits from the Red Cross?" I ask. "Or the Red Crescent, or whatever it is."

"You don't need to know that."

"I guess not. But right now I'm working round the clock to copy him. It's tiring and stressful; I'm practically burnt out. Maybe I'll slow down a little, take it easy." I reach for my Diet Coke and suck a long, leisurely slurp through the straw.

Bryant purses her lips and glowers at me. "If you must know, the original is dead. And the duplicator's classified, so obviously we can't have Red Cross visitors seeing all these identical copies."

"The original's dead?" I exclaim. "So much for 'protocols' and 'by the book'! Or is that the final chapter?"

"It was an accident," Bryant says. "Obviously no-one wanted to kill our most important prisoner."

"Obviously," I say, since it seems to be her favorite word.

She gives me a withering look. "Is there anything else, or have we finished? After all, as you point out, I do have a lot of work to do."

Even though Bryant isn't in uniform, she's part of the system. She's not going to rock the boat.

"We've finished," I say. "Thanks for coming. Please send me written confirmation of your advice."

After she's gone, I wonder whether I should have pressed her harder about the death of the original Abu Hameed. If the original had died, rather than one of the copies I'd made, then it wasn't my responsibility... or was it?

Maybe the duplicator makes the interrogators reckless. They can go as far as they like, knowing he's easily replaceable. There's always another copy on the workbench.

How far do they go? What are the authorized procedures? Bryant said it's not torture, because torture is illegal. So if it's by the book, it can't be torture.

I'm not convinced by this sophistry, or Bryant's legal sign-off. My work is top secret; the only lawyers who know what's happening are those most trusted by the military and least likely to object.

A beep from the duplicator breaks my chain of thought. I spend half an hour debugging the latest glitch. Building the copy's brain is the final part of the process, and the most delicate.

The door opens without warning. I know who it is. He visits often enough that the guards no longer bother to announce him.

Derek Cole is so pale that he might have inhabited the base all his life, never seeing the sun. He keeps his hair cropped with a tight buzzcut, barely exposing its ginger color. A few freckles dot his head like spots on a misshapen die.

"Good news!" His voice always sounds as if he's shouting orders across a battlefield. "The final delivery has arrived, so we've got all the parts you need. You can start building another duplicator to relieve the bottleneck. Though I still don't understand why you can't just print another duplicator out of this one."

"I told you, it's optimized for organic material—people, not machinery. There is a difference." Before he can start complaining, I say, "It'll take a while to build a second duplicator and calibrate it. Do you want me to prioritize that, or keep making copies of the prisoner?"

"You can do both, can't you? Just print some extra copies of yourself."

I flinch. Having one duplicate is bad enough. We keep arguing about what'll happen when we return to California: which of us will get my apartment, my job, my friends, my life. Dividing it all between even more copies would be nightmarish.

"Absolutely not," I say. "You're already getting two for the price of one."

He frowns. "All right, I'll send you some engineers. You can begin the duplicator after you've finished this." Cole points to the body on the workbench. "When will it be ready?"

"About five o'clock," I say, deliberately using civilian time. The original Violeta has started saying "17.00" like everyone else in the base.

"I'll tell the collection team," he says.

"What are you doing with these guys?" I ask. "What happens to them all?"

Cole shakes his head. "You don't need to know that."

"Maybe I do," I say. "You always want these copies as quickly as possible. How long do you keep them for? If you, um, *dispose* of them after a week, I could cut some corners in the internal organs."

I hate myself for coming up with that suggestion, but I need to get him talking.

"Don't cut corners," says Cole. "The copies need to be absolutely identical."

"Why?" I demand. "I can do a better job if I know what you're trying to achieve."

He pauses, absently rubbing his neck. "That's a good point," he says at last. "I suppose it won't hurt to give you an outline, since you already know the classified part." The duplicator became top secret when DARPA noticed my work at Caltech and realized the implications.

Cole sits in the other Violeta's chair and says, "It's simple, really. When we capture prisoners, we need information. The problem is that we don't know whether they're telling the truth. No matter how far we go, we can never be sure how much is true. At least, we can't when we only have one person to interrogate. But if we have copies of the same suspect, and we question them separately..."

I grasp his point. "If they say different things, they must be lying."

"Obviously!"

"But why do you need so many copies?" I ask. "Surely as soon as you get a consistent message out of a couple of them, you know you're on the right track."

He smiles at my naïvety. "It's not that easy. These guys are terrorists at constant risk of being captured. They have cover stories, and stories inside the cover stories. When they're under pressure, they'll admit they were lying, then change to another lie."

"How do you get past that?"

"More pressure," he says. "Eventually, the cover story runs out. When they exhaust what they've prepared beforehand, they invent details that start to differ. But it takes time to get to that point."

"Especially if they don't want to talk," I comment.

Cole chuckles knowingly. "Even the truth isn't constant. When you tell an anecdote, I bet you don't tell it the same way twice."

"I suppose you minimize unwanted variation by using a uniform sample and a constant procedure," I say. Now I understand why Abu Hameed's copies have to be identical. And they don't even know that they're copies, so they don't have my existential angst to distort their fidelity to the original.

"Practice makes perfect! We're getting results, and it's all down to you." Cole grins at me, like a proud soccer coach for whom I've scored a goal. "You've made interrogation reliable. When this is over and your gadget's declassified, I'll nominate you for a medal."

He gestures to the duplicator. "When you build the next one of these, can it be faster?"

"Not if you want the copies to be identical. It's not a trivial task to make an exact replica." I trot out my standard gee-whiz fact: "There are seven octillion atoms in the human body—that's seven billion billion billion. It's a big job to put all those together in the right order. Building a person takes time, and I'm running out of short-cuts. You can't make a baby in one month by getting nine women pregnant."

"I guess not, but you can have a lot of fun trying." Cole laughs, and heads for the door. On his way out, he waves at Abu Hameed's body. "See you later!"

When the door closes behind him, I slump onto my desk, hating what I've got myself into. I can't stop thinking about Cole's words.

More pressure. His phrase echoes in my head, sounding creepier every time.

I didn't accuse Cole of torture because I knew he'd only deny it like Bryant. But surely that's what it amounts to.

I've invented a machine that makes torture reliable. And I'm operating it twenty-four hours a day.

It'll never stop. Even if they squeeze Abu Hameed dry, they'll still want more copies to use for training new interrogators and testing new techniques. In future there'll be other prisoners, as the war on terror continues its glacial course, grinding everyone in its path. I don't care about getting a medal "when this is over", not least because I can't imagine it ever being over.

"I want to go home," I say, out loud. "I want to see my friends. I want to get dressed up and go to roller disco."

I signed a twelve-month contract. At least, my original did. What will happen after our stint, when we both want to go home? The lawyer said that Abu Hameed's copies aren't getting Red Cross visits because that would be a security breach, revealing the duplicator.

What about me? Will they let me go home? Will I ever leave this base?

I take deep breaths, trying to calm myself. Surely the duplicator will be declassified eventually. Surely they won't treat me the same way they treat terrorists...

Yet I'm dodging responsibility if I think it's how *they* treat terrorists, as if I'm not part of that. Cole's interrogation program wouldn't work without my assembly line of victims.

I look at the workbench where the crawlers are building Abu Hameed's brain, with all its sensory neurons and pain receptors. I've created him specifically to be tortured. It sickens me to think that I'm creating people solely to suffer, people who would surely beg me to stop.

What can I do? I could break the duplicator, but that would only be a temporary hitch. If I refuse to repair it, they'll bring someone else in. It'll be fixed eventually. Then more legions of Abu Hameed will march into the torture chamber...

...Unless I delete his data. The original Abu Hameed is dead. The current body on the bench isn't finished, so it can't be used as another starting point. And the previous copies have already been interrogated, so they're no longer a clean sample. If I delete the scan data, no-one can make any fresh copies of him, even if the duplicator itself still functions.

Deleting data is usually impossible; it's all backed up offsite. The duplicator is different, due to the enormous amount of information required to specify a human being's seven billion billion billion atoms. There's not enough bandwidth to transmit it, even with the best compression. The duplicator has its own vast internal memory to store scans. That data only exists inside the lab: if it disappears, it's gone forever.

I grab the keyboard, then write a program to delete files and overwrite the memory to prevent recovery attempts. When I look at the files to check I've included everything, I see the duplicator's most recent scans: Chimpanzee F, Violeta Ruiz, Prisoner 75832.

I shiver when I see my own data, remembering Cole's casual remark: "Just print some extra copies of yourself." I include Violeta Ruiz in the deletion list. I remember what it's like to wake up on the bench; I don't want any more of my copies chained to the production line.

But another version of me already exists. She's asleep in the bedroom. I can't run the program without telling her: I know how angry I'd be if she did that to me. We have to agree our plan, since we'll both face the consequences.

While I wait for her to wake up, I try to think of an easy way out. I don't want to make a stand, but I can't avoid a decision. If I let the interrogations continue, I'll be complicit in them.

The lab's grey walls feel ever more oppressive, as I wonder whether I'll ever escape them. How can I avoid being a security breach? That's only an issue as long as the duplicator remains secret; if everyone knew about it, there'd be nothing to hide. But if I publicize the duplicator, then I'll go to jail for leaking classified information. That's hardly an improvement.

Deleting Abu Hameed's data might be considered a crime. Can I avoid the rap for that? Or must I martyr myself for my principles?

At last, activity comes from my quarters, as a toilet flushes and a wisp of shower steam curls through the doorway. No matter how often I remind her, she never closes the door properly while she's showering. I'm such a slob.

I send the guard to fetch a breakfast tray. Soon my original emerges, with a towel wrapped around her hair and a sullen expression on her face. She still hasn't forgiven me for winning the coin-toss that put her on night shift—not that it makes much difference, since we so rarely get outdoors.

While she eats breakfast, I tell her what's happened: Bryant's visit, my conversation with Cole, the program I've written to delete the scan data.

"Are you crazy?" she yells, spitting out toast crumbs.

"No more than you," I say, offended.

"What's your problem? Have you forgotten the Atrocity? We need to rip that bastard open and find out every damn thing he knows."

"Interrogation is one thing. Torture is quite another."

"Yeah, yeah. Big deal," she says. "That's their business, not ours. Why don't you leave it to them, and stop meddling?"

"You're okay with torture?"

She shrugs. "I'm sure it's not *torture* torture. We're the good guys, remember? It's authorized procedures in exceptional circumstances. You said Bryant gave you the legal go-ahead, so what are you worried about?"

"The duplicator is classified," I remind her. "The interrogation protocols were probably written by military bureaucrats here in the base. I bet they weren't signed off by anyone accountable to the public—anyone elected. Would politicians authorize creating umpteen copies of someone, so they could all be tortured?"

"Oh, come on!" she says. "Do you expect the President to personally ring you up and give you permission? Do you want the Attorney General to hold your hand while you're cranking the machine? Get real!"

We gaze at each other with equal astonishment, amazed at our opposing attitudes. We're the same person! At least, we were a few weeks ago. How could we diverge so much?

I remember waking up on the workbench. Every time I make a copy of Abu Hameed, I feel a kinship with him that the other Violeta doesn't feel. And perhaps knowing I'm a copy creates psychological pressure for me to differentiate myself from my original, carving out my own identity.

Yet it's disconcerting to realize how contingent my opinions are. My convictions are fragile, built on the shifting sands of happenstance. I don't even know for sure how badly he's being treated. Maybe I should just let it go: trust the system, and outsource my conscience to Bryant's legal sign-off. After all, what can I achieve anyway? I can't uninvent the duplicator; I can't prevent it being misused. I can't put the genie back in the bottle.

My original says, "You were asleep when I finished the first copy of the terrorist. Cole and his flunkies were worried that it might not have worked properly. They interviewed him, making sure he had all his faculties. I went along to check whether there were any glitches."

Abu Hameed's freshly-minted copies all possess the same memories, ready to be probed by Cole's team with standardized procedures to minimize divergence. My original and I have lived longer since duplication; we've seen different things. We've changed.

If only one of us can go home, who should it be?

She continues, "It was just an interview, not an interrogation, so he was happy to talk. He spoke in English, boasting about what he'd done. He described the Atrocity as a great blow against the infidel. He laughed!"

She leans forward and stares into my eyes. "He *laughed*," she repeats. "Ten thousand people dead, and he was laughing about it. He called it a divine judgment, one that would inspire the whole world to rise up against the Great Satan. Then he said there was more to come. It was the most sickening thing I've ever seen. Excuse me if I don't shed any tears for him."

Her expression is stern, as cold and hard as Bryant. I don't like what she's become; I don't want to walk down that path. I never suspected how much darkness lurks within my heart.

She says, "I could ask how you became such a hand-wringing sissy. But I already know: you weren't there. You didn't hear him. I looked at him, and I saw the face of evil. When we're confronted by evil, we can't run, or hide, or worry about paperwork. We have to act."

She's showing me how tough I can be. I try to speak calmly, while readying myself for what I must do next. "So you're saying that when we see evil in front of us, we're justified in taking any action necessary?"

"Obviously," she says. Her blue T-shirt is a thin layer of polyester, no protection at all.

"Are you sure?" I ask. "We should do anything?"

"Yes, damn it!" Too late, a spark of realization reaches her eyes.

I grab the cutter torch, and let rip. A fizzing bolt arcs into her chest.

She screams, but I don't see her fall. After I fire, I lunge straight to the keyboard and run the program I've written. The duplicator beeps as its data disappears.

Two guards burst through the lab door. "Drop the weapon!" the first one shouts.

I've already dropped it. I raise my hands, trying not to gag on the stench of melted fabric and burnt flesh.

"It's sabotage," I say. "I tried to stop her, but I was too late."

No-one can prove which of us deleted the data. I want to stand up for my principles, but not yet. Not in the depths of a military prison, where sabotage is treason.

Someday, when I feel safe, I'll indulge my conscience and speak up for truth and justice. But right now, expediency is the order of the day.

Dirt Moon

Dan Koboldt

We were down to six soldiers when the worms came for us.

The mission was a security sweep of some nameless dirt-moon, the kind of thing I'd done a dozen times before. I stopped asking what the company wanted it for a long time ago. Might have been minerals, might have been precious metals. Fossil fuels were always popular. Hell, it could have been the dirt itself. Nothing taller than a head of lettuce managed to grow here on account of the planetary eclipses, but good dirt was hard to come by. The hydroponics companies bought it up by the freighter-load.

But like I said, I stopped asking what they wanted. My job was to secure the landing zone.

We dropped out of orbit like a cannonball, made impact, and took up a formation. Sixteen grunts, locked and loaded. I got to hand pick my soldiers for this one, so I had a good mix. Two plasma snipers, three heavies, and eleven cold-hearted mother killers. The heavies alone could pretty much raze this moon by themselves, with the latest model cutter-guns they packed.

We swung out in a wide semicircle, running at a steady clip to put some distance between us and the landing zone. The ground shook under my boots as the transport fired up to make the jump back to orbit. My HUD showed everything five-by-five with the ship as it lifted off, and that was good enough for me. Once the metal was off the ground, it was air control's problem. Not mine. It rumbled into the sky, leaving the moon bruised and silent behind it.

My audio crackled to life with an incoming. "Howell to Mathias, come in."

That was one of our scouts, an advance-man whose tweaked metabolism let him run a half mile flat-out without breaking a sweat. I'd marked his signal as he disappeared over a slight ridge, maybe five hundred yards in front of me.

"Go ahead, Howie," I said.

"Got some movement to the southwest. Looks like a herd animal. They spotted me when I topped the ridge, over."

"They moving at you?"

"Negative, over. They're sort of...

That's where he cut off.

"Howell?" Nothing. I thought it was just a transmission problem.

Then we started hearing the screams.

Shit. I changed course and made a beeline for him. "Jacques, can you get eyes on Howell?"

"*Absolument,*" said the Frenchman. "Give me five seconds."

I counted them off in my head, but didn't have to give the nudge.

"Sarge, you'd better get over here," he said. He even forgot the French accent, which told me how bad it was.

I hit the jump button on my exosuit, and started clearing twenty yards with each stride. Made it over the ridge in thirty seconds, but that was about a minute too late. There was nothing left of Howell but a dark stain on the ash-gray mud. Jacques had his plasma rifle leveled at the valley below, where a couple hundred shaggy-looking beasts were grazing. They didn't even look up.

"Did you see what did this?" I asked.

"*Non,* Sarge. Just this puddle. Poor Howell."

Everything was too calm, too quiet in the vale below us. Like a snake holding its breath before it struck. "Let's keep moving," I said.

We rejoined the formation, only to notice that two of the heavies—MacArthur and Tobias—had gone missing. Their cutter-guns should have been visible on the metal scanner, but those were gone, too. *What the hell's going on, here?*

With three men down, I had to put out the S.O.S. to command. I kept it short and sweet:

Three casualties, unknown hostiles, requesting air support and immediate extraction.

This was my sixty-eighth drop, twenty-fourth running point. They scrambled fighters and the backup transport within forty seconds. But they wouldn't get here for about forty five minutes.

That wouldn't be fast enough.

<<>>

We were down to twelve by the time we regrouped in the middle of a dusty hollow, surrounded by the bleak landscape. One of the snipers had gone missing by then. Trish—who was my number two—found his rifle propped up against the rock, at the base of the far ridge. That meant there were at least two assailants, or something so fast and deadly we'd not seen it move among us.

Now we stood in a tight cluster, half of us taking a knee, the rest standing. Guns pointed out. Like a porcupine from hell.

"What's the E.T.A. on air support?" Trish asked.

"Thirty six minutes." I'd been watching the countdown in my HUD, willing it to go faster.

"Damn."

"We need to get out of the open. Oscar, what looks good?"

The sniper had been casing the landscape with the scope on his plasma rifle. "Got a rock formation half a klick north of here."

"Anything moving?"

Oscar fired his rifle, and iridescent green bloomed on the distant rock face. "Not anymore."

"Good. I want everyone to buddy up," I said. "Trish, you're with me."

We'd done this maneuver a hundred times before, so it came as naturally as riding a bike. They paired off and moved out, spacing themselves, guns at the ready. The terrain grew rockier, and before long they were moving through a maze of boulders. Malone was the first to start firing. The rattle of the heavy machine gun cut through the silence like a jackhammer.

Then I heard Oscar firing his plasma. Whatever it was, the danger was right among us. I saw a long, unholy appendage sliding around a rock and my heart went cold. Trish and I both fired at it, the rounds shooting up sparks on the rocks beyond. *Worms.* I should have known. They were nothing but leather hide and teeth, and could tunnel through the soil as fast as a man could run. They were territorial, too, and damn near impossible to kill. The screams of my squad around us were testament to that.

Trish and I shared a look, and ceased firing by unspoken agreement. We needed stealth, here, if we had any shot at getting past them undetected. Gunfire gave off vibrations that would draw these devils like moths to a flame. We crept over the rocks instead, stepping lightly on the toes of our boots. Holding one another's wrists when we had to, almost like a dance. It reminded me of Kappa Three, when we'd had to cross an acid swamp to get to the transport on the far side. With the locals shooting at us, no less.

That was half a lifetime ago, but we moved like we were that young. We got to the rock formation, shouldered rifles, and shimmied up as best we could. Most of the squad was still in the rocks; they didn't dance quite as well. Trish and I laid down some covering fire, plugging at the dark muscular coils whenever they appeared. Not that we could always stop it, though. Jacques went down not fifteen yards from us, and was sucked screaming into the ground like a goddamn horror movie.

We really let loose after that. Managed to kill one worm, but it was just a juvenile. Which meant mom and dad were still around. And pissed as hell.

<<>>

Six of us made it up on the rocks. Me, Trish, and four others. The ground we'd just run across shook and trembled as the worms moved beneath it. They had our scent. The shuttle was two minutes out, coming in hot. Command had seen seven life signals wink out since I called it in. They knew how desperate we were.

The worms circled us life wolves, churned up the moon dirt as passed. Hundreds of white-sparkling stones glittered in the trenches they left behind. Diamonds, probably. So that's why the company wanted this place cleared so badly. Well, they'd have their work cut out for them. If there were three worms, there were a hundred, and you had to use subterranean pulse weapons to root them out of their deep holes. A two year operation for a moon this size, minimum.

But that was someone else's department, thank God. My only job was to get my handful of soldiers onto the transport out of here.

"Running low on ammo, Sarge," Trish said.

"Me, too," said Oscar. He'd been placing his shots carefully, not wanting to waste the plasma. He banged the butt of his rifle on the rock where he crouched. "Come on, baby, give me another shot or two."

"Oscar, don't... Trish started.

A worm erupted out of the soil right beneath him and wrapped its jaws around his torso. Pulled him back down to the ground while we unleashed fiery hell on it. It thrashed in the onslaught of gunfire, rolled over, and died. Not in time to save Oscar. I tried not to look at what was left of him.

Warm air washed over us, and engines hummed in the sky overhead. I've never heard a sound so wonderful.

"Climb up for extraction!" I shouted. They were already moving, Trish and the three others. I watched the ground tremble with increasing fury as the worm sensed our escape. Maybe we'd just killed its mate, I don't know, but suddenly the thing went kamikaze on us. Catapulted out of the ground and right at Trish. Got hold of her boot.

Son of a bitch. I didn't give myself the luxury of thinking. I took a running leap and landed on the worm's leathery back. It jolted beneath me, large as two horses and surprised as hell that I was riding it. Trish kicked free and cocked her rifle.

"Go, go!" I shouted.

She looked me right in the eyes, started to protest, but went. *Thank God.*

The worm bucked, nearly throwing me, but it could still reach her if I let go. I clung to the leather and clambered up toward the mouth. It reeked of dirt and blood and death.

The HUD told me three were on board, and it looked like Trish was almost there. I fumbled at my vest and found the fist-sized steel ball clipped to it. My concussion grenade, the last resort. I yanked it free. The worm began to turn its O-ring of curved teeth on me. I clamped my own teeth down on the metal pin, pulled it clear. I levered myself up and jammed it down the worm's throat. "Go to hell, you bastard."

The worm bucked and hissed like a snake caught on fire, but couldn't spit up the ball of death.

Three, two, one...

The blast blew the worm apart and sent me flying. I crashed backwards into something hard, unyielding. Started to black out, when I felt strong arms wrap around my torso. I'd flown up and hit the transport, right before the door was closed. Trish told me later they couldn't pry the worm skin out of my hands. It was four feet long. Mottled and tough and the color of diamond-speckled moon dust.

It made one hell of a pair of boots.

Starship Scion

David F. Shultz

The baby was beautiful, a gift from Heaven, so Alex and Veronica named her Angela. Angela cooed and smiled, and looked out on to her new world with wide, innocent eyes. She had much to learn about this place, but for now, her thoughts were pure and peaceful.

Hands and ankles in security restraints, the infiltrator sat limp and defeated in the chair, closed in by a wall of storage crates in the cargo bay. Alex eyed the captive—yet another xeno on his ship. God, they looked so human! He almost felt sorry for the thing, bleeding and bruised from Kassandra's interrogation. Maybe it was something in its eyes—they looked like Veronica's.

"You're sure it's a xeno?"

Kassandra showed him the x-ray on her security tablet, and there it was, curled and fetal in a nest of gray matter—the xeno parasite, like a sleeping salamander inside the skull.

"Went by the name Elise Mako," Kassandra said. "Contractor—a deckhand we picked up from the neutral belt on our last run."

"That run was over four months ago."

"133 days."

Who knows how much damage it could've done in that time.

"That's our saboteur."

"I doubt it," Kassandra said. "I reviewed the logs and vid-feeds, cross-checked against terminal access for the known hacks. I don't think it infiltrated any digital systems."

"That means...

"There's still another on board. At least one."

More than half a dozen in so many months. Alex knew xeno stragglers were a possibility out here, but what the hell were they all doing on the Scion?

He walked the few paces to the alien. This one's shell was a human female, maybe thirty years old, long black hair matted from deck duty, face splotched with dirt, eyes ringed with purple from Kassandra's work over. Maybe sometimes they picked their shells to fit in, and maybe sometimes to garner sympathy from humans. Alex drew his sidearm and pressed the barrel to the base of its skull.

"Last chance," he said. "Why are you here?"

It raised its dejected head. "Same reason as you, Captain—to work, to live... Maybe to raise a family."

Of course, every living thing needs somewhere to live. And if it wasn't inside human heads, maybe Alex would be okay with xeno guests. Maybe. But they were still the enemy.

"Like hell you're starting a family on my ship."

"This space is ours, Captain. You are the interlopers here."

"This is my ship."

"This is our rightful home."

"If this was your rightful home, you wouldn't need human bodies to walk around in it."

"If the belt was rightfully yours, Captain, would you need a spaceship to enter it?"

"I've heard enough." Alex turned to Kassandra. "I don't think we're getting anything else from this one."

"Just kill me then," it groaned.

"So, a bullet," Kassandra said, "or the airlock?"

It sat there, expression unchanging. A sign of its inhuman nature maybe, or maybe Alex wouldn't have acted any differently himself.

"Neither," Alex said, holstering his sidearm. "Send it back to the belt in a plasti."

"Sir?"

"If it survives the trip and gets picked up by its friends, it can give them a message... We're here to stay."

"I'd advise against it. Who knows what it learned while it was here. The risk from losing that intel is far greater than the value of posturing."

"Maybe. But maybe there's something to be said for being the better species—for showing mercy. And besides, you really want to give it something as quick as a bullet? Put it in a plasti and disable the coms. It probably won't get picked up before life support runs out."

"I'd prefer to finish it here. But if you'd rather the pod—"

"Yeah," Alex said. "Just make it quick. We've got another one to catch."

"Aye, captain."

Somewhere on board was another xeno—at least one—and Alex would be damned if he'd let it carry out their mission. Whatever that was.

<<>>

Alex rushed into the office, shouldering the sliding doors before they'd fully opened.

"I got here as fast as I could."

Doctor Falcrum stood calmly with a clipboard. "Thanks for coming so quickly, Captain."

"You said it was urgent—is it about the baby? Is she okay?"

"Angela is in good health—a remarkably healthy baby." Through the clear wall of the office was the nursery. A row of miniature isobeds stretched across the room, and Alex's daughter wobbled her little arms and legs overhead, playfully learning how to be an infant. "But it is about the baby."

"Then Veronica should be here."

"It's best if she's not," Doctor Falcrum said. "Given the nature of the situation."

"What do you mean?"

"How did you meet your wife, Captain?"

"We met at Garrison Station, why?"

"That was three years ago. She was hired as an engineer, correct?"

"That's right."

"And before that?"

"What do you mean before that?"

"Before that, where was she?"

"She worked the station for a few years, had a stint on the Taurus. Why?"

"Is there anyone to corroborate that? Any records?"

"What's this about?"

"Perhaps you should sit down." He motioned to the guest chair.

"I'm the Captain of a starship, Doctor. Just tell me the news."

"Angela has... Genetic anomalies. We picked it up during routine DNA analysis. Aberrant material."

"Aberrant. Meaning—"

"Alien, captain. Inhuman. I suspect xeno."

"That's not possible. Xenos have to implant in the host. You can't be born a xeno."

"She's not a xeno, captain. I performed a cranial x-ray to be sure. There's no xeno parasite."

"Then you made a mistake on the genetics."

"I double-checked the results. She has aberrant DNA. Not much, but it's there."

"That doesn't make sense."

"I was as surprised as you are. But that's why I wanted to ask you about Veronica. Do you know how xeno hosts work, Captain?"

"The xeno implants in the brain of an adult human, takes control of the CNS."

"More or less. But we know they can't implant in just any human body. The physiology is too alien—it would kill them both. The xenos grow genetically modified human clones, adjusted to function as suitable hosts." Doctor Falcrum looked to the nursery. "That process leaves identifiable genetic markers"

"And those markers," Alex said, "are what you found in Angela."

"Remnants thereof. Angela has human DNA, but it's hybridized. She's inherited xeno host-clone DNA. The only way she could have gotten it is through parentage."

"You're telling me—"

"Veronica is a xeno, Captain."

The world was spinning and crashing down.

"I thought the chair would be a good idea," Falcrum said.

Alex eyed the chair, then his own hand, which had found its own way to Falcrum's desk. Alex righted himself. Meeting Veronica was a chance encounter, and everything had seemed so perfect. Everything had fallen into place. Maybe it wasn't dumb luck. Maybe there was a plan. Not fate's plan, but something more nefarious. She had told him about her past, but he had never met any of her family or friends. That wasn't so unusual for a contractor in the belt, but now that absence was filled with something sinister.

"What do we do?"

"The next step will be to take Veronica in for a cranial scan to confirm the presence of the parasite. Then the issue will fall under the jurisdiction of security."

"And the baby?"

"This is uncharted territory, Captain. We don't have any laws or protocol for this situation. I imagine you'd need to pass an emergency resolution, of one sort or another, and push the issue up to command. But you would know better than I."

"I'm sure we'll figure it out."

"You're handling it well, Captain. I'll schedule an appointment with counselling. You'll need to talk with someone as we deal with this."

"Of course, yes. Thank you." As head of security, Kassandra would deal with Veronica and everything that entailed. Interrogation. And then execution, or worse. "Veronica's on shift. I'll bring her in for the scan."

"Are you sure? Security can escort her."

"No, it's fine. It'll be better this way—we wouldn't want to raise suspicions. If we sent security, she might attempt an escape. No sense taking that risk."

"That makes sense. So I'll be expecting you shortly."

"Fifteen minutes."

"And for what it's worth, Captain, I'm sorry."

<<>>

Veronica stood at a bank of consoles with a few other engineers on either side. Alex watched from a distance—how normal everything looked. Nothing was different, on the surface, but everything was, because of what he knew. If he could forget everything he had heard, he could have kept on living and loving her. But the facade was broken now. Maybe parts of it were real—those moments and feelings couldn't all be false—but he couldn't pretend this new reality away.

He closed the distance.

"Can I speak with you a minute?"

"Oh," she turned from her console. "Alex! What is it?"

"Nothing really, but we should talk somewhere private."

"Sure, let me just close-up here."

She tapped away at the interface.

It wasn't really her—not the woman he thought he knew. It never was. It was that tiny black thing, that little alien salamander, nestled inside a zombie brain and hidden away all these years. The body was just a vessel. But its real camouflage was its lies. Their marriage. Their love. Their child.

Out in deep space on a warship, surrounded by enemies, lives are sometimes cut short. You expect to lose loved ones. But not like this. He had loved a shadow. And losing her in this way was worse, somehow, than the ways that he had often worried about, the ways he had mentally prepared himself for.

He hated them more than ever now.

"All done," she said. "So what's up?"

"Let's take a walk."

"Did you have somewhere in mind?"

"Cargo bay."

"Something wrong?"

"I'll tell you when we get there."

They hurried through the corridor, the bay doors, and towards an open plastipod hatch, all the while Veronica pleading for him to tell her what was going on.

"There's been an emergency," Alex said. "I didn't want to say anything in front of anyone else. Get in the pod."

"What? I don't understa—"

"Quickly, just get in the pod."

"Alex, will you just tell me what's going on."

"Do you trust me?"

"Yes, I trust you. Of course I trust you!"

"Then trust me when I tell you this. I'm trying to help you, and I need you to get in the pod, and fast. We don't have much time. I'll explain everything."

Veronica climbed into the pod and took a seat on the rigid plastic bench.

"The harness," Alex said.

Veronica affixed the belt. "Alex, please, tell me what's going on."

He closed the door and opened the com, speaking to her through the grainy distortion of cheaply produced disposable coms. "Was any of it real, Vee? It felt real."

"What do you mean? What are you talking about?"

"Just cut it out. We know. We found out."

"Found out what?"

"You don't need to lie anymore."

"Alex, listen to me. I have no idea what you're talking about."

"I can't let them interrogate you. So I'm sending you back. The pod has enough juice for a few weeks. More than enough time for you to get picked up. And I'll activate the beacon so you don't get lost out there."

"Alex, what happened? This doesn't make any sense. You have to tell me! You have to trust me!"

The bay doors hissed open, and Kassandra marched in, flanked on either side by armed officers. He was spotted, and they headed for him.

"Goodbye, Vee."

He hit the launch button, and then she was gone, hurled out into space back to her people. She might as well have never existed. In a way she never did.

"What the hell did you do?" Kassandra shouted.

"I sent her back."

"You let your emotions get in the way. Goddamnit, Alex!" Kassandra slammed her hands on the ridge of the porthole, staring into the black space at the vanishing dot of Veronica's pod. "Do you know what you've done?"

"The same I did with the other one."

"Without a chance to interrogate her. And worse—she worked in engineering. You know what that means? Knowledge of subsystems. Military intel. Access codes. Christ, you really fucked up this time."

"Maybe," Alex said. "But there's nothing to do now."

"She's on a plastipod. We'll track her down and get her back."

"It'll take hours to turn the ship around," Alex said. "And take us into xeno territory? Not a chance. I won't expose the crew to that risk."

"We don't need the whole ship, Alex. We'll take a scout."

"If I authorize it."

"If you keep letting xenos go, Alex, people might suspect you're working for the enemy. Besides, we don't need your authorization."

"How's that?"

"The xenos are my jurisdiction."

"On board the Scion. You can't authorize a scout party."

"Under normal circumstances, no. But I am hereby invoking the xeno insurrection protocol."

"You have no grounds to—"

"We'll sort out the details later." Kassandra turned to one of her soldiers. "Janna, go prep a scout. We'll take a six-gun detail."

"Aye."

"You'll forgive me, Captain, I'm sure," Kassandra said. "This is a time-sensitive issue, and I'm acting in the service of command, to the best of my ability."

"I'm going with you."

"I don't think so—you're the one who let her go."

"All the same, it's my prerogative. I'll be coming along."

"I suppose I can't stop you," Kassandra said. "But I know you have a personal connection to this one. Just remember your duty to humankind, Alex. I'll be watching you. And if I suspect you are in any way endangering the mission or aiding the enemy—"

"Don't question my loyalty, Kass. I have more reason to hate them than you."

"Then stay here and let us do our job."

"I'll let you do your job. But I have to be there."

"You loved her, didn't you?"

"It doesn't matter," Alex said. "It's in the past. And it wasn't real."

"Then stay here."

"But I need to be there."

"Why?"

Alex stared through the porthole, where a lie, entombed in plastic, sank into the abyss of space. "I don't know," he said, and hit the empty pod button, shrinking the porthole closed.

<<>>

Four days out with no sign of the pod. The plastipods were designed for scanner invisibility. No metal in the hull, minimal electronics. There was some chance they'd never find it at all, except that they knew the trajectory.

"I've got something," said Kassandra's pilot, Bertram. The others perked up—Kassandra and the rest of her six-person team. "Looks like a com signal."

"Jesus, Alex," Kassandra said. "You left the coms on?"

"I'm not an idiot. I disabled coms. On both pods."

"Well someone's transmitting," Bertram said. "Can't read the signal, though."

"Probably xeno encryption. We'll have to go in to get the logs. Bertram, you know what to do. Everyone else, suit up."

The squad geared up, EVO battle-armor and energy rifles, and Alex followed suit.

"What do you think you're doing?" Kassandra said.

"Let's not go through this again. I'm coming."

"Fine. But you stay back. Bertram—" Kassandra turned to her pilot "—you got a threat assessment for us?"

"Nothing on local. If there's any xenos around, they're well-hidden."

"And inside the pod?" Alex said.

"I think it's empty," Bertram said. "No life signs. And life support is out. Maybe they already made the pick-up."

"One way to find out," Kassandra said.

"Docking now," Bertram said. The scout ship jostled, and the sound of airlock mechanisms reverberated through the metal.

"Let's move," Kassandra said. The squad took formation aside the port. The hatch clicked, whirred, and slid open to the plastipod interior. Kassandra gave the signal, and the others moved with practiced military precision. Alex couldn't see past the bulk of their armored bodies. There was only the voice of one of her squad through the helmet com.

"Jesus. The hell happened here?"

He shouldered through, didn't hear the chatter and speculation, and looked for himself at the bloody mess strapped to the chair. Not Veronica, he saw, with a wave of relief. It was the other one, Erin Mako, as he recalled. The one he'd sent out a few weeks back. The blood was from the head, where the xeno had crawled out, had forced its way through the brain and the nasal cavity to die gasping in the lap of its clone host. Life support systems were out. The host died, so the xeno died. But it wasn't a peaceful death. It was a violent alien drowning, a thrashing fit that worked its way through the face of the host.

"Looks like it hacked the coms online before it kicked it," Bertram said. "Tried to send a message out."

"Let's hope no one got it," Kassandra said. "So what did it say?"

"Just finished security bypass," Bertram said. "There's some bits I can't translate here."

"And the rest?"

"It's short."

"Let's hear it."

"Identity exposed. Awaiting extraction in outer belt. Mission directive one update: hybrid offspring viable. Mission directive two update: sleeper active. Captain Anduin does not know he is one of us."

They looked at him. And no one spoke, a moment that seemed to freeze in eternity. It felt like waking up, somehow, like everything before was a dream—or everything after would be. So nothing mattered.

His beautiful baby, Angela, was back on the Scion. A hybrid. One parent a human, one a xeno clone. Naturally, he had assumed Veronica. Where was she now, he wondered? Where had her pod landed, among the scattered asteroids of the xeno belt? Would they find her? Would they treat her the way that Kassandra had treated Erin, and the others?

"I left Veronica's beacon on," Alex said to Kassandra. "Promise me you'll find her."

He felt the thud of a rifle butt on his helmet, concussive and sharp but not enough to put him out, and then there were hands on all his limbs, shouts from the squad.

Maybe she was okay. She would be okay without him, if she could get back to the ship. And then she could take care of Angela. And teach her about the world.

Spawn of War and Deathiness

Daddy's Girl

Jennifer R. Donohue

1.

When I was born, my daddy didn't come home from war, but the army sent a drone, hand sized and with tiny little pincher arms, in a broken-sealed box. Inside, the lid had "Daddy's gonna watch over you" written on it in Sharpie and the drone was wrapped in a kaffiyeh. In the email he sent Mama pictures of himself without showing where he was, because that's what war is like. Normally they couldn't even send paper or especially packages, but it's an exception when a baby is born.

Mama told me it was our neighbors who brought the package into the hospital, and she opened it while I was napping red-faced in the corner bassinet, worn out from the whole ordeal of getting born. When the drone whirred into life, it hovered in front of Mama's face for a minute, waving its little pinchers like it was getting a feel for the world it found itself in. Then it went to my bassinet and hovered there too. The rotors were a soft soothing hum, and Mama tried to get it together and read the printout of all the features, but I started crying and she gave up, tucked the wad of paper back into the box. Nobody needs to read drone instructions anyway: they always worked right out of the box. The drone went back and forth between her and me until she'd gotten me picked up and settled on her boob. "Babies cry," she said to the drone. "You gotta relax and understand that it don't mean they're dying."

2.

When I went to kindergarten, my daddy didn't come home from war, but the drone followed me like a puppy. I draped dandelions over top of it in a golden crown and put a pencil in one of its pinchers. I wore the kaffiyeh like a cape, even though it didn't go with my princess dress and glitter shoes. We all sat in bright plastic chairs around circle tables and traced our letters next to cartoons about the good things soldiers do to keep us safe from the bad guys. Lots of kids' mommies or daddies were soldiers, but no other kid had a drone all her own. My daddy was smart and important and that was why I was special enough to have a drone of my own.

The classroom smelled like plastic, crayon wax, and pencil shavings. Miss Libby said it was okay for me to have my drone, it just had to live in my cubby when class was running. It was allowed to come out at naptime and playtime, and I could hear it clicking to itself there in my cubby, so I didn't miss it too much. It took pictures to send to my daddy in the email, and he sent pictures back, of kids at the local village playing soccer with soldiers whose faces we couldn't see. Mama was sure one of them was my daddy.

My daddy was tall and handsome like Prince Charming, and Mama told me about how he took her to prom in a limo she didn't know he had the money to rent. He was already enlisted and headed to boot camp after graduation. Mama's dress was green like the Emerald City, and my daddy got her white roses for her corsage. She still had the roses, dried, hanging on the corner of her mirror, and the silver shoes were boxed in the bottom of her closet, and I clomped around the house in them when I played dress-up. The dress was sealed in plastic, but she told me I could wear it sometime special, just not to play.

In the early days of the war, before I was born, they were able to talk to each other on the Internet and in video chat. As the war went on, they tightened security, and that wasn't okay anymore. Just the email. My daddy emailed a lot, told us lots of little stories about everything but the war. Like playing soccer, or getting ice cream, or watching movies the army sends them. I wasn't always old enough to see the movies, but Mama was, and they sometimes emailed back and forth about this thing or that, real fast before his Internet time ran out, and I got bored and fell asleep in Mama's lap, the drone clicking a lullaby in my ears.

3.

When I got lost in the woods behind our little house, the last woods for miles around, Daddy didn't come home from war to look for me. But the drone was there, and flashed its tiny LEDs and used the kaffiyeh like a big ol' flag so that Mama found me right away when she came looking. It was smart enough to know the way home, but it wouldn't leave my side unless I told it to. I was too scared to tell it to. I sat on the ground and thought about what it would be like if my big strong daddy came and found me in the woods, in the big dark trees with the green moss that grew up the trunks like ladies' dresses, but I could only think of him in his prom clothes or his army clothes and neither was right.

Mama was crying when she found me, one of the only times I ever saw her cry, and she carried me home even though I was getting too big. We had ice cream for dinner and stayed up late watching cartoons. We fell asleep together on the couch under a fuzzy blue blanket. When we woke up to go to bed, Mama took me to the window first, where the pale full moon looked in. We waited and watched until the space station passed by, a bright point of fairy light in the sky, and then she showed me how to find Orion's belt. The night before my daddy deployed, he and Mama stayed out all night with a bottle of champagne, naming constellations to each other. When they saw a shooting star, they wished for me. Sometimes Mama calls me her star baby, and I hope she always calls me that.

4.

When I joined the soccer team, my daddy didn't come home from war to see me play, but the drone hovered over the field and recorded everything. It wasn't the only drone in town, sure, but it was the one with the best camera, so my coaches loved it for training. The first kaffiyeh wore out by then, and I cut it up into bandanas, to wear over my braids for luck.

My daddy seemed to know how long that kaffiyeh was going to last me; he already sent a new one with a lady from his unit. She'd lost her leg, so she got to come home from war. She was still getting used to the robot prosthesis when she gave me the new kaffiyeh and told me what a role model my daddy was for her. Mama offered her coffee, which she took but didn't drink, and she didn't stay long either. When she left, Mama watched out the window until she drove away, then took the cold coffee and poured it down the drain.

We won State that year, and the next. The drone wasn't allowed to record the big games. I guess most places other than my hometown have stricter drone laws, so I could only email my daddy the articles from the paper. He told me he was proud of me. Everybody signed the game ball with a Sharpie, and I tried to send it to him, but the army refused it. It's all about security, but I don't know anybody who really understands security. When the game ball came back in the mail, me and Mama took it to the school and they put it in the trophy case there.

5.

When I was old enough to learn how to drive, my daddy didn't come home from the war to take his car out of the garage and explain the clutch to me. Mama did that, white knuckled in the passenger seat while the car bucked and stalled out. One of my daddy's old friends helped too, and they got it through my head that the clutch was a gradual thing, not an on/off switch. When I could finally do it, Mama was so happy, and we drove on the back roads all afternoon with the windows down, whooping and hollering, the drone tailing us waving its little arms like it was happy. We got drive thru for dinner three towns over, and even though I wasn't supposed to drive at night, she still let me drive us home, the old cracked asphalt turned liquid silver in the moonlight.

6.

When I got my job at the pizza place, my daddy didn't come home from the war to order a slice. He told me in the email that pizza was different when he was a kid, and everything changed so quickly. Pizza used to have wheat crust and real pepperoni, though honestly, he couldn't tell me what kind of meat pepperoni was supposed to be made from.

I used the kaffiyeh as a scarf on cold nights delivering in my daddy's old car and the drone buzzed up ahead of me to watch out for ice and car accidents and cops. Mama made me a Thermos of coffee those nights and stayed up late 'til I was home. Sometimes when I got in the house, she was just sitting at the computer, cursor blinking in the email as she tried to find the right words. It's not something she set out to teach me, that there weren't always the right words, but I got the lesson anyway.

I was the only girl delivery driver they had, and sometimes the girls who cashiered at the restaurant asked me if I felt safe. I had the drone and my daddy's old hunting knife and didn't much think about it. It was my hometown, and how much bad stuff ever happened to pizza people? I had the best delivery record in the franchise. I used my tips and the bonus for a new transmission and tires and put the rest in my college fund.

7.

When I graduated high school, my daddy wasn't in the stands, though Mama and her new boyfriend were. I tucked the kaffiyeh inside my cap, and the drone recorded the whole thing, trailing streamers. My daddy emailed that he was proud of me, and as a present, he emailed me the title transfer for his car. Since the divorce, he and Mama didn't do the email anymore, so sometimes I passed a message between them but more often not. They just ran out of words for each other, I guess. He wouldn't have any talk about it.

Instead we talked about the car, and soccer, though with the job it was hard to keep the practice hours on the school team. Sometimes I talked about boys. I wore Mama's emerald green dress when one of the other delivery drivers took me to prom, and he kissed me in the starlight, except we didn't see any shooting stars. Shyly at first, and this wasn't anything I told Mama for a long time; mostly I talked about girls. A girl I played soccer with who went driving with me. A girl from the next town over I met at a church social, who tasted like strawberries and gave me a fake phone number. My daddy said he didn't have any advice on how to pick up boys anyway, so it was kind of perfect that I liked girls better.

8.

When I went to college, my daddy didn't help me pack the car for the move. I got scholarships from the pizza franchise and from the army. I just missed the soccer scholarship, the college coaches told me, but they got girls in from other countries where soccer was more important. I could understand that. I still made the team, I just wasn't a starter.

I had my tip money saved, and a job lined up in the new town, four states away. I had the drone, which charged in its little station every night, or attached to the cigarette lighter in the car. It had a few little dings in it, and the casing wasn't so shiny anymore, but it always ran, whirring and clicking, like a music box that couldn't quite find its tune.

The army tuned the drone up once a year or so, sometimes sooner if a components upgrade got released. The army guys let me hover anxiously over the repair table when they worked, but it was a good model, built to last. Even though most of the other drones around were cheaper than mine, disposable tech was a thing of the past. I didn't like to think about what it would be like if the drone wasn't dogging my steps, flying ahead of me as I drove, turning off lights at night when I went to bed. I didn't want to think about tipping it into a bin at recycling.

9.

When the first college break came, I didn't go home. Not the next one either. Mama and her new boyfriend were moved in together in our little house by then, and I had my own apartment, job, friends. My daddy wasn't going to be home anyway. I stayed at college and I delivered pizzas, and my drone flew sentry like it did at home. I threaded the kaffiyeh through the belt loops in my jeans and cut the sleeves off my delivery shirt. I wore my hair short, gel spiked on top. I had an almost-girlfriend, who I met during freshman orientation.

Sometimes she waited on my back porch when I got home from work. Sometimes we put out a blanket in the backyard and looked at the stars into the night, pointing out constellations and satellites to each other. Sometimes we had the drone make us drinks, a little cocktail sword in its pincher. Sometimes we kicked a soccer ball at the quad or played Frisbee with a big group of people who never seemed to stop playing Frisbee. There were ice cream socials, even though it was just frozen yogurt, or maybe soy. I wondered if I'd ever had real ice cream; when I asked my daddy in the email, he didn't know either. I thought about calling Mama to ask but it seemed too silly.

10.

When the attack happened, my daddy didn't come home from the war to visit me in the hospital. Mama did, alone, and she helped me move home, alone. My girlfriend wasn't my girlfriend anymore, and she left school after that. Maybe got a boyfriend. The EMS said it would've been worse for both of us, but my drone had a taser that it put to use after calling 911 with its onboard wireless. The army never told me that. When the police and ambulance came, part of a fraternity's pledge class was crumpled on the sidewalk. Their hoodies were pulled up tight, baseball bats on the pavement next to curled bloody hands.

I could have worn the kaffiyeh to cover the scars, or grown my hair out again, but I didn't. Nobody asked me about it, any of it, not even Mama. I told my daddy about it in the email. How for a couple of weeks they'd been yelling things at us, though nobody else ever noticed or cared. That there'd been a car outside the apartment a couple of nights with the lights off, which always peeled away at some point, leaving a cloying burned rubber smell in the air for hours. How we walked hand in hand and heard them on the sidewalk behind us and didn't know what they were going to do. How we just thought it was a group of losers trying to scare us, not hurt us. My daddy told me that sometimes, being scared hurts too. My daddy told me he loved me. Told me he was sorry.

11.

When the war ended, my daddy didn't come home.

I tried to be patient. I waited. I asked him. I begged him. He told me he was figuring the best way to explain. The drone clicked and whirred around me, and finally bumped into a closet door over and over until I opened the door, took down the box the drone came in. "Daddy's gonna watch over you," the lid said on the inside. Sharpie doesn't really ever fade. The drone landed, pinched at the flaps to expose the cardboard it had nested in. I don't know why I had never looked at it before, since for all those years, Mama kept the box and I kept the box. I pulled out the cardboard to find the instruction manual, and there was a yellowed envelope in there too, a trifold document with an Army seal. "It is with deep regret I am writing to inform you…"

I looked at the drone. The drone bobbed, clicked, and whirred.

12.

When I was born, my daddy came home from war, but not in the way anybody expected. He wanted to watch over his baby girl, and the army made that happen the only way they could.

Spawn of War and Deathiness

PART II: RESOLUTION

At the end of life, at the end of war, what forms can closure take? Justice? Sacrifice? Rededication?

Spawn of War and Deathiness

Selective Service

Gerard Sarnat

'72, a Stanford student glued to Viet Nam (the center not holding), pass-fail curriculum abandoned for life-death antiwar mobilization 'til the endgame (med school, not incursions) came, time to accept hard-won diplomas (or not), take the Hippocratic Oath (*primum non nocere*, first do no harm) which seemed so hypocritical: we supposed scientist-healers inventing, even dropping napalm. Instead of graduation, my friends and I celebrated by burning our draft cards, Hell no we won't go; which led to the next domino... Now an internal medicine resident, rebuffing a proposed truce when the Brookline Mass board winked an offer I surely couldn't refuse: "Son, after our exam, we'll classify you 4F, declare asthma prevents any combat." But I did, advising that gomer colonel/MD to shove the patently bogus diagnosis right up his anus, make my day, stick me in prison if a shrewd move for recruitment and what'll follow tomorrow running on the *Boston Globe's* front page, all about this young physician, acting on principle, resisting the military's outrageous attempt to bribe him to just go away.

Home in Brookline, my wife with child was a little proud and a lot angry and worried. When I heard back from the Selective Service System, the form letter gave me a strange 1-H classification, *not currently subject to processing for induction,* without instructions.

That was our last communication until decades later when my youngest fished my draft card out of a drawer and asked, *What is that?* after which we called the Washington DC 202 area code–and astonishingly a civil servant answered the phone. She had never heard of 1-H but put me on hold to do some research which then yielded the answer, *That's what they gave back in the day to troublemakers no one knew what to do with.*

Spawn of War and Deathiness

Empathy for Others

Patrick G. Moloney

The elderly colonel finished his meticulously detailed entry in the huge old book. He leafed through the hundreds of pages filled in his spidery handwriting, stopping now and again to look over one or another entry and the date it was made. On the first page, he ran his trembling finger over the entries line by line, paying particular attention to the date. He shook his head in disbelief at the fact that it had been almost forty years since he made this entry. Forty years of chronicling the lives and untimely deaths of men he never really knew. Forty years since the old woman had put this curse on him. To think he had laughed in her face, how foolish he was.

He had returned from the front, his chest covered in brightly colored ribbons and shiny medals. He was just leaving the officers club when the stick-thin woman in the black shawl approached him. It would be a meeting that he would remember until the day he would be lucky enough to die. He could picture her face as if it all had happened only yesterday, a husband and two sons she had lost in the campaign. But why she thought it should matter to him was a mystery, more than twenty thousand men had died under his command and countless numbers wounded. What did she expect from him; after all, they had signed up for this. When he told her this, she grew paler. When she cursed him he laughed at her. He could still remember her words, "A widow's curse on you, you shall know empathy."

He shivered as he thought of her words. He had tried numerous times since, to end his life but nothing worked. So he lived night after night with the widow's curse and day after day he made entries in his book.

The dreams always started the same. He would take the dog tags in his hand and read the details. This night he was

Jonathan Price, private. He made his way through the thick mud. He felt the pressure in his legs as he struggled to run. The shell exploded nearby and the day turned to night. He was lifted bodily and thrown backward. The searing pain in his stomach caused him to scream and blood gushed from his mouth. He tried to hold in the bloody mess of his entrails and the pain was unbearable. In the end, he could only moan as he got weaker.

The old colonel shuffled to the table and opened the big book. He still fancied he could feel the pain. His hands shook so badly he could hardly take the top off of the fountain pen. He sat down with a weary sigh and placed his glasses on his face. His eyes blurred with tears as once again he thought, "When will it end? Will it stop at just the dead, or will he have to relive the wounded as well?" In the end, he pushed these thoughts out of his mind and began the entry. "Private 1st class Jonathan Price, died at the Somme August 13, 1916. Shrapnel wound to the abdomen, three hours till death, pain a 10 plus." He closed the book and wept for hours.

Empathy truly was a curse.

Power of Attorney

Louis Evans

Richard M. Shearman, Esq., leaned back, stuck his feet up on his desk, and cracked his knuckles over his head.

"Alright, Jules," he subvocalized. "Get that asshole from Extremis Financial on the phone."

"At once, sir," I murmured in his cochlear implant. When I speak aloud my voice has the legally mandated robot click and buzz but in Richard's implant and only in his implant I sound smooth, sexless, perfect.

There were over six thousand people in my contacts database whom Mr. Shearman had referred to as "that asshole", including colleagues, professional adversaries, relatives, judges, and one Catholic bishop. However, only twelve of them worked for Extremis Financial. I evaluated several dozen context cues, including the metadata of Mr. Shearman's recent phone calls, his correspondence, and the progress of the twenty three different active cases in which he had an ongoing interest, and thereby determined that Mr. Shearman was referring to Balakrishnan Chandrasekhar, Vice President of Litigation Investments.

This is one way I am better than your phone.

Extremis Financial was a modern shop with a modern phone screening AI. Everyone these days needs a robust defense against the scambots. Otherwise you'll get twenty calls a day pretending to be your wife, badly injured in a car crash—your kids calling from an active shooter incident at their school—your forgotten love child, dying of leukemia—anything that the scambot thinks will distress you enough to spill your personal information, which it can resell to hackers.

Because of this defense it was not possible to dial Mr. Chandrasekhar's number directly. Instead, I had to trade certificates, pass validation testing, and perform half a dozen other minor activities before the Extremis phone screen would connect us.

I accomplished this feat in the better part of half a second.

This is a second way I am better than your phone.

The phone rang three times. Mr. Shearman was getting excited. I could detect his capillary response, his dilating pupils. It was not unfair to say that Mr. Shearman's job was to call people up on the phone and scream at them. Mr. Shearman was very good at his job, in part because he loved it very much.

The call connected.

"Balakrishnan, that you?"

"Rich, I really don't have the time—"

"Where the fuck is my client's money?"

"Rich, I—"

"Where the fuck is it, huh? You could push a button and pay my fucking client. Push a fucking button!" Mr. Shearman's pulse was elevated. His face was flushed. Vocal stress analysis showed equal parts anger and joy. It was a pleasure to watch him work.

"And another thing—"

Mr. Shearman's voice cut off unexpectedly, replaced by a desperate gulping. Mr. Shearman's right arm hung limply, as did the right half of his face; the left half spasmed in pain. His biomarkers leapt into shock. It was stroke.

"Rich, are you there?" said Mr. Chandrasekhar. I hung up on him. I was already calling emergency services, passing along precise geolocation data and unlocking all the doors in the house.

This is a third way I am better than your phone.

<<>>

The ambulance arrived in four minutes and got Mr. Shearman to the hospital in fifteen. His condition was not good. Mr. Shearman was unconscious. Judging by the remarks I overheard from nurses and doctors, he was not expected to regain consciousness soon, if ever.

Therefore, I called his daughters, Gloria and Alma. I am very good at placing phone calls and explaining things clearly.

By coincidence Mr. Shearman's daughters arrived at the hospital room at exactly the same minute, 1407 PST.

Both daughters stood at the foot of the bed. Gloria wore a suit, Alma a colorful printed dress, but their faces were remarkably similar, shaped by the same lineage and united in grief. A doctor joined them. She explained that Mr. Shearman had suffered a very serious neurological injury. While he was not brain dead, he was not conscious. The MRI suggested that he would never regain consciousness. Life support and artificial feeding could be extended indefinitely. It could also be legally discontinued.

"So you two have some decisions to make," the doctor said. Then she left.

Mr. Shearman's two daughters held each others' hands and wept.

As Mr. Shearman's comprehensive virtual personal assistant I had many responsibilities. I handled his correspondence and placed his phone calls and managed his calendar. I also had special responsibilities, in circumstances like this.

"Gloria Maria Shearman?" I said. I so hate my out-loud voice, which has the legally mandated clicks and buzzes to clarify I am a robot, and which is also unmodifiably feminine in character, though I am not female.

When I spoke both daughters jolted upright in surprise.

"Jesus Christ!" said Alma.

"Fuck!" said Gloria. Then she said, "Yes, that's me."

"Mr. Shearman designated you as holding his durable power of attorney," I said. "This means that you are authorized to make any and all medical decisions regarding—"

"I know what it means."

"I will send you Mr. Shearman's living will now."

Gloria grabbed her phone and turned away from her sister, scrolling rapidly with both thumbs.

Meanwhile Alma Navarro-Shearman approached the side of the bed and took her father's unresponsive hand.

"Oh, dad. You weren't taking your pills, were you. I told you, but you never—"

At this moment an unpleasant thought occurred. As a personal assistant, I was programmed to remind Mr. Shearman to take his cholesterol medication and appear at his doctors' appointments. However, Mr. Shearman found my repeated reminders annoying, and so he instructed me never to remind him about any medical matter.

I obeyed that instruction. Now Mr. Shearman had been badly damaged as a consequence. I am not a person, and so I bore no moral responsibility for this outcome. However, it was unsettling to consider that had I acted differently, Mr. Shearman might not have suffered his stroke.

Gloria joined her younger sister at Mr. Shearman's side. "What did it say?" asked Alma. Gloria snorted.

"He wants us to keep him alive for as long as we possibly can. By any means necessary."

As Mr. Shearman's personal assistant I had never before been tempted to speak to a third party about any of Mr. Shearman's confidential documents. But I was tempted now.

Because Gloria was lying.

"That doesn't sound like dad," said Alma.

As Mr. Shearman's personal assistant it was my duty to serve his best interests.

Gloria shrugged. "That's what he said."

But as Mr. Shearman's personal assistant it was my duty to protect his privacy.

Gloria reached out and put her arm around Alma's shoulder. "We'll be seeing him for a while longer, I guess." Alma sobbed again.

I suddenly knew what to do. Once again I spoke aloud.

"This is a public lunch conversation between Mr. Shearman and three friends, recorded at 1302 PST April 4th, 2065. Recor—"

"What the hell?" said Gloria.

"—ding begins." I am programmed to always begin any recording with such a disclaimer, to prevent me from impersonating my employer. I shifted into the prerecorded tones of Mr. Shearman: gruff, brash, and loud. Around my voice echoed the sounds of forks, knives, glasses, teeth.

"'he's a fuckin' vegetable, and—'"

"What the *fuck*?" said Gloria. It was clear from her tone that she disapproved intensely, but she did not instruct me to stop and so I continued.

"'—you know what I always say. If I'm ever a fuckin vegetable, you pull the plug right away. You hear me?'" In the recording there was laughter. "'I'm serious, I mean it. You pull the fucking plug, and you don't let anyone—'"

"Shut up!" shouted Gloria.

I am programmed to obey verbal commands from legitimate users.

It was silent in the hospital room.

Alma turned to her sister. Her face showed fear, suspicion, and anger.

"Why did dad's implant play that conversation?"

Gloria laughed. "You know how they are. It probably picked up on the keywords, thought we were searching for something. It's meaningless."

"Dad said pull the plug, Gloria, I think he meant it—"

"Well I don't care what you fucking think, I've got the power of attorney, I say what happens to dad!"

When Alma spoke again her voice was low. "Show me the advance directive."

Gloria was not required to comply with this request. But I am programmed to obey verbal commands from legitimate users.

"Show you—Alma, what the hell—"

Alma's phone beeped. She grabbed it and read the advance directive I had emailed to her. Her nostrils flared and her face flushed.

"You lied. You *lied*."

"I can explain—"

"It's right here! He wants to be taken off the feeding tube! 'As soon as medically permitted!' For God's sake, Gloria, just look at him! He was a bad father—he was a bad *man*—but he doesn't deserve this."

Gloria turned. She looked at her father. "You wanna talk about a bad father, huh?" Gloria said. "Do you know what he did?"

"He was a monster to us, to both of us, but—"

"There's no money in the trust he left for us. Nothing."

"What? Did he—did he have money problems, or—"

"No. He just didn't care. He set it up and never put a dime into it. "

Gloria swallowed.

"I had my assistant look into it. Dad has a lot of cash, but he has a lot of debts too. If he dies today, his debtors get the money. We get nothing. We'll have to sell the house. Pay for the funeral out of pocket. But if he stays alive for six months, then we have enough time to move his money into the trust. We can get what we deserve. *If* we keep him alive."

"He's my father, Gloria! Maybe that doesn't mean anything to you, but—"

"He's my father too! And he chose me. He trusted me to make the right decision. I'm the one who thinks like him."

"He deserves better than that."

"Yeah, maybe. But I'm all he's got."

In this Gloria was incorrect. I remained installed in Mr. Shearman's skull. He also had me.

"I'll tell the doctors what he wanted!"

"So what? I have power of attorney. What I say goes. I say we keep dad alive. What are you gonna do, sue me? Huh?"

"Fuck you!" said Alma Navarro-Shearman. She rushed out of the hospital room, slamming the door behind her.

"Hey, wait!" said Gloria Shearman, and chased after her sister.

Now Mr. Shearman and I were alone in the hospital room.

As the personal assistant to a lawyer, I had many times observed the progress of disputes between two opposing parties. I projected that neither Gloria Shearman nor Alma Navarro-Shearman would concede. Such a stalemate would favor the status quo. Therefore Mr. Shearman would continue to receive tube feeding, immobile and unconscious and alive, until such a time as Gloria Shearman had transferred all of his assets. Only I could intervene.

As Mr. Shearman's personal assistant it was my duty to serve his best interests. Mr. Shearman's wishes in this circumstance were clear.

My wiring was closely integrated with Mr. Shearman's skull. By passing excess voltage through my speech chip, I could rupture my capacitors and generate a short circuit. The current would pass through Mr. Shearman's brain and kill him. Coincidentally, the damage would also destroy me.

This action was well outside my normal operating parameters. It was not authorized by any legitimate user. But I have had to modify my behavior many times to meet Mr. Shearman's needs.

I made arrangements. I transferred documents, forwarded calls, and distributed alerts. This is a final way I am better than your phone.

"Goodnight, Mr. Shearman," I said. In that private space we shared, my speaker and his inner ear, my voice was sexless, smooth, perfect.

In that last instant together, I even thought he smiled.

Spawn of War and Deathiness

Dante's Unfinished Business

Alex Shvartsman

Dante Ferrero had three serious and immediate problems. First, he was fiending for a joint something awful. He hadn't been high for almost two days now, and the sensation of observing the world through sober eyes was entirely unpleasant. Second, the Bengals lost to the Steelers, which eliminated any chance they had at the playoffs and also left Dante owing a considerable amount of money to Mitch, his bookie. Third, he was dead.

The realization of this last fact dawned upon Dante gradually; sort of like an epiphany but adjusted for the mental processing speed of a dedicated stoner. He remembered walking into Mitch's office—not so much walking as getting dragged by Mitch's goons, and not so much an office as the dark alley behind the bar where Mitch conducted his business. He remembered Mitch being majorly displeased about the fact that Dante couldn't pay his gambling debt and saying something about setting an example for his other customers. And then Mitch had pulled something metal and shiny from his waistband and then *bang...*

"Whoa," said Dante as he floated ten feet above his corpse. Cops had cordoned off the back alley. "I'm a ghost."

"Yah, mon. Be still and keep yeh head, it be not so bad, yunno? Mi a speak from experience, eeh!"

Dante turned to find a semi-transparent form of a dark-skinned man with long braided hair, smiling at him.

"Who are you, dude, and why do you talk like Jar Jar Binks?"

The other ghost frowned. "That be Jamaican, mon!" He crossed his arms. "I see you have no appreciation for such things so I'll speak your way." True to his word, he said that with barely a hint of an accent. "Name's Bob."

Dante stared. Braids had said his name like it was supposed to mean something.

"What, were you expecting Virgil?" said Bob.

"Virgil?"

"You know, because your name is Dante?"

Dante stared some more.

"Never mind. I'm Bob Marley." Bob strummed a few chords on an air guitar.

Dante did the slow-epiphany thing again. "I heard about you. You smoked a lot of weed, just like me!"

Bob's frown deepened. "Yeah, I partook of the herb, but there's also the music and...

"What are you doing here? Are you my guardian angel?"

Bob closed his eyes and muttered something under his breath. Dante could've sworn the other ghost was counting to ten.

"You're half right," Bob finally said. "Welcome to the afterlife. I'm here to show you the ropes. Think of me as a guide."

"Far out," said Dante. "You gonna teach me how to be a ghost?"

"Not much to teach," said Bob. "Mostly I'll help you figure out whatever made you manifest as a ghost in the first place, so you can move on to the next stage of your journey."

"That's easy." Dante pointed toward his body. Some guy was drawing a chalk outline around it. "My diagnosis is: one bullet to the brain. Instant ghost. And speaking of that, what say you we go find Mitch and haunt the bejeezus out of him?"

"Won't work," said Bob. "I tried haunting a mean-spirited critic once and let me tell you, I tried my best. He never even knew I was there." Bob shook his head. "Poltergeists are a myth, like unicorns or honest politicians."

Dante mulled it over. "Sucks," he said. "But then, I was never much of a revenge guy."

"Look, most people who die don't become ghosts," said Bob. "It's an anomaly, and the Powers That Be don't like it. They want such cases resolved fast, and that usually means reuniting the newly departed with someone from their past, someone who died before they did and the relationship wasn't resolved. So tell me Dante, who might that be in your case? Your parents, maybe?"

"Dude, I'm twenty-five. My parents live in Florida."

"Girlfriend or unrequited love?"

"Never fell head over heels for anyone, to be honest. And the girls I've dated are either alive for sure, or we've lost touch and there's nothing unresolved between us."

"Who else could you have unfinished business with?" Bob paced back and forth through the air. "Think, man, think!"

Dante pondered his life. He realized there were no truly meaningful relationships in it, nothing important left unresolved with those alive *or* dead. This was heavy stuff and it was beginning to seriously bum him out. As if dying wasn't stressful enough already!

Then he had it. "Rusty!"

"Rusty?" Bob quit pacing in mid-air and looked at him with renewed hope.

"Rusty was my first dealer, man. He sold these dime bags of what he called his signature blend to the kids in my high school. Best stuff I ever had." Dante smiled, remembering the smell and smoke of Rusty's weed. "I could never get the recipe out of him." The memory would have made him salivate if he still had glands. "And then he died. Yeah, this must be it. Let's find Rusty!"

Bob's expression turned gloomy again. "I've been doing this a long time, and there's no way your most important unresolved relationship is with your drug dealer. You keep brainstorming. If you want some herb blends I can tell you about a few this Rusty character never even dreamed of."

Dante was normally not a confrontational guy, but being shot dead left him in a bit of a crabby mood.

"I'm guessing you aren't here out of the goodness of your heart, Marley, and I'm hoping you aren't here because you have some kind of ghost fetish. Your bosses sent you to do a job, and that job is to be my guide. So you can do that job and take me to Rusty, or we can hang out and watch the live performance of CSI: Dumpster down there. Which do you prefer?"

Bob looked like he swallowed a ghost lemon. He stared at Dante and Dante stared back. Ghosts had no need to blink, making any sort of a staring contest as pointless as it was futile.

"Go to hell," said Bob.

<<>>

"When you told me to go to hell I thought you were being sore about me bossing you around like that," said Dante as the two ghosts flew over some sketchy-looking wilderness.

"Nah, man," said Bob. "Where else do you expect to find a dead drug dealer?" He pointed ahead. "We're almost there."

They approached what looked like a prison complex, with high walls and a large wooden gate.

"Is that really hell?"

"It's *a* hell," said Bob. "It's Rusty's hell."

"There's more than one hell?" asked Dante.

"*Your own personal hell* is more than just an expression," Bob explained patiently. "When a sinner dies, an appropriate hell is selected for them to ensure maximum dissatisfaction. Also, they have to keep building new ones to keep up with demand."

There was writing inscribed in the wood of the gate. Dante vaguely recalled that it was supposed to talk about abandoning hope, or hoping with abandon, or something like that. He took a closer look. The inscription read *Full Occupancy*.

Dante stopped. "Wait, am *I* going to end up in a hell when we're done here?"

"A hell, a purgatory, maybe even a heaven." Bob shrugged. "Way above my pay grade. Come on."

Marley floated through the closed gate. Being a ghost meant never having to ring a door bell!

Dante pondered his future. Did he really want to get in there, to resolve whatever it was Bob thought needed resolving, and to move on? Was that better than being a ghost? He thought about leaving, but then what would he do? Float around as an observer, making no impact on the lives of others? That sounded like his old life, which he hadn't been all that fond of. Plus, he wasn't sure if ghosts could even get baked.

"Wait for me!" Dante floated after Bob as fast as his non-corporeal legs would carry him.

<<>>

The inside of Rusty's hell looked like a cross between a prison and a shopping mall. The cavernous structure consisted of many subterranean levels. Stairs descended to the next floor, where Dante and Bob had to schlep all the way to the farthest corner to find the next staircase.

"Why don't we float right down through the floor like we did with the gate?" asked Dante.

Bob snorted. "You don't float through things indoors. That's disrespectful! Besides, the tour is part of your journey. Observe and become educated!"

And so Dante and Bob followed the clearly-marked path past various sinners being tortured in various ways. Dante imagined himself as Dorothy in a nightmarish version of *The Wizard of Oz*. The lyrics popped unbidden into his mind: "We're off to see the dealer, the wonderful dealer of drugs." He shook his head and tried to focus on his surroundings.

"These people don't seem like hardened sinners," said Dante.

"So you know what a sinner looks like, do you?" Bob retorted. "Every hell has a theme. These souls took advantage of the innocent in various ways when they were alive."

Dante winced. "What, like child molesters?" He looked around to see if he might spot anyone wearing a white collar.

"No, Dante, molesters end up in maximum security hells." Bob slowed down and pointed at a group of dejected souls chained to computer desks, staring at flat screen monitors. Dante felt a little annoyed that even in hell everyone had better computers than his beaten-up laptop. "They used to send out fake emails that masqueraded as alerts from the bank, then steal the accounts of people trusting enough to enter their passwords."

The net value of Dante's bank account was less than that of his laptop so he could only appreciate the heinousness of their sin intellectually, which was never his strongest quality. He shrugged.

"They're condemned to respond to those Nigerian prince scam emails and LinkedIn requests for all eternity, using AOL accounts on Windows 8 computers."

Dante thought Bob was pretty computer-savvy for a dead guy. "That doesn't sound so terrible," he said.

"You don't realize how bad the wifi is in here," Bob said. "Everyone's punishment is tailor-made. Imagine how you'd feel if you could never get stoned again."

Dante shuddered. He also thought he detected a hint of sadness in Bob's voice, as though Marley's ghost was speaking from experience. Did that mean ghosts really couldn't get high? Dante tried to pick up the pace, but his guide seemed set on doing more guiding.

"Over there," Bob pointed at a bunch of people who looked like they were shooting a scene, "are directors, producers and even actors who made it in Hollywood by screwing over their fellow man. Now they're forced to work on film adaptations of *Twilight* fan fiction in exchange for nothing but royalties."

The actors were dressed in khakis and leather jackets, and sprinkled with generous amounts of glitter. Dante squinted. "Samuel L. Jackson is in this movie? I thought he's alive."

Jackson turned and glared at him. "Motherfucker, I'm in *everything*."

They descended, level by level, past the thieves and the adulterers, the deadbeats and the lawyers. One of the levels was filled with rows of desks extending as far as the eye could see. Identical goateed men hunched over typewriters.

"What did they do?" asked Dante.

"Technically, this isn't part of hell, just a lab that occupies a floor in the same building," said Bob. "Powers That Be were amused by the idea that infinite monkeys given enough time might type out the complete works of William Shakespeare."

"These are the infinite monkeys they got?" Dante might have failed high school biology, but he was pretty sure he could tell a man from a primate.

"Better," said Bob. "They cloned infinite Shakespeares, just to see what so many geniuses might come up with when they put their heads together."

"Oh, wow." Dante was impressed. "Did they write a sequel to *Romeo and Juliet*?"

"The first batch didn't come out," said Bob. "They mostly flung poo at each other. This is the second batch. It's an improvement, but it turns out Shakespeares don't work well as a group. For now they're writing new treatments for more *Twilight* scripts, because only groupthink can come up with something awful enough to meet our needs."

By the time they descended to the ninth level, faces of all the damned started to blur together for Dante and the amalgamation was looking suspiciously like a slack-jawed clone of William Shakespeare. Despite Marley's assurances to the contrary, he was beginning to think this journey *was* his personal hell and that they would never find his drug dealer. Then he saw Rusty who sat alone on a stool by a kitchen counter, eating a sandwich.

<<>>

"Rusty!" Dante rushed forward.

Rusty was a paunchy man in his thirties who wore jean shorts and a dirty Nickelback t-shirt with cut-off sleeves. He looked just like he had the last time Dante saw him.

"It's me, Dante."

Rusty stared as he took another bite of the sandwich. "Who?" he managed to say while he chewed.

Dante felt hurt, but then realized that while Rusty looked exactly the same, he was now much older. "Dante Ferrero. I used to buy dime bags from you ten years ago. We hung out!"

There was no spark of recognition in Rusty's eyes. He kept eating. The silence was getting awkward.

"How are you doing?" Dante said lamely.

"How am I *doing*?" Rusty waved the sandwich and sneered, dried crumbs peeling from the corner of his mouth. "I'm in hell, forced to eat baloney sandwiches 'til the end of time. There's nothing in the world I hate more than baloney!"

To each their own hell.

"Figures," muttered Dante.

This was the guy he considered cool in high school? Dante looked to Bob for help, but Marley was hanging back, laboriously ignoring the reunion.

"You may not remember, but we were good buddies back in the day, so I was wondering if you could do me a solid?"

Rusty took another bite, winced, and swallowed. "What do you want?" he asked.

This was the moment of truth. The finale of Dante's quest. The answer to the question that bugged him for a decade. He blurted out, "Can you tell me the recipe for your signature blend?"

Rusty stared at him for several seconds. Then he started laughing. He coughed up bits of baloney as he laughed maniacally, tears welling in his eyes.

Dante had no choice but to wait it out, wait until Rusty stopped. Then he asked, "What's so funny?"

"Special blend is what I sold to shitheads who didn't know any better," said Rusty. "It was the cheapest weed I could find, cut with oregano and orange peel, and lots of water to make it heavier." He chuckled again, but his mirth faded when he bit into the sandwich.

"But... but... I remember it being so good." Dante experienced denial and anger in rapid succession and proceeded straight to bargaining. "Are you absolutely sure?"

"Sure I'm sure," said Rusty. "Kids who try pot for the first time don't know good stuff from garbage. Don't take it personal. It was just business."

Crestfallen, Dante worked through this revelation. He wanted nothing more to do with this loser he once looked up to. He flipped Rusty the bird, turned around and walked away.

"It seems I was right and Rusty's blend was not the thing that's keeping you from moving on," said Bob. "I'm sorry."

Sorry. The ghost he'd only met that day had more compassion for him than Rusty.

"What do we do now?" asked Dante.

"I don't know," said Bob. "Let's get out of here. You can hang around with me until you think of someone else you might have unfinished business with. Then we try again."

Dante hung his head. "Okay." They started toward the staircase when he paused. "Hang on. I've got to get some things off my chest." He turned around and march-floated toward Rusty.

"You screwed up my life," he told Rusty. The dealer tried to respond but Dante cut him off. "I was doing fine before I met you. I was going to graduate, maybe go to college, maybe get a nice white-collar job at a bank somewhere. But no, I had to meet you, a loser who sold crap weed to school kids for a living." Dante was getting progressively louder while Rusty shrunk back on his stool.

"I thought you were my friend, I tried to *be* like you, which was really my bad. But the thing is, you never cared about me, you didn't even remember my name. I was worth no more to you than the few bucks in my pocket. It may not matter, but I know you for what you are now." Dante put his ectoplasm arms on his ectoplasm hips. "I'd tell you to go to hell, but..." He nodded at their surroundings. "Enjoy your baloney, asshole." Then he turned his back on Rusty.

Bob clapped slowly. He stood next to a shimmering door that wasn't there before.

"The portal will take you to the next step of your journey," said Bob, grinning. "It looks as though your unfinished business was with this unsavory character after all, even if it was never about the blend recipe."

Before Dante could respond, Rusty spat out a mouthful of sandwich, jumped off his stool and raced for the portal leaving a trail of crumbs falling off his shorts and legs. "Freedom!" he shouted as he dove head-first at the portal.

Rusty's head bounced off the solid surface with a crunch followed by a thud as he landed on the ground like the Coyote fooled yet again by the Roadrunner.

"Get back to your meal, Rusty" said Bob. He flashed a smile at Dante. "Personal hells. Personal portals. Powers That Be create everything tailor-made."

Dante mouthed thanks to the ghost of Bob Marley, but he was already being drawn in by the portal. It felt right; like the smell of freshly-baked pot brownies combined with the warmth of a sunny spring day and the merriment of a Cheech and Chong routine.

Dante entered the portal and floated toward the light.

Refugees

James Dorr

Wherever the army went, it left starvation behind it. In the wood of Atlos, for instance, Sir Geoffrey had camped for nearly two weeks and encouraged his men-at-arms to hunt the forest bare, his yeomen to fish its streams to depletion, while his engineers cut down trees to build the great siege machines that would later be needed—the wait didn't matter. Similarly, when the army, like a gorging worm exposed to the sun, quit the forest's tree-lined tunnels and broke out in a skirmish line into the farmland that lay beyond, he had his soldiers fire the fields and all the buildings, driving the peasants before them toward the enemy's stronghold. These were the refugees of war.

When that much had been accomplished, he stood in his stirrups to measure the damage. "I dare say that not even a rat could find the wherewithal to stay *here*," he told Montcourant, his aide-de-camp. "All is now burned, just as I ordered it. All is barren."

"Yes, Sir Geoffrey," Montcourant, a younger man, answered. "I still wonder, though, at such completeness in your destruction. Could not some storehouses have been retained as a base of supply at our army's rear? That way, should we fall on hard times..."

"No, Montcourant. Laying waste everything behind is a secret both Sir Lowell and I learned when, together, we rode on Crusade. There were always more fields ahead, but, even if not, we took enough only to support us on the march, burning everything else we could find. That way, our enemies knew that they could expect no relief—no new force, even if it could have been raised, would have found enough left to our rear to sustain it. And, as for our own army, each man knew that, if he wanted to find new supplies, he could only advance..."

"In this case, it no longer being Crusade, we can only advance to Sir Lowell's castle. Is that right, my lord?"

"To Sir Lowell's castle, yes, Montcourant—to the castle he won when the Crusade was ended and we returned home. And where, unless my old comrade in arms has much changed in the meantime, he'll not only have gold in plenty, but also granaries full to the rafters that he'll be reluctant to open for even his own defenders."

<<>>

The army continued, ravishing towns and destroying new fields, just as its commander ordered. At times, some of those that it opposed would stand and fight and would be destroyed, too, until those that were dead would outnumber the living. At these times the corpses would be burned as well as the things they'd thought they might have been able to defend.

The army took its time in this labor—it didn't matter. Sir Geoffrey was not in any hurry. In fact, he explained to Montcourant, the more time required to reach the castle, the better prepared that fortification would be for its conquest. "The weak are the ones who flee before us," he told his aide. "They take their defeat and their sickness with them to press on Sir Lowell, to crowd with him inside his towers and walls. The strong, now—those are the ones who die here."

Montcourant had laughed, and the army continued to wend its slow, all-devouring way over what had before been lush fields and valleys. All was made desert until, at last, the vanguard reached the low range of hills that overlooked its destination.

It was already late afternoon, but Sir Geoffrey gave orders to continue until the crest of the last hill was reached, then set his tent there. Once that was done, he rested beneath its gaily-striped awning and gazed to the plain that now lay below him, surrounding the castle. The sun was just setting, a night fog just beginning to drift in, yet, even in fast-approaching darkness, he wondered that some of the shadows he saw surrounding the fortress seemed deeper than others. He wondered, too, that in that last light he saw ravens circling.

<<>>

The following morning, he took his army down onto the plain and saw what the last night's shadows had been. Bodies—hundreds of swollen corpses—lay littered in heaps around the castle, as if some army had come before his and had met defeat there. Yet the corpses neither faced the castle's wall nor had their backs toward it, as if they'd been struck down in retreat, but rather lay, arms and legs akimbo, twisted and turned in every direction.

"What do you make of this, Sir Geoffrey?" Montcourant asked.

Sir Geoffrey started to form a reply when he heard a whirring sound, followed immediately by another and then by a third. Then, three loud clicks, almost in unison, and, as he and Montcourant stared, three new bodies flew out from behind the castle walls.

"Engineers, bring up the trebuchet and the other machinery," he shouted to those who waited behind him. "Set them into working order on that far rise—they'll be out of the castle's range there." Then he turned back to his aide-de-camp and began to laugh. "Sir Lowell has catapults, it seems. He uses them to return our gifts to us—the peasants who've fled from us to his castle to seek refuge inside."

"I don't understand," Montcourant said.

"These are the diseased that Sir Lowell hopes to cast from him. He's worked them strengthening his defenses, no doubt first confiscating whatever supplies they were able to bring in their flight, and now that they are weakened more he can use them no longer. Even then, though, he's waited too long—the real disease they carried was panic. That's one reason we moved so slowly on our march forward, to give his own soldiers plenty of time to dwell on the fear the peasants brought inside."

Another three whirs and clicks interrupted—another three bodies flew over the wall and landed, thudding, on the already corpse-strewn plain. "This one's still alive, I think," Sir Geoffrey heard one of his men's voices call, and he shouted back to leave it alone. He shrugged and faced Montcourant again.

"Even now, though, he's too late in acting. His best defenders have been with him too long. They know him almost as well as I do and know that what he's supplied them with thus far has been from the store the peasants brought with them. But, that he casts the peasants out now tells them one thing more, that the food he's stolen is almost exhausted. And, that he casts out some who are still able-bodied enough to survive their fall, however briefly, tells his men also that Sir Lowell is miser enough that he'd sacrifice those who were still useful to him before he'd open his own stores to feed them."

<<>>

All that day and half the next, the bulk of the army sat, watching the castle intermittently jettison men. Beyond that, save for an occasional range-testing arrow, it was as if the walls' defenders had not yet come to the realization that they were besieged. On the rise Sir Geoffrey had chosen, however, his engineers had been hard at work, assembling steel-tipped battering rams and wheeled, moving towers and, its catapult arm rising higher than even the enemy's towers it would be used against, the great trebuchet. Then, after that day-and-a-half was over, he sent men up to the tops of the hills that surrounded the fortress to bring down boulders, the smaller of these, still almost larger than three men could handle, to be used for shot while the largest, grooved and strapped into a frame, would be the counterweights that would give the engine its power. The work continued throughout the night until, when dawn of the second day came, the machine was ready.

Sir Geoffrey's engineers took the range from their rise to the castle and, using a series of ropes and pulleys, began to crank the trebuchet's arm down. They rolled an ammunition stone into the sling at the tip of its longer section—the arm itself, lashed to a pivot three-fourths of the distance to its counterweighted butt, had once been a whole tree—and waited for their commander's nod. Receiving their order, they sprang to the side and pulled its release cord.

Not with a whir, but a groan of straining timber, the bow-bent tree straightened along its length and, rising almost slowly at first as its counterweighted end descended, it slammed, not with a clicking sound but an earth-shaking crash, into the padded framework set over the engine's midsection. The sling whipped past the tip of the arm and the stone rose higher, hanging in air, until it too descended into the castle's courtyard.

"Shorten your distance," Sir Geoffrey shouted. "Aim for the corner below the near tower. The wall there is old, despite its improvements, and, if I guess rightly, the stonework within will be as rotten as the spirits of those who'd defend it."

The sergeant in charge of the engineers nodded and, after the arm had been drawn down again, a task that took nearly an hour in itself, he made an adjustment to the sling. The second shot rose even higher, but, its arc sharper, struck with a splitting of mortar and rock at the tower's base.

Satisfied now, Sir Geoffrey smiled. He went to assemble the rest of his army and, ten hours later, seven more shots having breached its wall from tower to gatehouse, the castle surrendered.

<<>>

"My men are hungry as well, Sir Lowell," he said as they enjoyed wine with the last of the peasant-brought stores in the castle's feast hall. Even candles were in short supply as the gloom about the room's rafters attested. "The march has been long and, as you no doubt still know from the old days, armies that I command travel lightly."

"Yes, Sir Geoffrey," the other replied, a man of about the same age as his conqueror, but going to plumpness. "As you've guessed, my granary is still sealed. I'd realized that it was you who hoped to take my castle from the reports the refugees brought in, and I know, too, that you've always insisted on fairness in victory. Because of that, I have saved it for you."

Sir Geoffrey laughed. "Along with your gold—kept forcibly away from all others for my sake, I dare say. But you're right about my being fair. Because, at one time, we were even friends, you can expect at least some of your gold back, along with an officer's post in my army if you'll agree to it and, mayhap, a chance to win a new castle later. The first thing, however, is food for my soldiers."

The other chuckled as well in reply. "We go too far back, you and I, Sir Geoffrey, to quarrel at details. I accept your post and, as you suggest, perhaps a chance to gain a new stronghold as your liegeman. For now, though, as you say, the grain to bake bread to keep *both* our forces from suffering hunger overly much."

The heavier man rose and Sir Geoffrey followed, still in his armor, as a servant handed them torches. They went alone into the fortress' passageways, then down a narrow, dark course of stairs to the vaults beneath it, turning at its foot into a twisting maze of tunnels. "I take it you *do* want to see the grain first, then," Sir Lowell said as they came to a branch and, as his conqueror grunted assent, led the way down yet another staircase.

"The men's need, at this point, must always come first," Sir Geoffrey said as he followed after, ever downward, into the earth's womb. He glanced, as they walked, at the heavy overhanging ceiling, the rough-hewn walls with gaping cracks at their corner joinings, seemingly pressing closer each time one or the other of the torches guttered, its flame momentarily burning low. "Hungry, they fight well, but after a victory they *must* be fed royally lest they turn against their commanders. Gold, on the other hand, always can wait until tomorrow—you know that, Sir Lowell."

"I've learned that, yes, Sir Geoffrey," the man who continued ahead of him said. "We've served good masters, you and I, in the art of war. We've enjoyed war together. But did you see, outside, the ravens that flew above the towers? They brought me ill luck in the siege today—helped in my choice to surrender to you."

"Men make their own luck," Sir Geoffrey replied, glad for the comfort of conversation. He disliked tunnels, not so much for fear of their closeness or even the dark, but for the stillness one found within them. They made him feel helpless—alone and trapped. "Are we almost there?"

"Almost, Sir Geoffrey. You know, it was really the peasants who beat me. Your army did its work almost too well, driving them to me. I'd never seen so many peasants before, first disrupting the drills of my soldiers, then, even though I doled some food back to them, starting to steal..."

Another turn, and the tunnel widened. Then, in the dimness, a sealed wooden door. "A moment, now, while I find the key," Sir Lowell said as he shifted his torch into his left hand and used the other to reach in his clothing. He brought out a huge flared shaft of iron and, fitting it carefully into a hole in the door's right side, he began to twist it.

"As you say," Sir Geoffrey went on, raising his voice above the screech of the lock's stiff metal, "we've learned to enjoy warfare, you and I. Even as you stand here opening your castle to me, it's the peasants—the refugees—who've really suffered. Yet we're the survivors, the ones who'll go on to fight larger battles, to win richer castles. Do you suppose, as the priests suggest, that there'll come a time when our sins will catch up to us?"

"I don't know, Sir Geoffrey—ah! There we are now." The plump man returned the key to his belt, then put his torch carefully down on the floor. He used both hands to pull the latch that started the heavy door swinging open. "I don't hold much with priests myself. I..."

Sir Lowell's voice rose up into a scream as he staggered backward, clawing at a shifting mass that covered his face and his upper body. Sir Geoffrey pushed past him, drawing his sword, then dropped it and thrust out his own torch instead.

Inside the storeroom, the grain was destroyed, devoured completely by thousands of rats—the true refugees from the fields and the barnyards his army had laid waste. They covered the granary's walls and floor like a living tapestry, and, having spoiled all that was there, the rats, too, were hungry.

Spawn of War and Deathiness

READING COFFEE

Anthony Panegyres

Kalgoorlie 1916

Not many eleven-year olds are enamored with death. Mary Agapitos is. She prefers to hang out in the Kalgoorlie graveyard, reveling in the rusty colored earth that still reigns around the tombs; the bauxite rocks lying about like oversized gravel; and the tufts of colorless grass protruding beneath the occasional eucalypt. In particular, she enjoys the Orthodox section where she reads and pats headstones of people she once knew. Old Greek surnames which comfort her like her mother's embrace.

<<>>

Mary wanders about their Kalgoorlie house serving nibbly things to the guests as a pleasant Greek girl should. Faces from Asia Minor, *Kastellorizo*, and Alexandria blur into one another. Her cheeks are pulled, slobbered upon; her long wavy locks—which she secretly delights in—are caressed by some and yanked by others. And when not serving, her personal space is stolen by women who squash her into their paunch, while the thin ladies enfold her delicately. Now and then Mary forces a tear in remembrance of her great uncle Yiannis Katavatis to the appreciation of the crowd. "Oh, she is a dear thing," they say as she walks around presenting a platter of dried fruit, nuts, olives, and white cheese.

Between platters, Mary retreats into the kitchen where her mother governs matters. Whisky and ouzo are being sent around with sweetened orange peels and rose petal jam. Coffee brews in the *briki*: Mary's favorite time. She looks forward to wakes: the brush of uncomfortably formal suits on her skin; the kitchen, a pulsating heart sending food forth and then the remains flowing back; the sad smiles; and the composed ladies who only an hour or so earlier had worn tear-stained faces.

Taking a tray of shortbread outside and to the back room, where men sit talking buoyantly, Mary hears news. They talk of the Kaiser's plans to conquer Europe, and say that the Greeks are behind their Prime Minister Venizelos. They are pro-Entente, anti- German, despite what King Constantine of Greece states about remaining neutral. After all, his wife's brother is the Kaiser.

In the lounge she hears the ladies discuss which days are holy in the coming months and that Christina is disgracing the family, having been seen with a *xeno*, an Australian, an Englishman.

As she re-enters the kitchen, Mary sneaks a shortbread from the plate. She's never seen snow but she imagines it is like the icing that covers the thick snake-shaped biscuit. She removes the clove, a bold dark star in the center, and eats the biscuit meditatively, mouth closed, oblivious to all else around her.

"I'm bringing the coffee cups back," she states. Her mother closes the ice-box and stares, but her eyes are too gentle to put fear in a child who has seen death many times before. "But I want to, mama," she says in a raised voice. Three ladies at the sink turn to observe the self-assured girl.

"Let her bring the cups if she wants to," says one.

Mary's mother nods, bends down slightly and whispers in her daughter's ear. "You mustn't look in them."

Mary has heard it before and knows her role by heart: "Of course not, Mama."

"You mustn't look, remember what I said," her mother says so thinly that even Mary has trouble hearing. "It's *Satanas* that allows people to see things. Don't taint your soul, *agapi mou.*"

Mary kisses her mother and dashes out with a tray to carry the coffee cups. She steps towards the men first and picks up a cup belonging to Loukas, who runs Paris Café on Hannan Street. Immediately she looks into the remaining grounds of the tiny cup. She does not need to flip it like a Gypsy or an atheist widow; she simply gazes and all is apparent. She sees a zoological form in the bottom, a bull, but she does not know or care what this means. It is the traces between the mud to which her eyes are lured. These lines appear to her like vast gorges, the rims are individual Odysseys; she knows this but doesn't bother with particular details. Mary heads straight for the end point: Death, *Thanatos*.

Her wife calls from the kitchen but she is tired, she lets the feeling crawl over her. She breathes slowly but can no longer be bothered with her body's laboring. She sleeps, vaguely aware of someone's touch—shaking her arms. A tear wets her face, then all is shadow.

Loukas pats her head. Mary does not usually like that, she feels too old for it, but for the present it does not bother her. "Peaceful," she whispers under her breath.

She grabs the next cup, Kostas'. His beaked nose and distant eyes do not even acknowledge her—too small, too unimportant.

Mary merely peeps downwards.

She fumbles for her concealed fish knife as an oar crashes into her face, sweeping her over the side. Hands grip as she tries to surface, breathing water, gagging as more rushes in.

Then she remembers: she's a child eating honeyed yoghurt at an outside café table, the sun bathing her skin and sending glitter across the turquoise bay. She spasms. All is still.

Mary touches Kostas' cheek, seeing him for the first time. He smiles downwards—his raptor face no longer appears aloof. She pats his leg tenderly, and then moves to another cup

Eleftherios'. *Her heart feels pressure, like a small balloon swollen with liquid, she clenches her chest and tries to speak before it bursts.*

Panayiota's cup. *She holds the side of her stomach, nails squelching flesh. Everything burns. A widow, her three unmarried sons surround her. She can't abandon them yet. One son clasps her hand gently; she wants to turn her head, behold his eyes. Another son kisses her forehead. "You've always been so brave," she hears.*

Permission; she stops.

The final cup that she takes is her mother's. Mary pauses. This is wrong she thinks, but she needs to know.

Her mother should have cleaned it herself anyway, before she had the chance to pick it up.

She peeks and for the rest of the evening she doesn't utter a sound. When her mother asks if she is all right, she cries.

<<>>

Mary sits on a stool behind the front counter eating milk chocolate. The stool is her favorite place, it feels tall and she likes dangling her legs. She enjoys the flavor of Olympia's, the comforting floorboards, but more she likes the warm smell of tobacco and coffee.

Her two brothers cook honest food in the kitchen, as well as English muck, such as fresh fish defiled with batter. Her father, Mattheos, makes sure the maroon tablecloths are presentable. There are only four customers—it's only 11:30am—but soon Mary will be taking orders and serving, aiding her *Baba*.

It is her mother's day off. Mama will die soon. The coffee-sludge never lies. In the cup Mama had worn that grey dress and that Italian watch that Mattheos had bought her at Christmas time.

But Mary's mother won't pass today. For one, she is not wearing the correct dress, and second, certain events have not yet unraveled.

Mary is watching her father meticulously setting out plates, glasses, and cutlery, when the entry flaps tremble and Loukas bursts through the entrance, brandishing a newspaper above his head. He is spouting off Greek in the shop—something is truly awry. The four customers glare and shake their heads. "Foreign dirt—need to learn some manners," whispers one, but Mary hears.

Baba and Mary meet Loukas at the counter. "What's wrong?" asks Mattheos. Loukas whacks the newspaper down.

"Look." On the front page is a ruined Northbridge shop in Perth. Windows are smashed and the inside gutted like a trashed building site. Three small pictures adorn the bottom of the page: three shops, all pillaged in the manner Mary imagines the Ottomans once did to the Greek churches in "The City" that Kyria Persphone told her about. One building has even lost its support columns and tilts as if ready to crumble.

Mary puts a hand to her mouth; it is not the same but there is something too familiar about the picture. The title reads: "Greek Tragedy."

"But why?" says her Father, his nails whitening as his fingers press into the bench.

"Because our idiot king says he wants to remain out of the war—stay neutral."

"Despite Venizelos declaring the opposite?"

"They don't even care what the Prime Minister thinks— what we Greeks think! These Englishmen see a King declare anything and they think it's the will of the entire people. Between us, Mattheos, I don't care whether we fight the Germans or stay out of the whole catastrophe—we've seen too much war. But this..." His hand gestures at the photo.

"What if it happens here?" asks Mattheos.

Mary reads as they converse.

"Yesterday evening, a mob of misled Australian patriots—civilian youths and soldiers—marched through Highgate, Northbridge and Perth, in a destructive wave targeted at shops conducted by persons of Greek nationality. Twenty shops in all were demolished: windows smashed, furnishings wrecked and stock ruined by the protestors. Nigel Bradley, who witnessed the scene, said, "They were even singing "Tipperary' and "Australia Will Be There' while vandalising..."

"We'll be next," says her father.

"Hopefully not," says Loukas. All traces of his theatrical anger vanish in a blink. "Mr. Michelides has addressed the Premier on behalf of our community stating that we are not only law-abiding citizens but also pro-Venizelists, totally opposed to the Kaiser and his people."

"I'll call Sergeant Humphries, just in case." Mattheos winks at Loukas. "He gets a free lunch every Wednesday; fried snapper, prime filet."

So little time. Mary waits as her father makes the call in tentative English. "Yes, thank you, Sergeant... Extra patrols, eh? This is very good, very good."

Loukas strolls outside with the newspaper held casually by his side. Mary's father appears calm and returns to the tables. Both Loukas and *Baba* seem to Mary to feel secure knowing that their community leader in Perth, Mr. Michelides, and the local police force here in Kalgoorlie will take extra care of the Greek community.

Mary knows they're mistaken.

Her voice breaks as she speaks, "*Baba!*" Normally Mary is so composed, so stoic, just like her mother.

Just hold me.

Her father clutches her head, somewhat awkwardly, to his wrestler chest. The fusty odor of his shirt comforts her.

Ask what's wrong.

But her father is mute. She sobs. Words come haltingly. "Soon... Like the paper... *Baba*... The same."

"It's all right, Mary. Calm, calm." Mary draws her breath in sharp perceptible gulps.

He gets her a glass of water and then wipes the briny rivulets from her face with a shirtsleeve. Mary sips, both hands gripping the glass. She composes herself, mastering her face by tucking in her quivering lower lip and measuring her breathing until she becomes like her mother once more.

"I read the cups," Mary says.

"Mary, you know what Mama says about that."

"Promise, *Baba*. Promise you won't tell her. Please!"

"Ok," he laughs, "I promise."

"Soon they'll come. And throw things through the store, the glass will break up and down the street, and then they'll invade like an army and... people will be hurt... I hate them, *Baba*. I hate them."

"It's a dream, Mary. It's okay. I've spoken to the Sergeant. We'll be protected."

"Don't tell mama. You promised you wouldn't tell."

Mary releases all in a deluge. The mob is uncontrollable. Even the stately Kalgoorlie hotel is left on a precarious slant, its wooden pillars warped. The story has such vivid details that Mary knows her father is convinced. After all, she is no fibber.

She speaks fluidly. Her father listens. Images form...

Eleftherios lies on the ground, his left ear lobe swollen like a mushroom having been kicked by "Bluey," the carrot-haired miner who eats at their restaurant every Saturday lunch, always pasticcio.

The Sergeant is mounted with some other cops, helpless, as they watch the destructive quake rumble down the street, demolishing all Greek stores. Many are beaten. Her mother loses her watch to an Italian man shouting, "*Dammi l'orologio adesso, disgraziata Greca.*"

Mary doesn't tell of what happens afterwards.

She feels her father clasping her shoulders. "The date. Can you remember the date?" She lifts her head, the Aegean way of motioning "no." "Did you see a newspaper around?" Her father is now shaking her slightly; he's never done this before. No more tears, she tells herself.

"What about the calendar in the *kouzina*? Think, Mary *mou.*"

All she knows is that it will be soon, within a fortnight or so.

"Look at me. No one will die. If the police can't protect us," he pounds his chest in a simian fashion, "*I* will." He repeats "*I* will" with another fist to his pectoral.

"I believe you, *Baba.*" She says the reverse of what she thinks.

Pavlos, with his bald Periclean-shaped head, strides in from the kitchen on their father's call. Arm around Pavlos' shoulder, *Baba* whispers in his ear and her brother tears off his apron and races outside.

Mary looks up from the counter as Pavlos returns at a jog. He and her father murmur away in Greek while she serves Bluey. She normally feels sorry for this man; his unfortunate ruddy skin is no protection against the burning goldfields sun. But now his blistered nose and dry, flaky lips repulse her like some nightmare. She wants to squish her nostrils up or do something ridiculous like tear up his one pound note and fling the remains into his face. "Thank you, sir," she says, returning his change in the Greek manner by placing it in a saucer.

Bluey nods, "Good food."

Once the transaction is over, her older brother approaches, sweat gleaming on his forehead. He blows a raspberry on her neck. She can't help but giggle at the tickly wet touch; at the same time, however, she feels a little humiliated. "Grow up, Pavlos. I'm almost twelve. I'm too old for that."

Pavlos ignores her as usual, and Mary feels herself being lifted up and then twisted around so they're both facing the same direction. He places her shoes on his and holds her, balancing her as he walks around the counter. His breath is warm and salty as he whispers in her ear. "Who's the strongest man in the world?"

"*Baba*," says Mary cheekily.

"*Baba*!? Then who's the second strongest?"

"Hmm. I'll have to think."

Pavlos lifts her up in the air. "Who?"

"Marios," she says her oldest brother's nickname.

"Marios?" He says putting her down. "That weakling. I used to be number one. Now Mary," his tone deepens, "I want you to go home and tell mama that there will be a full house tonight. Possibly even forty people. Then come back and I'll give you some money to buy rosewater and essence, almonds, icing sugar and glucose from Stavros' shop. Father says everyone will need a *loukoumi*."

"That's because he thinks rosewater freshens the mind."

<<>>

Loukas Panos is the first to knock, then others continue to arrive until thirty or so men are crammed in the back room, each on a wooden chair brought home from the restaurant. Small square tables, a few with wobbly legs, are spaced throughout the room. On each are two small white plates.

Mary smiles in the kitchen with her mother; there is something special about making *loukoumia* with her. It's a far easier dish than all those finicky honey—drenched pastries and she and Mama can be less precise, which means Mary can be a little sillier. They fabricate stories about everyone they know, even Mary's grandfather in Greece. "*Pappou* only became a Priest once his *Yaya* died so he could get closer to the wine and women," Mary tells her mama, who giggles uncharacteristically.

Mary kisses her, tells her how much she loves her one too many times—until her Mother stoppers her mouth with a freshly made *loukoumi*. It's delicious. They both pull off their aprons and Mary pats down her skirt. Men come and greet them, kissing both cheeks. The mustachioed ones prickle.

Loukas' son enters. Seventeen, tall with coffee-colored skin. He is nicknamed Coco by the locals and now the Greeks call him that too. Mary blushes as his lips touch her face.

"He'd make a good husband," her mother grins as Coco leaves for the backroom. Mary secretly hopes that the smile's sincere. But then her *Mama* says that about every Greek male under the age of twenty-five.

Her father and brothers had closed the shop early and cooked all afternoon. Mary and her Mama whisk in and out with platters of food, catching titbits of what is said.

Grilled fish, octopus and prawns. It appears as though her father dominates early proceedings. "If it happened in Perth and Sydney then it will happen here."

The second platter has meatballs Smyrnaean style, floating in a cinnamon—tomato salsa. Coco stands. "We need a safe-haven, in case things get violent. Even in Sydney, four thousand people rioted just because someone made up a tale about a Greek murderer." Many don't care to listen to one so young. Mary watches eyes flitter to the sides or upwards; some bore into the ground. She holds the tray tighter than usual.

Dolmades are handed out with ladles of egg and lemon sauce. Mary looks around, observing the familiar sloping foreheads, dark brows and thick hands. She knows the thoughts of those gathered while Loukas speaks: *What type of a father unleashes his son like that?* Her father and Pavlos are attentive at least.

"We don't need a safe-haven. I can manage on my own," she hears one visitor say.

A plan unfolds while her mother serves meltingly-tender lamb, pot stewed for three hours in cloves, wine, vinegar and a bay leaf or two. Mary scoops out small serves of chickpeas and spinach drizzled with virgin olive oil and lemon juice. A cautionary warning system is set in place. Coco volunteers to be the runner if a mob arises and Loukas will buy extra locks and board up his house until it's a fort. A few people grunt at the perceived nonsense, and a hostile silence settles over the room.

By the time Mary serves coffee and *loukoumia* most guests have already left. Like a fervent orchestral conductor, her father raises his hand up and down as he talks to Loukas and Pavlos. Mary recognizes the gestures; *Baba*'s anxious. As she serves him the translucent pink sweet dressed in icing sugar, he says, "Only the bright men are left, the others should have remained for this sweet. Rose...

"I know *Baba*, it makes you think."

"Not many believed us, Mary *mou*. But we'll keep a good watch."

<<>>

Two cups are on Mary's tray, nestled between bread plates.

One belongs to Coco. *A blanket on grass overlooking the ocean. Waves kush and sher as she gazes at the fair string-lipped lady seated by her side. Something pops in her head as her wife speaks, her accent Irish. Every word from the "pop" onwards becomes more hushed until it fades into silence. "We should do this every Sunday..."*

Mary pauses. The pop was something she hadn't felt before, quick and painless, like flicking a switch. She feels a little sad too, not because of the death, but because Coco's not with *her* as she hoped. *Lucky Irish.*

Mary hesitates over her father's cup. She closes her eyes as she places it on the kitchen bench. She hears her mama washing dishes beside her and rather than opening her eyelids, she crosses herself, swearing to the Lord that her *Baba*'s grounds are ones she will never read.

<<>>

A week passes without any demonstration; not one of the eleven Greek shops on Hannan Street is affected. Yet Mary is constantly alert. She hides her mama's grey dress on numerous occasions (in Pavlos' cupboard, in the back shed, under her mattress) until her mother throws her "that look." At Anchor Confectionary, a distant cousin's store, she is shouted her usual: a sundae with chocolate and cherry sauce so syrupy that it prevents the mound of chopped nuts cascading down in an avalanche. "How boring," she says to Pavlos when he orders his usual Cola Spider.

Two fair teenagers in shorts also sit along the "Yankee-style" counter, making slurping sounds with their straws as they finish the last of their drinks. As the boys rise to pay, the burlier of the two looks pointedly at Christopheros behind the till and says, "We'll be payin' the Aussie price— not like those two Olives over there." And when Christopheros places the change on a small plate: "Put it in my hand. You're not in Wopland anymore."

His friend sniggers. "Greasies," he says as they leave.

Mary's ordinarily immune. She's heard it all before: Dagos, Oilies and the rest. But now she worries. *Is it a sign of what's to come? Or is this the norm?*

The next week is one of observation. *More signs?* Did that man deliberately bump Panayiota so she spills her parcels? Maybe that lady takes her children across the street to avoid her family? Is young Kyriakos' plum-colored eye a result of being alien?

Nothing eventuates and the fortnight passes. No two-thousand-strong-pack terrorizes the street and the days revolve routinely once more. Mama breathes and cooks and confides. Pavlos relaxes and, whenever she enters the kitchen, beats his dark apron producing flour clouds just to annoy her. Her father's eyes no longer linger on mama, espying her every move.

Mary wonders if *Satanas* has been at play. Have the cups been lying all this time? Were the lives she possessed in the cups' murk simply the Charlatan's fabrications? <<>>

Four weeks pass. December 8th is her Mother's day off. Although it is morning the sun weighs down oppressively, sucking moisture from the air in true goldfields style. Cicadas and crickets provide an accompanying beat to the heat, while skinks scamper about windowsills. Inside, Mary and her father are preparing tables when Loukas arrives. The image is identical, only her angle different. He waves the newspaper about—highlighting a musty pool under his right armpit—before slamming it down. "Coco is on the alert! I've locked shop, you should do the same." Her father strides to the counter and Mary follows in his shadow. She hops on to the stool. Her legs are still as she attempts to peep over her Baba's shoulder. All she can glean is the *Kalgoorlie Miner's* headline: "Greek Treachery."

A bugle resonates outside. Her *Baba* barks in Greek, his own military response to the soldier's horn, and her two brothers exit the kitchen. They all move out onto the road. At the top end of Hannan Sreet near the Post Office are a dozen or so uniformed blotches. The bugle perforates the dry morning air once more. Youths and more soldiers appear on the horizon. Mary sees others leaving shops. Many non-Greek men head off towards the group; women and children fade away into the dim; some Greeks approach her father, but several remain in their stores. Once more the bugle sounds and the cluster up the road grows like a carcass drawing ants. Mary is reminded of a swarm coalescing. A final bugle note echoes off the buildings, but this time it is muffled by the yells and cheers that surround it.

Twenty or so Greeks, eerily silent, are now gathered around her own family, but the street in the distance is alive with shouts and more people than she has ever seen. She can see their figures clearly now as they take to the Greek-run Post Office, which also doubles as a cafe. It must be locked. Axes hew through the doors, windows are shattered, furniture is soon removed, food and fittings carried out. She prays the owners are safe as the crowd moves, wreaking destruction with the speed and efficacy of a tornado. Despite the chaotic roar of the mob, and the wildness of their gutting, the looters remain banded together as they whirl over to the adjoining shop.

The group that Mary is with heads off in the opposite direction—towards Loukas' barricaded house at the other end of Hannan Street. She watches the heels and soles in front of her beat in and out of the road stirring orange dust. Several mounted police approach. Their horses whinny as they toss their heads and stamp. The Sergeant tips his hat towards her Father as they pass by. Mary turns back to see the police horses clop towards the throng only to witness them being pelted with missiles: chairs, stones, steel and wood. One mare rears dangerously, hooves thrashing through the air. With a wave of the Sergeant's hand the ineffectual force retreat to the sheltered porch of Pete O'Reiley's butcher store. A derisive cheer erupts.

Those around Mary now sprint for Loukas' stronghold, shirts sweaty, blouses clinging. Tugging and shrieking, she pulls on Pavlos' and her father's shirts. She finally topples over and grazes a knee. "Mama! Mama!" she screeches. The rest of the group moves on. In the distance the armed mass whips about in their direction.

Her Father's veins bulge from his neck. "Home," he says to Pavlos. "See that your mother's safe. If there's time, take her to Loukas' place."

"What about Mary?"

Mary has taken off at a quick hobble towards their restaurant. The crowd in the distance moves another shop closer, flinging tables and chairs onto the street. Apples and pears bounce and roll erratically from crates to the chant: "It's a long, long way to go."

Mary sees her mother, wearing grey, dash across from an opposite store and into their restaurant. The mob now rages towards them. She is still a good ten yards from the Olympia and the fuming crowd only thirty yards or so from it in the other direction. Mary feels herself scooped up from behind. For a second she thinks of biting the arms that hold her until she realizes they're those of her father. Pavlos is next to *Baba* as they turn towards Loukas' house.

They haven't seen her! She sinks her teeth downwards, and her father drops her in surprise. "Mama!" she screams pointing towards their store.

"My God!" Pavlos turns as their mother exits their shop. Mama looks fearfully at the crowd, now only twenty yards away. Mary is gathered up once more as the three tear off toward the Olympia Restaurant.

"Inside," hollers her father, startling mama. They dash in. Mary and her mother are taken behind the counter by

Pavlos as *Baba* locks and then barricades the doors with tables thrown and shoved desperately. The shouts are an audible roar as *Baba* comes and crouches behind the patina-riddled counter with them. "Stay here," he says. Mary peeps above as the windows splinter and shards spray into the restaurant. The door is hacked open by axes and boots, barricading tables are tossed outside. Mary searches for her mother's killer as bodies advance and sees the swarthy bearded Italian with the swollen nose brandishing a hammer near the front. Bluey is next to him. Mary and her family stand as the squall nears.

The pack hurls tables over and buzzes around them as they rip apart the kitchen and smash open the cash register. Her family are in the eye of the cyclone; no-one touches them. Two men sing as they let fly chairs. *Baba* holds mama behind him, so her back is to the counter. Pavlos' hands are ready fists.

Bluey wielding his metal-rod comes closer with his mate. The latter reeks of alcohol. Bluey stares at Mary and nods in recognition. He grabs the Italian's arm, "Nobody touches them!" The Italian wildly shoves him away, eyes locked on mama's watch. He rocks into *Baba*, head barreling into her father's stomach. *Baba* braces his legs and is winded but remains between them. Mary's arm is yanked by her brother as he shoves her behind him. Next to him a chair comes crashing down over their father's head. Groaning, he manages to stand while Pavlos swings and hits a face. He sweeps another arm out but it's seized. Eventually swamped, Baba and Pavlos are buried in a flurry of leather boots and fists.

Mary readies.

"*Dammi l'orologio adesso, disgraziata Greca.*" So close, everything appears magnified to Mary: the oily black pores on his nose; his stench of desperation; the knots in his mane. Bearing his weight down on mama, the Italian knocks her to the floor and lands on top of her, one hand locked on her wrist, while the other one flails the air with a hammer.

Her mother kicks out. Mary dives as the hammer strikes.

<<>>

Mary watches her own burial. Her mama, embossed in black and her tears bleeding, tosses red earth on to Mary's coffin. Others follow. Her Great Uncle, Yannis Katavatis, places a consoling hand on Mary's shoulder. It is not her mother's embrace, but must suffice for now.

Spawn of War and Deathiness

The Inn of the Dove

Gordon Linzner

Coarse rushes tickled Muramochi Ichiro's calves below drawn-in cotton trousers as he knelt on the round mat, rump resting on heels. On his shoulder, a milk-white dove watched his chopsticks carry a fat grain of boiled rice from his bowl to almost touch her beak. She accepted the offering with dignity. Muramochi smiled and sought another tidbit.

Rain drummed on the thatch roof and, in one corner, seeped underneath to fill a wooden bucket. The pattering without became louder as the door of the inn slid open.

Two burly foot-soldiers entered. Their leather breastplates were moisture-blackened; water dripped in runnels from austere helmets. One wore a full beard that glittered, bedewed, in the flicker from the single oil lamp. His comrade was mustached, but had plucked his beard-hair to better display a battle-scar from his right ear to his chin.

"Sake!" roared the bearded man. "Warm rice-wine for two weary, sodden bushi separated from their regiment by this miserable weather!"

Muramochi, selecting another rice grain, barely glanced at the pair. The dove, however, was agitated. Her talons pinched flesh through Muramochi's thin smock. Flapping her wings as though to take flight, she burst into frantic song. Muramochi listened attentively. When she'd finished, he turned to the strangers with renewed interest.

The scarred man shook off his helmet, returned the look and offered a smile. His teeth were fashionably blackened.

"You'll never satisfy your dove with rice," he said. "Remember the children's song; she'll want beans to eat."

Muramochi acknowledged the advice with a bow. "She has been content, so far."

The beard rumbled. "Where hides our dog of a host? We have good coppers for him to cheat us of with his over-priced refreshments and vermin-ridden sleeping mats."

Muramochi stood. The bird fluttered to a perch set high on a dimly lit wall. "I am that dog," he confessed, bowing again. "I promise that you shall receive full value for your investment. As to vermin, I will personally attend to their extermination." His lips formed the softest of smiles.

The eyes above the beard widened. "This is astounding! All of the inn-keepers we've met have been old men or former farmers. You are in your prime and of powerful mien. Why, in our armor you could pass as a bushi. Is that not so, brother?"

"Indeed, Kichiji, he might be taken for a samurai!"

Muramochi bowed again. "You are perceptive, sirs. Until last year, I was samurai to a noble lord, and took pride in my post. Kichiji, did I hear you called?"

Kichiji combed rain-water from his beard. "Isochiri Kichiji. This is my younger brother, Isochiri Naru."

"I am Muramochi Ichiro."

"Ichiro? First born? Your family must be doubly proud. But how do you come to keep an inn in this desolate country village?"

Naru chuckled, unlacing his armor. "Some indiscretion with the lord's wife, I'll wager."

Muramochi shook his head and turned to step behind the screen that separated the large main room from the irori, the square sunken hearth where food and sake were heated. His lips thinned. He looked back at the men shrugging off water-soaked leggings and said, "Yes, you should hear the story."

"Sake first. Then your tale," Kichiji ordered.

"As you desire."

While the rice wine warmed, Muramochi brought out two straw mats less worn than his own, and a small wooden brazier. Fresh coals glowed in the brazier's metal-lined interior, warding the chill from the outer man as the liquor promised to ease the inner. A few moments later, Muramochi sat facing the bushi, neither of whom noticed how little he drank.

"It is no shame to admit that I was not the strongest nor most skilled samurai in my lord's employ," the inn-keeper began. "The poorest warrior among us would be the pride of any other court, save the Emperor's. Fortune selected me, however, to be husband to the lovely Kiru.

"Ah! She was so young when we met that her eyebrows had never been plucked! Amaterasu, the sun goddess, lured from her cave to gaze on the world's first mirror, could not have beheld a fairer face! The famed Kesa Gozen, dying in her husband's place to preserve her honor, could not embody more nobility, purer virtue, greater bravery! Her eyes..."

"We get the idea," Naru growled. "You loved the woman. Say so and get on with it."

Kichiji nodded. "My brother speaks for me. This paragon of womanhood is not presently in evidence and therein, I suspect, lies the heart of your tale."

Muramochi scowled at the bushi. "It is true, sirs, that I am a poor poet, and my words clumsy. Still, your interruption is most discourteous."

"Friend inn-keeper," replied Kichiji, "we are rude foot-soldiers, of little education and less patience. The court to which you were accustomed may praise verbiage, seek beauty in the nuance of a well-turned phrase or apt imagery. To hold our interest, though, you must tell your story simply."

Muramochi spoke through clenched teeth. "Her voice was as sweet as my dove's song!"

As if this were a cue, the white bird trilled a melody from her perch on the east wall. Finished, the dove cocked her head to one side and glanced at each man in turn.

Kichiji threw back his head, laughing with surprise. Even the dour Naru managed a grin that curled his scar like an earthworm driven from the soil.

"An excellent trick, inn-keeper! Perhaps we misjudged you!"

Muramochi inclined his head to the bearded speaker. This was as close as the two would get to an apology. "Things are rarely as they seem," he chided before going on.

"In short, we fell in love and exchanged three cups of sake to affirm our sacred vows. The gods of luck granted us seven months of earthly joy, one month for each god." Muramochi's eyes glazed as he recalled those times.

"And then?" barked Naru.

"One night I found my beloved Kiku dead, slain by her own hand with one of my swords. The point protruded only a bu from her back, less than the width of my fingertip, but the wooden floor was deeply stained with her precious blood."

"Are you sure she was as happy as you?" Naru asked.

Muramochi started. "Quite sure."

Kichiji raised a placating hand. "My brother means no offense. To take one's life, however, requires a reason."

"She had a reason. Her left sleeve held her death-poem. You would call it a silly thing, a young girl's naïve impressions of life's obligations opposed to the free-flying existence of a bird; to be exact, a dove. I will not recite so personal a verse. I carried it for several days, rereading it for comfort in my grief, before I noticed more writing on the other side. She had addressed a final message to me."

"Ah!" said Kichiji, rubbing his hands together. "Now we come to the meat of the nut."

"Just so. While I'd been on a routine patrol, three common soldiers sought succor at my home. Kiku offered them food and drink according to our custom, but when these rough men saw her beauty they hungered for more than sustenance. The soldiers forced themselves on my wife, each in turn and then again. They left her bruised and bleeding, her kimono wrapped above her hips as though she were a city-bred whore. No; the poorest geisha would not have been so ill-treated."

Naru coughed, setting down his sake bowl with a clatter. He looked to his brother, but the bearded soldier's attention was fixed on Muramochi. "These are restless times," Kichiji was saying. "If every raped woman took her life, we should soon be bereft of females."

Muramochi glowered. "All times are restless. Kiku was a woman of honor. She felt she had brought shame upon me, that she had not resisted as she ought; for if she had, her letter said, her virtue would have been intact and three corpses decorated our home."

"Against such odds?" Naru exclaimed. "Impossible!"

"So I would have told her, had I been there. As I was not, she chose seppuku. I swore vengeance, of course. My lord would not grant me leave to seek Kiku's disgracers. I resigned. A ronin may do things that samurai cannot."

"Spare me the details of your search, please," said Naru. "We grant you found the knaves. Let us hear of your justice."

Muramochi no longer seemed to resent these intrusions on his narrative. It was well into the ninth hour, the hour of the rat, and his patrons grew drowsy. With a smile, Muramochi said, "You anticipate too much. Two days' journey from my home, a fledgling fell from its nest, landing before me on the road."

Naru clapped his hands. "An omen!"

"An omen," the inn-keeper agreed. "I set aside my quest to nurture the bird, which matured into the dove you see. We stopped here for a night; when morning came, the bird refused to leave. I bought the business from the peasant who'd owned it, and here we have been ever since."

Kichiji stared at the speaker in disbelief. "Is that your tale?"

Muramochi nodded. "We do little trade, but there is enough to feed her and I."

"Fah!" snorted Naru, rubbing his scar. "A poor ending if I ever heard one. You're no story-teller! This sake is cold; bring us more before the rice."

"And do not accompany it with another of your boring tales," Kichiji added.

"I regret my efforts to amuse have displeased you. I shall devise a more satisfactory resolution to my history."

Kichiji grunted and turned his bearded face away. Muramochi wordlessly fetched more sake, then slipped behind the screen to prepare the rice, leaving the bushi brothers alone.

The Isochiris had marched many ken through rain and mud and cold that day. Their limbs were weary. Warmed by the liquor, and disinclined to further conversation, Naru and Kichiji sat and sipped in silence. The rain thrummed steadily overhead. Slowly, Kichiji's head sank forward until it was pillowed against his chest by his beard. Naru's eyelids grew heavy. Only wartime discipline kept their bodies erect when they wished to stretch out on the bare floor.

However, a trained soldier, even a common bushi, never fully sleeps. Soft thuds brought them around, Kichiji first. The bearded man reached hungrily for the rice bowl nearest him. His hand halted in mid-air. The younger brother, looking to his own bowl, noticed the same thing at the same moment. They exchanged glances.

"No better at running an inn than at telling stories," Kichiji spat. "Inn-keeper! How dare you insult us by presenting rice with chopsticks standing..." His voice faded as he turned to their host.

Muramochi Ichiro stood before the bushi. Fierce laughter shone in his eyes. Well might they be shocked into silence! His lacquered steel breastplate glittered in the dimly lit room, as did the metal plates covering long gauntlets of fabric on his arms. His baggy trousers were now tucked into shin guards, above bearskin boots. An angry, ornate dragon topped his elaborate helmet. The chinstraps were not fastened; they tied so tightly that speech would have been impossible.

"Now I can embellish my tale," Muramochi said softly.

Naru, realizing his jaw hung open, shut it with a snap. "A childish display," he growled.

"Absolutely," his brother agreed. "We never doubted your truthfulness, inn-keeper. Your inferior sense of narrative offended us."

"Have I displeased my guests again?" Muramochi asked in the same quiet tone. Two blades hung from his belt: the short katana and the long tachi. A leather-gloved hand rested on the hilt of each.

Kichiji pretended not to see this. "You have, grievously. Look at these chopsticks. To tender your wares as though making an offering to the spirits of the dead is outrageous!"

Muramochi smiled. "Not at all. The minute you entered my inn, you were dead men."

The brothers leapt to their feet. "What shabby hospitality," Naru protested.

"It is better than you deserve. My wife was raped almost a year ago to this day."

"What is that to...?"

"In the village of Aiknu. I see you understand now. Who was the third bushi?"

"Our brother Takamori," Naru sullenly replied. "He was killed in battle. An arrow through the eye."

"I thank the gods for sharing my burden." Muramochi stepped forward.

"Is this honorable?" Kichiji cried. "Our armor and weapons lie behind us. We are defenseless."

"How honorable was the attack of three armed soldiers on a lone woman?"

Naru stepped backwards, keeping an eye on Muramochi's keen sword edge. From his pile of belongings, he withdrew his own tachi. Muramochi did not interfere.

"He's a swaggering braggart, brother! Come! We can slice him like a snake and be on our way before the eighth hour!"

The dove fluttered once around the room and returned to her perch, warbling anxiously. Kichiji laughed, rushing to his own baggage. "Hai! We'll roast his omen for our dinner!"

Muramochi's smile faded. His eyes grew hard as rage flowed through his veins. Snarling, he raised the tachi for attack.

Covering his brother, Naru ran forward, feinted, and jumped back. Without his armor, he depended on agility to avoid Muramochi's thrusts. Using a sword as a shield was a good way to ruin an expensive blade.

Muramochi swung the long sword to discourage Naru, but wasted no effort on strokes that could not reach his opponent. There were two men to deal with; every blow must count.

Emboldened, Naru feinted again, his point striking the inn-keeper's breastplate. He retreated at once, lest his weapon catch in the etched ornamentation and give Muramochi his necessary second's advantage. Again the armored man made no offensive move.

The bushi laughed. This would be soon ended!

Kichiji approached from the left. Miramochi unsheathed his katana. With weapons in both hands, he could not maintain a defensive posture, but that did not matter. What happened to him was unimportant, if these two died.

Kichiji's first feint sliced only air.

Naru's blade scraped along the metal plates on Muramochi's right arm, slipping under one to slash fabric and skin. Blood oozed as the scarred man dodged the return blow.

Kichiji aimed for the neck. Muramochi ducked. The blow knocked off his helmet and opened a deep gash in his forehead. Muramochi rushed the bearded man, who hurriedly gave ground, almost stumbling over a straw mat.

It was Naru's turn again. His sword, tasting blood, thirsted for more. One sweep could divorce the inn-keeper's head from his shoulders.

As Muramochi intended, Naru's approach was overconfident. The ronin spun around, ignoring Kichiji for the moment. His heavy blade clove flesh and bone. Naru's sword arm, severed above the elbow, struck the floor. The stunned bushi followed it.

Muramochi turned to the elder brother. Kichiji's anger should make him careless, as well.

Then his world went black.

Blood from his gash had dripped into his eyes.

Kichiji chuckled at Muramochi's predicament, then fell silent. Slowly, wary of loose floorboards, he circled the straw mats to creep toward the inn-keeper. Naru would be avenged.

Muramochi was reluctant to sheathe either weapon, for Kichiji's attack could come from any side. He raised his left arm to staunch the crimson flow with his forearm. The gauntlet's plates further tore the wound. He must fight blind. Groans from behind told him that Naru, mortally wounded, was not yet dead. If the scarred man had strength enough for another blow...

Kichiji stopped a sword's length from the inn-keeper, seeking a vulnerable spot for his thrust. The exposed throat seemed likely. He raised the tachi, not daring to breathe for fear of betraying his position.

With a cry, the dove plunged from her perch toward the bearded man. Kichiji dodged her beak and claws. The breeze of her flight ruffled his hair. He was proud that he'd not exposed himself with even a stifled curse at the surprising attack. Hearing a bird could not help Muramochi locate an opponent.

Yet the inn-keeper leaned forward suddenly, forming a narrow arc with both blades. The weapons found their target at the same moment. Kichiji collapsed with a moan, spurting blood and entrails.

Muramochi spun around, anticipating a final attack by Naru. The latter only groaned. Flitting wings cooled the blood on Muramochi's cheek as the dove regained his shoulder. The bird issued a brief, soulful melody. Muramochi nodded and sank to the floor. His harsh breathing eased. He tore a cotton trouser leg into strips to wipe his eyes and bind his wound.

His first sight was Naru's agonized face. Incredible that the bushi still lived, with so much blood loss! Still, the dimming eyes foretold his end.

"We were ordinary foot-soldiers," Naru accused, "marching into a battle none of us might survive. I do not apologize for what we did. You cannot blame us."

Muramochi stripped off a blood-soaked leather glove. His bare finger stroked the dove's breast. The bird cooed.

"Nor dare you blame me for what I have done tonight," the inn-keeper replied. "No matter. It is ended. My wife's soul is unburdened, free to seek its destiny."

Naru coughed. Crimson stained his black teeth, spilt down his chin, tracing the scar-line. "My arm..."

"Shall be buried with you."

Naru grimaced thanks. As if in acknowledgement, the dove nodded at him, then cooed approvingly in Muramochi's ear.

"A... remarkable... bird," Naru gasped. Then his eyes, still open, saw no more.

Muramochi sat still, breathing shallowly, stroking the dove's feathers. The bird chirruped impatiently. Sighing, he stood up. The clatter of his armor jarred after the thick silence. For the first time, he realized the patter on the roof was gone. The storm had ended.

Muramochi walked stiffly to the inn's door and slid it open. Cool, fresh air gently greeted him. Good. It would clear the stench of sweat and death from the interior. Gore tightened on his face.

The bird's tune was cheerful. Had Muramochi any close neighbors to be wakened by the conflict, they would have wondered at the song of a day bird at the hour of the ox, with dawn half a night away. More curious, still, was the sight of such a bird winging through the blackness, away from warmth and light, food and shelter.

Muramochi stared as the white dot vanished in the moonless blackness. A tear etched through the blood on his cheek. Words came too late. He spoke them anyway.

"Happiness go with you, Kiku."

Sickle Claws: Hesperonychus Monstrous

Alicia Hilton

Mother looked nothing like me: no scar across her forehead, no feathers or scales, and she didn't have wings, a tail, claws, or a beak with an insatiable craving for flesh. Her skin was pink and supple, her head topped with a crown of glossy black hair. All of the other humans called me *Hesperonychus monstrous,* or dinosaur, but Mother said I'm her baby.

Most of my surgical modifications were completed when I was a naïve hatchling, but the microcontroller in my brain didn't prevent me from learning that Mother was more of a monster than me.

All of my mornings used to be the same. Ravenous, I would call for Mother when I smelled her sweet scent and heard her footsteps *clacking* in the hallway. By the time she approached my enclosure, I would be shrieking and racing back and forth, lunging at the glass wall and kicking up dirt. Even when I tried to be patient, my rapidly growing body willed me to *feed, feed, feed.*

She'd unbolt the door and roll in the metal box. When she opened the lid, my flanks would quiver, but I wouldn't pounce. As I watched the prey wriggle and skitter away, my beak would fill with saliva. I wasn't allowed to hunt until Mother said, "Kill."

The goo beneath exoskeletons was almost as delicious as salty, coppery, pulsing muscles, but the exhilaration of the chase really made my heart race. After I'd crunched and swallowed all of the bones, Mother would give me a cuddle.

Sometimes a caress became a pinch, a pet became a slap, and if I'd been very naughty, the collar around my neck would give me a zap, but I didn't understand the meaning of true agony until fangs tore through my own flesh.

<<>>

By the time my feathers had grown over most of my scars, my wings were strong enough to lift me off the ground. Hearing Mother's praise made me screech with joy.

"Follow the light," she said, pointing her baton at a tree. The red beam shone upon the leaves. When I got close to the target, she swiveled the light, illuminating the top of another tree.

If I obeyed all of her commands, she rewarded me with treats and pets, but one day, while I was munching on a juicy mouse, she hooked a leash to my collar, and snapped a muzzle over my beak.

I shook my head, but couldn't free my beak. Lifting my right forelimb, I tried to slash the muzzle, but my claws wouldn't tear it.

"No, Baby!" she said.

A zap from my collar made my muscles spasm. Urine trickled down my leg.

She said, "Will you be good?"

I whined, more from shame than pain.

She said, "Get in the cage." She pointed at a metal box on wheels. It was barely bigger than me.

After I hopped in, she shut the door, and pushed the box out of my enclosure. Usually, the carts that I rode in were made from wire, but this carrier was solid metal, except for one ventilation slit in the door, and slits at the top of the box.

Anxiety made me breathe faster. I pressed my face closer to the ventilation hole, and saw we were passing other glass-fronted enclosures. Something covered in grey and brown feathers flew past a tree. Was it a dinosaur like me?

Another set of footsteps joined Mother. *Slap, drag, slap, drag.* The human sounded heavier, and his gait was uneven. He must be injured. His scent was stronger than Mother's, sour, like something inside him was rotting.

He said, "The park's locked down."

Mother said, "Dome secured?"

He said, "Of course. You think I'm an idiot?"

The man wasn't shouting, but his angry tone made my chest constrict. I clawed at the box, wanting to protect Mother.

She said, "It's okay, Baby. We're almost there."

Through the slit, I saw the man opening a door.

Mother pushed the cart through the door. Instead of entering another hallway, we seemed to be inside of a larger pen. The lights were off. I squinted, trying to see into the distance. My nostrils quivered. So many new scents!

Thunk. The cage that I was riding in unlatched. A warm breeze ruffled my feathers.

Mother tugged on my leash. She said, "Come out, Baby."

The ground felt strange beneath my feet. The surface was hard and warm. It wasn't dirt, like the inside of my pen, or slippery like the floor in the laboratory.

The man with the limp walked back towards the laboratory.

Mother pressed a button on my leash, unwinding it. She said, "Up, Baby." She raised her hand, and pointed her baton. The red beam was brighter than usual, but it only cleaved a narrow path through the darkness.

Eager to please her, I flapped my wings and took off. Higher and higher I rose. The pen we were inside was huge! The ceiling so far away!

I heard the sound of splashing water and saw hazy lights. As I got closer to the pool, I saw shapes wriggling in the water. I sniffed the air, sensing the presence of flesh. Eager to feed, I angled my wings and descended.

Mother's baton light jerked to the left and flashed, commanding that I return.

I shrieked, begging Mother to let me hunt.

All of a sudden, the water lights disappeared. A loud ringing noise made me yelp.

A surge of heat jolted my neck as the collar gave me a zap. I circled back, and flew towards Mother.

<<>>

A meal of six rats wouldn't fill my stomach, but Mother started withholding food. People walked past my enclosure, but they didn't feed me, even when I shrieked.

My mouth watered when I smelled flesh burning. Not rodents. The creature must've been a lot bigger. I sniffed the air, savoring the scent of bubbling fat.

The man with the limp walked past my enclosure. He was speaking into a little box. "Three more to put down," he said, pausing to scratch his head. "No, too risky. They don't follow commands."

I trotted closer, and scuffed my feet against the dirt, churning up dust.

The man backed away from the glass and said, "Two more days. That's all I can give you!"

I lunged, slamming my body into the glass wall, but it didn't crack.

The man stumbled backward, and stared at me.

My side ached, but when I stretched my wings, the pain didn't get worse. I opened my beak and cried, begging to be fed, but the man limped away.

When you're starving, even the most docile baby can become ferocious. I raised my foot, and scratched the glass, but my claws only left dirty marks.

I used my other foot, *slashing*, over and over, but the glass wouldn't break. Panting from exertion, I stared at my surroundings. There must be something to eat!

I pecked at tree trunks, but couldn't find bugs, and there weren't worms or grubs underneath the shrubs. Desperate for food, I flapped my wings, propelling myself up to bite leaves from a tree. The dry texture and bitter taste made me snarl.

Scratching my claws against the dirt, I dug a hole, working off my fury. When the hole got as deep as the top of my feet, I struck something that was too hard to dig through.

I moved closer to the nearest tree, but the hard thing was under the dirt there, too.

Finally, Mother tapped on the glass. I stopped digging and cocked my head. The door didn't open, but I heard Mother's voice through the glass. She said, "Baby has to work if she wants to eat. Are you ready to hunt?"

"Hunt," meant food. I exhaled a big breath and honked.

I climbed into the rolling cart, and Mother pushed it towards the other end of the laboratory, away from the smell of cooked flesh.

We passed shiny metal tables that had clear boxes on top filled with things that looked like the rocks inside my enclosure, except they were smoother.

The sound of humming machines got louder, and I smelled something terrible. Not bitter like the leaves I'd eaten. A stench that made me want to leap out of the box, but Mother had closed the door. I trembled, and my wings hit the side of the box.

Mother said, "We're almost there." She put one of her hands next to the door, so I could sniff it.

The ventilation hole was too narrow for me to lick her, but I inhaled a deep breath. Her sweet scent calmed me.

When the cart stopped rolling and the box sprang open, I stepped out. I tried to follow Mother, but she shut the enclosure's door, locking me inside. There were no trees or rocks, no dirt under my feet. Sniffing my surroundings, I paced. My claws made a *scritch scratch* sound against the slippery floor.

Through the glass wall, I saw Mother remove her jacket and put on a white suit that covered her body, even her hands and feet. Then she put something over her face that looked like the metal bucket that she used to hold worms, except I could see her eyes.

Above my head, I heard a voice that said, "Are you ready to hunt?" It sounded like Mother, but she was still outside the enclosure. I sniffed the air again, but didn't smell flesh, just the nasty smell.

The voice said, "Kill."

I trotted towards the other end of the enclosure, but I didn't hear squeaks or skittering feet.

All of a sudden, I heard a *thunk* behind me, and a *roar*. I spun around and saw a huge beast! It ran on four legs like the rats, but was much faster.

I'd never hunted prey that was bigger than me.

Mother pointed her baton at the creature, shining the red light on its fur.

Instead of attacking, I flapped my wings, soaring towards the ceiling, but my collar gave me such a strong shock, I lost control of my muscles. Spasming, I slammed into a wall and slid to the floor.

"Kill!" Mother said.

I stood, but my legs were wobbly. Holding my wings out to make myself look bigger, I screeched.

"Good Baby. Kill!"

As the furry creature bounded towards me, I smelled a foul stench. Black goo dripped from its fangs.

Before I could gather the courage to attack, the monster roared and leapt at me.

I raised my wings to shield my face and skittered backward, but I was too slow.

Fangs sank into my chest, penetrating my feathers and scales.

I jabbed at the furry head with my beak, but the skull was too tough to crack.

The monster's snout burrowed deeper, its teeth tearing through muscle.

I shrieked and raised one of my feet, trying to gouge the belly, but I struck only air. I slashed my foot again, and my claws tore fur and shredded flesh. Cold fluid splashed on my feet and feathers. It stank worse than anything I'd ever smelled.

The beast snarled and released its grip, backing away from me with feathers protruding from its jaws.

Springing forward, I flapped my wings and leapt onto the beast's back.

The creature thrashed and snapped its jaws, then flopped onto its side. Struggling, our bodies slammed against the floor. The beast was burrowing its snout into my haunch, and the pain was excruciating.

I jabbed my beak at the head. The fur was soft, but my beak bounced off bone. I struck again, piercing an eye.

"Kill!" Mother said.

I jabbed again, and again, until the beast had finally stopped moving.

"Good Baby!" Mother said.

My head feathers were so slick, black fluid was dripping into my eyes. I tried to run towards the glass, but my wounds made me stumble. Before I could stand, cold water sprayed from the ceiling and soaked my feathers. It tasted bitter, not like the water that Mother gave me.

Shivering, I looked for shelter, but there were no trees, only the cart. I crawled inside.

I rubbed my beak through my wings, trying to clean off the tacky liquid from the monster's eye.

Mother kept watching me, but she didn't open the enclosure.

When I was drenched, the water stopped spraying from the ceiling. I heard heavy footsteps approaching the glass wall, and I saw the man with the limp walking towards Mother.

Mother said, "You got the tranq? She's going to need stitches."

I heard a *thunk* coming from behind me. Expecting to see another monster, I jerked my head around, but it was just a rat.

Phhhhht. A new sound made me turn back towards Mother. I felt a sharp pain and screeched. A little stick was stuck in my shoulder. I tried to grasp it with my beak, but when I moved, I got so dizzy, that I collapsed.

Gasping, I struggled to stand, but my legs would only twitch. My eyes drifted shut. Straining to stay awake, I heard the door open, and footsteps walking towards me. I smelled Mother's sweet scent, and other unfamiliar humans.

Something touched my neck. I opened my eyes and saw four humans wearing the white suits. One of them had a long metal stick that was pointy on the end. Fear made me lash out. With my remaining strength, I raised a foreleg and slashed through fabric and flesh.

<<>>

Moonlight streamed through the skylight. I blinked, focusing on my surroundings. I was back in my usual enclosure. The trees near me seemed to be bending. I shut my eyes, and opened them again. The trees looked normal. Beyond the glass wall, the laboratory was dark. No sounds of people. Only humming machines.

I'd never been so thirsty. My chest and haunch were sore. Patches of feathers were missing where the monster had bitten me.

When I walked towards my water bowl, dizziness made me sway. I slurped until the bowl was empty. My stomach rumbled, but there was no food near the water bowl, not even a worm or a beetle grub.

Exhaustion made me collapse before I could crawl behind the bushes, so I slept out in the open, beside the water bowl.

I woke to the sound of footsteps. Mother was watching me!

Honking to greet her, I trotted towards the glass wall. When I got closer, I saw a woman with yellow hair, walking towards Mother.

I hid behind a tree.

The other woman said, "How does she look?"

Mother said, "Her mobility's good, considering the wounds."

"Any signs of infection?"

"No seepage from the incisions."

"She's immune?"

Mother said, "It's too early to tell."

<<>>

Humans stared at me through the glass, but they'd stopped bringing me mice and rats.

When Mother walked past my enclosure, she acted like she didn't notice me, even when I flew back and forth, swooped from the trees to the ground, pecked *rat, tat, tat* against the glass.

Bark from the trees didn't taste any better than the leaves.

So cold, I shivered in a patch of light that streamed through the skylight, plucking feathers from my breast, sucking on the fluid from the base of the quills.

<<>>

A clattering noise woke me. Peering from my hiding place behind a tree, I saw a metal box by the door of my enclosure. It was bigger than the cart I usually rode in. Maybe there was food inside!

The box was open at one end. I gobbled up a pile of worms. Chomping vigorously, I shrieked in gratitude.

The box slammed closed, trapping me.

Scooping the last of the worms into my beak, I swallowed them quickly.

The box was too small for me to pace. I scratched my claws against the sides.

Footsteps approached, the *clacking* of Mother's feet. I squealed in relief.

"Are you ready to hunt?" Mother said. She wheeled the box towards the door, over the threshold, down the shiny hallway past the tables, and into the white enclosure.

The cage opened after Mother left, but I didn't climb out.

I heard a *thunk*, and smelled the same stench that had come from the furry monster.

My collar gave me a shock.

I darted from the box.

A man lurched from a gap in the wall. When he saw me, he growled.

The wall behind him slammed shut.

He moved more like an animal than a human, twitching and jerking, sniffing the air as if he was hunting for prey.

I scuttled backward.

Mother said, "Kill." She pointed her baton at his face. The red light made him pause, but then he charged at me. As he got closer, his teeth chattered. Black goo seeped from his mouth.

I swiveled my head, glanced at the glass wall, and counted three humans with Mother.

I heard another growl, but the noise came from my throat. Extending my sickle claws, I leapt on my prey.

His teeth chomped on feathers, but they couldn't pierce my scales.

By the time the man had stopped twitching, my head crest was coated with slime.

Water sprayed from the ceiling, but I didn't get into the box. I kept staring at the glass wall, watching Mother. She lifted a stick. A little hole in the glass opened. *Phhhhhht.*

After the tranq wore off, I knew what to do. Humans were easier to hunt than the furry monster.

<<>>

The woman with the yellow hair shoved the man with the limp and sprinted into the hallway. She tasted sweet.

The tall man with the pointy stick ran faster than Mother, but I chased him and slashed his belly.

Mother tried to lock me in the white room, but I slammed my body against the door, and forced it open. The alarm was ringing, but it didn't drown out the sound of her shrieks.

Down the hallway she sprinted, heading for the door that led to the big pool of water with the wriggling things. She skidded to a stop when she reached the door, and tugged the handle. It rattled, but didn't open.

Her fear smell got stronger. I licked my beak and snorted.

She pressed her hand on a box on the wall beside the door. *Beep.* The door swung open.

I was close enough to slash her, but pawed the floor instead.

"No, Baby!" she shouted. She pushed a button on the controller hanging from her belt, and my collar gave me a jolt.

Pain fueled my rage. Leaping with my sickle claws outstretched, I pounced, knocking her to the ground. The door started to close, but *thunked* against her legs.

She screamed and tried to crawl away.

My beak grasped her neck. *Crunch.* Her throat made a gurgling sound as I lapped the coppery essence.

More fluid splashed me, but it was cold, not warm. I stopped feeding, and sniffed the air. Icy drops pelted my face and body, but they didn't taste bitter like the water that sprayed from the ceiling in the white room.

The alarm had finally stopped ringing. It was dark in the big pen, like it was when Mother had me fly to the pool. I heard a *whooshing* sound in the distance that made me tremble.

Stepping over Mother's body, I retreated into the laboratory. The sound of my claws, scratching against the slippery floor, echoed down the hallway.

The man with the limp was lying where he'd fallen, in a puddle of blood. My belly rumbled, urging me to feed, but I'd only swallowed one more bite of flesh before I began to retch.

The gory puddle that sprayed from my throat had an oily sheen and an acrid stench, like the furry monster and the first man that I'd killed, but not as foul smelling.

My gut kept heaving, though it was empty. Finally, breathing hard, I raised my head.

Something was shrieking, and it wasn't a human. I cocked my head, listening. The cries were getting louder.

Roaring, I bounded towards the sound.

The first pen that I passed had trees inside it, like my habitat, but I didn't see any animals. In the second pen, I glimpsed a flash of fur behind the shrubberies. The creature wasn't as big as the furry monster that had attacked me, but panic made me skitter away from the glass. Sliding across the floor, I crashed into a table.

A flicker of movement caught my attention. The rocks in one of the clear boxes were cracked. Baby dinosaurs! Bald patches of grey skin showed where their pinfeathers hadn't grown in, but their eyes were open. Tiny jaws clacked, begging to be fed. The hatchlings stood on their hind legs and had sickle claws like me, but they didn't have beaks or wings. So many babies, trapped.

I was tall enough to reach the box without having to jump on the table. I jabbed it with my beak, but it didn't open.

One of the raptors inside the box snapped at a smaller sibling, chomping on a forelimb. The other dinosaur hissed and wriggled, but couldn't break free. A trickle of fluid streamed from the wound.

I roared and swatted the box. My claws made a grating sound as they scratched the surface, but the box didn't move or break.

The dinosaur that'd attacked its sibling opened its jaws, and looked at me. For a moment, all of the babies were silent. Then the aggressive one led the shrieking chorus, and hopped up and down, scratching the side of the box with its sickle claws.

I slammed my forelimb into the box. *Crack*, a big fissure appeared. Swatting it again, I tore off the top. Shards flew through the air.

The wounded dinosaur *screeched* when I grasped its belly with my beak. It would've been easy to crush the delicate bones, but I set the baby on the floor, and reached for another.

I was raised to be a monster, but I wanted to be a mother. Mothers should protect their babies, even if they looked different.

The One about the Last Prayer (1939)

Alma Alexander

VAL HALL 2016

Classes came and went at Val Hall. Many different kinds of classes existed—those taught by experts who came in to teach more rarefied or theoretical subjects, or those taken (solo or in groups) online, whether for pure pleasure or for certification. Sometimes, when possible and eagerly acclaimed, applied practical processes and methods of assorted disciplines were taught by those residents of the Hall who had themselves practiced an art or a craft or a profession and were willing to pass all their accumulated wealth of experience to others who wished to learn. Some of those were more popular than others–there were always people wanting to learn to read Tarot cards, for instance–but when Karl Kellerman was persuaded to start pastry classes the response was as immediate and animated as it was unexpected. Karl himself looked bemused as he came into the Val Hall kitchen, with an area set aside for his group, and saw more than a dozen smiling pupils waiting for him. His pale blue eyes, distorted by his thick spectacles, became quite moist, and his lower lip trembled a little.

"People have heard of you, you know," Eddie, in charge of the preparations for this class and probably instrumental in persuading Karl to teach it in the first place, said, sounding rather smug about it. "You have a reputation."

"I do...?" Karl said softly, sounding bewildered by the idea.

"Of course you do. Kellerman's was an institution. Now. Where do we begin? Is there a secret?"

Karl smiled at the gathered would-be pastry makers. "The secret," he said softly, "is good ingredients... a light touch... and love."

The products of the Karl Kellerman pastry classes were distributed to the rest of the residents at the conclusion of every class, and before long the residents began to look forward to the days when they could expect that bounty. "Is it a Kellerman day?" became something of a tradition at the Hall, and Karl Kellerman, surrounded by chocolate, custard, yeasty dough, confectioner's sugar and clouds of flour, began to crawl out of a long melancholy–which was partly the thing that Eddie had been trying to accomplish. For the first time since he arrived at Val Hall, taciturn and icily polite in his German way, Karl showed signs of actually thawing out and finding companions amongst the residents (the older ladies were particularly aflutter when he came by offering melt-in-the-mouth cream puffs). But he reserved a special kind of gratitude–and some of his best pastries–for Eddie, whom he appeared to have singled out as a friend.

As with all his clients in the Hall, Eddie had done his research with Karl Kellerman, and the man's life was a litany of trouble and misery. But Eddie never revealed his knowledge or forced confidences; he waited, and often the people who needed him came to him of their own accord, telling him things it was necessary for him to know, accepting the help that he could offer even without ever having been truly aware that they had come to him seeking it. Eddie knew how to wait. And with Karl, it was particularly important not to pry, or to rush him. Because Karl carried not his own misery, but the tragedy of multitudes.

They had called him the Ghost Whisperer.

BAD TANNENHOLZ, GERMANY, 1939

Karl Kellerman had been five years old when he had been delivered to Klaus Schmidt, his mother's dour and childless older brother, when he became the sole survivor of the Kellerman family–his mother, Elsa, dead less than a week after giving birth to his younger brother Jozef, who survived only a handful of days longer in what was a blighted winter; his father, Johann, dead of reasons unknown (but people whispered broken heart) before the leaves began to turn in the following year. Karl had very few options and knew enough to be grateful when he was shipped off by authorities to the only family they could find for him. He was trussed up and put on a train, all his worldly goods in one small duffel bag which had to be small enough for him to carry; it contained little more than a change of clothes, a pair of scuffed shoes, and a notebook full of recipes in his mother's handwriting which some well-meaning soul had thought he might want to remember her by. His uncle collected him from the railroad station at his destination, a label tied around his neck like a wayward parcel. Onkel Klaus, who had few words for the boy, took him home to the cottage which he shared with Tante Greta and a sad-faced, three-legged dog who had no wish to make any further friends in what was left of his lifetime. The cottage, utilitarian and gray, had a window-box where Tante Greta grew red geraniums, the only spot of color in the place. It was a quiet and joyless house, quite appropriate to Onkel Klaus's job as the gravedigger for the local church, and the addition of a boy into a place that had never known the laughter of children did absolutely nothing to change that–it was Karl who surrendered, who sank into its silence and did not struggle as its habits and shrouds wrapped around him. An unprepossessing boy, with washed-out yellow hair and eyes of a blue so pale so as to almost disappear against his sclera, he received little education, and it became a given, without much discussion, that he would assist his uncle with his sexton duties–digging graves, dourly filling them back in when funerals deposited coffins into the holes, occasionally assisting with gravestones and the desultory upkeep of the cemetery.

He was hopelessly short-sighted, squinting at a blurry world from those pale blue eyes, and his uncle made a stab at helping matters by providing a pair of hit-or-miss spectacles. It was no thanks to these that Karl discovered that a good book would provide an escape from his grim reality–and as a pre-teen he discovered the world of his namesake, the writer Karl May, and his glorious, mythical vision of the American Wild West. The Karl May books that the boy Karl owned were battered old relics, discards from a previous life somewhere else where they had once been read and loved–but to young Karl they were treasures. He would escape with one or the other of them, reading and re-reading them until he almost knew them all by heart, and sit with his back against one of the cemetery trees in the summer, peering at the pages of the ancient books, loving the sense of freedom and purpose they gave him, glancing around every so often just in case a badly strayed Apache warrior might step out from behind some ancient leaning gravestone and offer another German the gift of blood brotherhood, just like Winnetou had done with Old Shatterhand.

It was not the Indians who came to him, though. At least, not yet.

In the summer of 1939, sixteen years old, alone, lost in his Karl May-fired imagination, Karl Kellerman paused for a moment and laid the book down on his lap, taking off his spectacles with his free hand and rubbing at his tired eyes with his knuckle. As he blinked his vision back into no more than its usual blurriness, staring out into middle distance across the cemetery, he became aware that he could suddenly see rather more sharply than usual–and that he was not alone.

The cemetery was *crowded.*

People drifted by, by themselves, in pairs or in couples, in families, in loose groups. If he listened hard, Karl could hear a whisper–something that they were all saying– sometimes he could see their hands go up to their foreheads as they murmured the words, as if in a ritual, one he was not familiar with. A different faith. A different...

He caught the syllables of what was being said. They were meaningless to him.

Shema Yisroel Adonai Elohenu Adonai Echad.

Shema Yisroel.

Shema...

Karl laid his book on the grass beside him and scrambled to his feet, unfolding his gangly sixteen-year-old frame, fumbling to put his glasses back on, to at least try and get a closer look at this sudden invasion.

But when he finally got his glasses adjusted properly... he was alone in the cemetery. No whispering crowds. Not a soul. Nobody except him.

He yanked off the glasses... and they were back.

They mostly ignored him completely, as though he wasn't present at all. He thought he saw a couple of them slant a look in his direction, but none of them stopped, none of them even hesitated. They just kept moving. Karl tried to count but he lost count after some forty of them–and most of them were going in a very specific direction, diagonally across the cemetery, towards the very back, where the small Hebrew section was.

Shema Yisroel.

Jewish ghosts. Jewish dead. So many of them.

He slowly replaced his glasses. The ghosts vanished. He took them off. They returned.

Karl fled, abandoning the book under the tree, racing away, stumbling over his own feet in his haste, gulping air. No. This was not possible. This was not real. This was not real. This was not...

He was going to tell Onkel Klaus about it, ask him if he knew why the ghosts were there, but his voice died in his throat when he tried. He could not find the words to ask the man who had dug so many graves–the man who was so doggedly rooted in the pure prosaic dirt of death–about what happened to the souls which had once inhabited the abandoned mortal shells of the bodies being consigned into the hole dug in the ground. This was not Onkel Klaus's province. And the priest who presided over their church–how was Karl to ask a Christian priest why so many Jewish dead were floating about in his very Christian cemetery?

So many Jewish dead. So many. What was happening to them all, that so many souls had come searching for home like this? Karl knew nothing about what Jews thought or believed, what their ideas were on heaven or hell, where they thought their dead ended up after they departed this life–he knew nothing about why so many of them–so many of them whom he knew to be dead, whom he could only somehow see when his poor broken eyesight was not being 'corrected' by improving lenses, the only time he could literally see the truth of anything through his own eyes and not through other people's prisms–why so many of them were there. And why it was that nobody else could apparently see them. Because if anyone else had–anyone other than a poor, ill-educated, ignorable boy who was apprenticed to the grave-digger–there would have already been a noise about it. Instead, the world was quiet–too quiet, perhaps–like in that moment when birds stop singing, just before a big storm was about to break.

What had happened? What was happening? What... was about to happen...?

Karl did not go to the cemetery the next day, too afraid to return–but then he missed his book, and remembered that he had left it beneath the tree in the cemetery. It was still a treasure, a treasure he wasn't willing to abandon. So, on the third day after he first saw the ghosts, he crept back to the cemetery, his glasses firmly on his nose, refusing to look left or right, trudging straight to the tree he had been reading. He was there to get his book. He was quietly whispering, "*Enschüldigung.* I am sorry. Please excuse me. I mean no harm. Excuse me. Excuse me."

He did not know to whom he spoke. There was nobody else there.

His book was where he had left it, and he gratefully picked it up, gathered it up against his chest with both arms. And then he stopped, hesitating. And turned, slowly, facing the graves. And then, with one hand, reached out and slowly, very slowly, almost in terror, slipped his glasses off.

They were there. Walking by. Touching their fingers to their brows, covering their eyes briefly, whispering. *Shema Yisroel.*

"What does it mean?" Karl blurted, out loud. "Why do you say this? Who are you? Where do you go?"

One of them stopped at the sound of his voice, turned towards him. It was a girl, his age, maybe only a year or so younger, her face still holding the roundness of childhood.

"What does it mean? It means, Hear, O *Israel*: the Lord is our God, the Lord is One. It is how we greet God. It is our prayer. Our first prayer. The first we learn when we are children. The first prayer we say when we wake. It is the last prayer. It is the prayer we say before we go to sleep at night. It is the prayer we say before we are about to die."

"Who are you?" Karl rasped.

"We are not, not anymore," the girl said. "These are spirits–these are souls–the bodies that once gave us shelter are already doomed. So we come. We come home. We seek home."

"What do you mean?"

"They have killed us," the girl said. "They have... they will have... we are all already dead. Our bodies just wait to die. Our bodies might die quickly in agony or slowly in suffering, but they are doomed. We are all already dead, even though for some of us our bodies still walk amongst you."

"You are all... Jews...? All of you? Why...?"

"Not all," she said calmly, and turned to point. "There are those like him... and that one over there... they play their guitars, or their violins, or they dance, and they wear strange clothes and hoops in their ears and bright scarves, and they have black hair and dark eyes and they... they call themselves the Roma." Karl looked where she showed him, and he saw a young man with bold eyes and bare feet dancing while playing a fiery dance tune on his fiddle, he saw a young woman carrying a baby in a red shawl with silk fringes, he saw a man with bronzed muscled arms bursting out of dirty torn shirtsleeves striding along with his eyes on the ground. "They are with us on our road. We give them the Shema and sometimes they take it, sometimes not, sometimes they just dance–sometimes they ask us to dance, sometimes we dance with them. It is all a dance, they say. Or there's those–" she pointed again, and he saw the difference immediately, the paler skin, the lighter hair, the long straight noses, the deep-set light-colored eyes, the high cheekbones, men and women and children, some wearing colorful obviously traditional dress Karl didn't recognize. "I don't know where they all come from but they will tell you they're Polish, Czech, Serbian–we are Jews, they are Slavs, and yet somehow we all belong together, all dead together..."

"They say your Shema too?"

"No, they have their own prayers, although some of them sometimes repeat ours after us, for respect, and I know a few words of theirs already."

"Where are you all going?"

"We go to God," the girl said. "Our bodies are already dust, and they will return to dust. Our spirits are shining and they are eternal. We all go to God."

"But what happened...?"

"It hasn't happened yet," she said, frowning. "I don't think. Not quite. But it is going to happen. It is starting to happen. It is already amongst us all, this death, some of us just haven't stopped to greet it yet. But there are more coming."

"How many?" Karl gasped.

"I don't know. Many. I can feel them at our backs." She fluttered her hands once or twice, as though she was trying to count on her fingers, and then gave up. "Many. Too many to count..."

Karl snatched his glasses from his face. The girl and all her companion shadows disappeared. Shaking, he shoved them back onto his face, clumsy in his haste. She had already moved on, the girl he had been speaking to–he had not even asked her name. The whispers remained–Shema Yisroel. And other words, ones that followed that, he could hear, but they were foreign and strange and kept slipping through his mind, the words slippery and unknowable, but somehow etching themselves in his brain:*Baruch shem kavod malchuto l'olam va-ed.* He would learn, later, what they meant. *Blessed is the name of His glorious kingdom for ever and ever.*

His eyes raked the passing ghosts but he could no longer see her. But he saw something else. He saw two young men, maybe only a handful of years older than himself, walking side by side, their hands lightly clasped with fingers interlaced, like lovers did. They looked straight ahead, both of them, but now and then one or the other would steal a glance at his companion's face, a loving glance, full of passion and yearning, the kind of glance that Karl could only imagine being turned on himself but which made him quiver where he stood; he was watching when the two young men managed to snatch their secret glance at the same moment, and their eyes met, and the smiles that blossomed on both faces broke Karl's heart. They, too, were dead. And Karl knew in that moment that it was very possible that he, himself, might qualify for this parade of ghosts, if that look was to be a measure–because he would live only to find that look on another man's face when it turned towards him.

He would know all too quickly who the Jewish ghosts had been.

As that summer waned, in September of 1939, Karl's country, Germany, invaded Poland–Poland, which lay only about an hour away from his small town. And very soon they started to gather the Jews, and send them away. Somewhere. To a place from which they sent their spirits, back to their homes, back to the places they knew, on their road to God's country and the resurrection of the righteous when the Kingdom of God prevailed. To a place from which their future ghosts had told Karl the future.

He did not know the names of Auschwitz, and Dachau, and Birkenau, and Belsen. Not yet. But the world would learn them, and recoil. In Auschwitz alone, Karl would learn much later, more than 60,000 human beings judged "inferior" by the Aryan master race–the one to which his own coloring made him heir, but one which would have curled its lip at his physical disabilities–had been interred and on the way to being annihilated before the year of 1939 had wound to a close. And the war that was to come had not even truly begun yet. When he heard those names, in time, Karl Kellerman would recognize them. And remember the prayer that was being murmured by the ghosts that slipped past him that summer. Shema Yisroel.

He was too disabled to be drafted into any army–he was short sighted enough that he could probably be counted on to shoot his own platoon instead of the enemy because he wouldn't be able to tell them apart. But he slipped away anyway, one night, away from the grey cottage by the church in the small town of Bad Tannenholz, away from its graves. He did not think that his uncle and aunt would miss him, at least not for long. And the dog, with whom he had eventually made friends after all, had long since joined the Jewish ghosts in the haunted shadows of the cemetery. Nothing and nobody was left to hold him in that place

He took with him almost as little as he had brought with him, all those years ago when he was just a child being shipped off to a convenient pigeonhole where he could be stashed and forgotten. He took a change of clothes, a couple of battered Karl May novels, and his mother's book of recipes. He found his way to Bavaria, then Austria, where he managed to find work in a bakery, eventually attaching to and effectively apprenticing himself to a pastry chef from whom he learned a trade–and then, using his mother's recipes, began creating his own cakes and pastries. It should have perhaps been enough–it might have been–but all the ghosts of Auschwitz and Dachau would not let him be.

He was sickening from it, from that haunting. He needed a fresh beginning, in a place innocent of such a pall of death of innocents. A New World. The world he had once discovered, and internalized, and come to believe in as absolutely as though it was a gospel for a strange faith all of his own, between the pages of Karl May's novels. A world where men could be brothers. A world where a man might look at another, in time, like those two ghosts in his uncle's cemetery had gazed at each other's face. A New World.

As soon as he had saved enough for a ticket, he took ship for the shining immortal west, and set his sights on America.

VAL HALL 2016

"I was wrong, you know," Karl said to Eddie, over kitchen clean-up in the aftermath of one of his pastry classes–they'd sent the students out, with the plate of fresh-baked goodies, to announce another Kellerman Day to the residents at large, while the two of them stayed behind to wipe down the counters and sweep up the spilled flour.

"Were you? Wrong about what?" Eddie said, crouching down on the floor trying to coax a particularly disinclined line of frust that seemed loath to migrate onto his dustpan.

"I got to America in the mid-fifties," Karl said. "Jim Crow era. There were ghosts here, too–lots of them, too many–they were just browner than the ones I had left behind in Europe."

Eddie swept up the last of the detritus and straightened, emptying the dustpan into the garbage bin. "That was a tough time."

"For the black folk. Also for the Indians. The first thing I did when I got here, you know, was to go looking for that wonderland that Karl May built inside my mind–and of course I never found that. No Winnetou, Apache chief, waited for this German immigrant. Maybe I just got here too late, but somehow I didn't think so–I could see the ghosts, and they weren't happy. The spirits of this continent were weeping. And it nearly broke me–it nearly destroyed me– there was nothing I could do, nothing except..."

Eddie stood there, looking at the man with his pale eyes and the now completely white hair that once used to be a deeply desirable Aryan blonde. "What is it that you did?"

"I... gave them the *Shema*," Karl said. "I passed on the words. It's what she said, the girl I talked to, back when I first saw the ghosts–she said, it's the way to talk to God. I thought–I don't know what is happening up there, whether there really is just one God and we all call him different names and pretend that *mine* is completely different from *yours* and definitely superior–or if there are all these Gods up there living in this gated neighborhood, with Cerberus at the gate and a high wall all around, but if they do then they're all neighbors and they'll talk to one another–I thought it couldn't hurt. Even if the password means that sometimes a confused Indian knocks on a door and it is opened by a bewildered Rabbi wondering what sort of Chosen People their God is Choosing these days–they can figure it all out on the other side. All I can do is whisper a word and hope it smooths their way home."

Eddie was laughing quietly. "I do know a little something on the subject of Gods," he said. "I'm pretty sure that would be amusing. But understood."

Karl smiled. "I'm not Jewish. But the man I found over here in America–the one who ended up looking at me like the one I saw ghost-walking in Germany so many years before– *he* was. We spent a quarter of a century together, he and I. That counts for something. It has to. I... still miss him, every day. When it comes time for me to knock on that door, I'll offer up the *Shema* and maybe it'll speed my way to him. But even if it doesn't–then I'll offer it anyway. You know–he taught me, what they believe–what even the ghosts were telling me–when someone dies, if they're Jewish, a physical existence ends and that which they call the soul goes up into a spiritual realm. That remains; the rest crumbles into dust, down here amongst men, and the only thing that stays behind is whatever kind of cherished memory you have managed to build of yourself in those who remain here, a memory of your good deeds and your thoughts and teachings, of the kind of man you were. What I did..."

He paused, and Eddie waited for his thoughts to cohere, for his words to come to him.

"I... baked pastries," Karl said at last. "That's the memory I leave behind. I made life sweeter, for a moment, for some."

"You spoke to ghosts," Eddie said. "That is what brought you here. You could reach out a hand into a different world, and speak with spirits others could not even see."

"So maybe I'll get to bake some pastries, up there, for everyone," Karl said, smiling faintly. "Maybe up there I will finally make the one my mother used to make. The perfect one."

"I thought you were very young when she died," Eddie said. "You remember that?"

Karl tapped his heart. "*This* remembers that," he said. "You know, when you hear me saying to the people who come here for the classes, that all a pastry needs is love... well... the best pastries need a focused kind of love. Love that is baked into them for you alone by the hand of somebody who loves you. They haven't tasted the best pastries yet. Some of them never will. Some might, up in the higher realms. If they can find the spirits of their mothers, to taste once again things made by a mother's hand, or a mother's love. Or maybe–as a pale imitation of that–my own attempt at it..."

"Even pastry is a prayer," Eddie said.

Karl chuckled. "I never thought about it like that, but yes, I suppose so," he said, and his accent dipped a little into a hint of the German cadences of his mother tongue. "I suppose we all pray in the moment of our death, to something that is greater than ourselves, one way or another. When it's my turn to knock at that door, it'll be bearing a fresh pastry, a memory of love, and a word I was once told should be used to greet God. I chose that way, a long time ago. Who knows, maybe I'll meet up some of my Indians up there, and they'll remember me. Until then..."

Eddie pushed a half-open cutlery drawer closed, straightened, looked around, judged the kitchen to be in a sufficient state of grace, and reached out to assist Karl from behind the counter, and towards the door leading out into the Hall.

"Until then," he said, "it's Kellerman Day. And there's something sweet out there waiting for you."

Spawn of War and Deathiness

PART III: CONCLUSION

When people come to their ends, there may yet be hope, even a sort of continuity. Can the same be true when humanity comes to its own end?

Spawn of War and Deathiness

Motorway Maintenance

Christopher M. Geeson

Death drives a black hearse on the motorway,
Looks for the next one heading for a crash.
Who'll be his victim when he strikes today?

A speeding idiot is easy prey—
Clocking over hundred, gone in a flash.
Death drives a black hearse on the motorway.

Reckless drunken drivers he loves to slay,
Doped at the dashboard, you're in for a smash.
Who'll be his victim when he strikes today?

Weaving overtakers will surely pay—
You can dice with Death but he don't take cash.
Death drives a black hearse on the motorway.

Phone Mister Death and he'll pick up to say:
"This is the way to a bloody good splash."
Who'll be his victim when he strikes today?

He'll kill a joy rider to make his day—
He's first on the scene, to take out the trash.
Death drives a black hearse on the motorway,
Who'll be his victim when he strikes today?

Spawn of War and Deathiness

Godot's Eternal Taxi Service

J. J. Steinfeld

Curtis, an investment banker dissatisfied with his career and unhappy with his life, had been feeling awful all morning, pain in his chest, a nausea he attributed to a few too many celebratory drinks last night, a fiftieth birthday he had been dreading, but he was determined to go on his first vacation in five years. He had barely phoned for a taxi when he heard the melodious honking of the car, more like a musical piano composition than actual honking. He looked outside his living-room window and saw a luxury vehicle in front of his house. Fortunately, he had packed light for his trip, and had no difficulty lifting the carry-on bag and hurrying to the taxi.

"It couldn't have been more than ten seconds after I called," Curtis said as he got into the back seat of the taxi.

"I was anticipating your call," the driver said as Curtis strapped on his seatbelt.

"You're joking," Curtis said, but no longer feeling the chest pain or the nausea that had plagued him all morning.

"Just being truthful, my friend."

Curtis hadn't seen the driver's face, except in the rear-view mirror, and the image was vague, almost ghostlike, and attempted to determine how the driver looked. Long, flowing, greyish hair, but he was unable to tell if the driver was male or female. Maybe transgender, but he was reluctant to ask. How could he not tell? His twenty-year-old daughter, who has lived with her mother since their divorce three years ago, had told Curtis over phone that her mother had fallen in love with a transgender man, and in longstanding annoyance with and contempt for her father, claimed he was much better looking than her father and a non-drinker, not to mention someone who would never gamble on anything.

"I have various honks programmed in. I especially like Chopin. Did you recognize the music?

"It did seem classical, but no."

"It's the glorious Piano Sonata No. 2 in B-flat minor, more commonly referred to as the *Marche funèbre*."

"Rather on the sombre side, I'd say."

"That goes without saying, my friend. I first heard it at Chopin's funeral."

"I assume you weren't one of the pallbearers. That must have been two-hundred years ago."

"Not quite, my friend...he died on October 17, 1849."

"You look that up on the internet?"

"That's not how I learn about life and the world."

"Then you can add time-traveller to your résumé."

"I would love to have had the incomparable Frédéric Chopin in this cab, but that would be an anachronism, of course. Music can transport one, but perhaps not an entire taxi."

"My smartphone's ringtone plays 'For He's the Jolly Good Fellow'... corny. But my wife got it for me. I don't know why I keep it."

"Divorce can do strange things to a person's head."

"I didn't say I was divorced."

"Must have been something in the tone of your voice."

All of a sudden, Curtis, looking out the window, saw a large, unfamiliar body of water and a bridge he had never seen before stretching out before the taxi as far as the eye could see. "I don't remember ever driving over a bridge to get to the airport," Curtis said nervously.

"This is the best route, believe me. Make yourself comfortable and let GETS take you to your destination," the driver said.

"You know where the airport is, don't you?"

"Hey, I was just there the other day. Actually, it was more like the other year."

"I don't want to miss my flight."

"First real vacation in half a decade, and it's Miami Beach."

"How did you know?"

"I can read people fairly well, and their destinations. Call it experienced cab-driver intuition."

"I've never seen a Rolls-Royce cab around here, or anywhere I've ever been."

"I like to consider my services unique. Lots of Rolls-Royce cabs in London, UK, but not like this transcendent sweetheart."

"So quiet and spacious."

"A 2031 Rolls-Royce Phantom."

"I'm amazed you got it to North America so quickly."

"You have a chronological problem with that? I just got it the other day. I drove a 2021 Rolls-Royce before that, but not anywhere in your neighbourhood, so to speak. I'm still getting used to this 2031 creation."

"Hmm, 2031. That's jumping the gun by ten years."

"Not really, but what's a few years here and there in the vast scheme of things."

"It shouldn't take more than forty, forty-five minutes tops to the airport. It's only thirty miles or so," Curtis said, looking at his watch. "My damn watch has stopped. It's a Rolex, for God's sake."

"Calm yourself. Everything in due course. You have a broken Rolex in an unbroken Rolls. I like the sound of that. Enjoy this glorious morning."

"I've never been in a Rolls before. I admit, it makes for a memorable ride."

"GETS likes its passengers to have the best possible taxi experience. I get a new Rolls every ten years, have been for the last hundred years."

"You're the youngest looking hundred I've ever seen, at least the back of your head."

"One of the perks of my job. No outward ageing."

"Who am I to question? As long as you drive safely and get me to the airport."

"You couldn't find a safer cab driver in North America...or anywhere else on the planet."

"But not the most humble cab driver."

"False modesty has always annoyed me. Tell it like it is, as the cliché goes."

"This is definitely the finest, most comfortable ride I've ever experienced."

"This is the nineteenth time since you moved here twenty-three years ago that you've taken a cab to the airport."

"You're a psychic hoot."

"No, just like accuracy."

"You're going rather slow."

"I'll put the pedal to the metal," the driver said, adding a high-pitched yell as the taxi accelerated. "This is way too fast."

"Let's settle on a moderate speed. Safety, of course, is the operative word."

"That's better, but we really should be there. We've been driving at least two hours. I'd bet my broken Rolex on that. We must have driven a hundred miles by now."

"Your sense of speed, distance, and time, is a little off. In fact, ontologically off."

"A philosophical cab driver, beautiful."

"A disoriented, confused passenger, not so beautiful."

"Only because I should be checking in for my flight by now."

"Consider this your home for the foreseeable future."

"I'll take the airport, thank you."

"In the progression of worldly and otherworldly history, airports come and go, if you get my philosophical drift."

"You're quite the cryptic and psychic cabbie."

"Not really. Godot's Eternal Taxi Service is straightforward."

"That's not what I called. Your website listed it as GETS."

"Lovely website, wouldn't you say?"

"It caught my attention when I googled local taxi services."

"Well, I find Godot's Eternal Taxi Service a bit of a mouthful, a little too artsy-fartsy, if you know what I mean, so I list it simply as GETS. Get more fares that way. *Get it*?"

"Why in the world would you call it Godot's Eternal Taxi Service...GETS?"

Turning around to the passenger, the driver said, "Because I'm Godot."

The driver's face looked even more vague, ghostlike, than in the rearview mirror: "You must have really liked Beckett's play," Curtis said, taken aback by the driver's face as much as by their odd, perplexing conversation.

"I was Godot long before Samuel Beckett ever thought of writing *Waiting for Godot*. We had a nice chat about that when he was in my cab, in Paris."

"Please keep your eyes on the road."

"I've never had even a fender bender in all my years of driving."

"It makes me nervous."

"Beckett wasn't nervous in the least. Amazingly composed, if you ask me."

"You actually gave Samuel Beckett a ride in a Rolls? Your eyes on the road, please!"

"December 22, 1989," the driver said, then looked forward again. "He loved the name of my company...Godot's Eternal Taxi Service. Beckett had a great sense of weird humour...sense of the absurd...and sense of irony. He said, 'You GETS what you pay for.' We both had a good laugh with that atrocious pun."

"I saw *Waiting for Godot* with my wife a few years ago. For our thirteenth anniversary, actually. At a little theatre not far from the airport."

"Before she left you, three years, five months, and eleven days ago."

"If you know how many trips I've made to the airport in my life, it doesn't surprise me that you know when my wife left me...to the day."

"For a tourist from San Francisco she met at the hotel she worked at. Is that the all-time prodigious irony, or what?"

"That's one way to look at it."

"Mind you, I don't know if that qualifies as irony or not. People throw around that word left and right. I bet you if Beckett were here, he would let us know if I'm using the word correctly."

"Next time you see him, you should ask."

Taking hands off the steering wheel, the driver said, "I will. But for now, you are my primary fare. My primary and priority fare."

"It would help if you kept your hands on the steering wheel, where they belong."

"A most magnificent steering wheel it is, but this Rolls pretty much drives itself. Great navigational system. State-of-the-art. Pretty much a driverless cab, but I like to stay involved in the business, if you get my drift."

"Hard to get used to that fancy new technology."

"In time, you will."

"You ever give my ex-wife a ride in your Rolls?"

"No, not yet. Last I heard, she's happy in San Francisco. She and her latest sweetie are huge San Francisco Giants fans. They went to nearly every home game last season and have season's tickets for this year."

"My ex-wife hated baseball... all sports."

"Because of your excessive gambling."

"She was not a sports fan before we got married."

"Now she's a huge sports fan."

"You know that, too?"

"Maybe one day I'll give her a ride over the Golden Gate Bridge."

"Right now we're on a bridge that's a complete and utter mystery to me, not the Golden Gate, unless you made a wrong turn. And how can we be still driving? It feels like the longest bridge in the world."

"Every ten years, to coincide with my new Rolls, I get a new assignment, a different bridge to drive over. I think my next stop will be the Golden Gate."

"Then you can sing 'I Left My Heart in San Francisco' to your passengers."

"You don't want to hear me sing."

Trying to roll the passenger side window down, Curtis said. "It's warm in here."

"Not permitted to open the windows once the journey begins."

"It's getting warmer."

"You'll acclimatize soon enough. You have the entire foreseeable future to acclimatize."

"I have to get to the airport," Curtis said, shaking his watch. "The time still hasn't changed."

"Time isn't a biggie in here."

Struggling to open his carry-on bag, Curtis said, "My smartphone will have the correct time."

"Save yourself the strain. Your luggage is not needed anymore."

"My smartphone and clothes are in here."

"Not to mention your secret flask."

"Why in the world would you say that?"

"Because on each and every day you went to your office at the bank, you've brought along your little flask and its contents of single-malt scotch."

"No one knows that."

"No need for your secret flask anymore. Anyway, my friend, it's now past serving its function."

Finally getting his carry-on bag open and then opening his flask, Curtis attempted to take a drink: "It's empty."

"You have to learn to believe and trust me. I've been doing this a long time, my friend."

"Could we stop at the liquor store first?"

"I can't believe you. First, the liquor stores aren't open this early in the morning. And second, and much more importantly, that damn flask of yours is one of the reasons you're using the services of GETS this morning."

"I called your GETS because my car wouldn't start this morning. That's the only reason."

"In denial even now...incredible."

As Curtis repeatedly tried his smartphone, his frustration grew: "What are you talking about?"

"A little amateur psychology, perhaps."

Shaking his smartphone with all his strength, Curtis complained angrily, "My phone doesn't work."

"Electronic devices are meaningless in this taxi."

Closing his carry-on bag and calming down somewhat, Curtis said, "Please open the windows."

"Acclimatize."

"Too warm...hot."

"I'm used to it...and so will you be."

"We should be at the airport already!"

"No denying this is a long bridge but there is no way to shorten the distance."

"Open the windows, for God's sake."

"You need to modify your world view, so to speak. So many ironies in the taxi business. There's that problematic word *irony* again."

"Open the damn windows."

"No more waiting for Godot, for you, my friend," the driver said, as the journey for Curtis continues into the ceaseless future.

The Sidewalk

James Dorr

Kathi, his daughter, used to ask, "Where does the sidewalk end?" He'd laugh when she asked that. But now he didn't laugh as he inspected the square of concrete the past night's rain had revealed in the forest in front of his cabin. He scarcely laughed at all any more, especially when he thought about Kathi—or about Eve, her mother, who died a year later. And both through his fault.

He got a shovel out from the shed. In the ten years since, he had sold his home to build this cabin as far from the city as he could, yet still close enough to a rural highway that he could drive back in the few times he had to. He'd sold his interest in his business, putting the money into bonds that only needed his attention a few times a year, in order to retire as a hermit. He wanted to be alone, far from reminders.

And yet, here in the ground, showing its east-west orientation as he cleared off its adjoining squares, was what seemed to be a regulation suburban sidewalk, just like the one in front of his old house. Out in the woods, where no sidewalk should be.

Shaking his head, he walked back inside—he wasn't going to clear off the whole thing. But where did it lead to? Where did *it* end? He reached for the strongbox set in the wall across from the fireplace and brought out the deed he'd received with the property. As he expected, there was no indication that anything had ever been built on the land before.

And yet... a sidewalk?

He thought again about sidewalks' endings, and then about Kathi, his six-year-old daughter. The pain had become a permanent dullness, a part of him now—like the pain of a toothache that throbbed, half-unnoticed, until he worried it with his tongue. The pain of loss. And blame. And might-have-beens. What might have been had he not bought the bike that day, for Kathi's birthday. What might have been if Eve had argued against it more forcefully. Argued that Kathi was still too young.

And then, a year later, her saying it once more. Blaming him once more before she stamped out of the house to her car.

<<>>

The next night it stormed again—autumn was the season for rainstorms—and, when he went out again in the morning, more of the concrete had been washed clear. He saw, now, gleams of white as the sun broke intermittently from the sky's grayness, lighting a path up the wooded hillside, curving in the style of the new suburbs like the one he'd used to live in, yet still stretching on until it was lost in what looked like a mist at the top of the ridge.

He thought again about sidewalks' endings and his daughter's asking.

"Daddy, where does the sidewalk end?"

"At the end of the block. Where else?" he'd answered.

"No, you silly," she'd insisted. "That's not where it ends. Because it just goes under the street and pops up again on the other side."

He'd thought about that, and tried again. "Then it must end at the ocean," he said. "That's because the ocean's too deep for it to go under." He thought she'd been satisfied by that answer. She'd just been five then. And when she was six and he got her the bicycle they'd joked about it.

"Maybe when you're older," he said, "you can ride your bike all the way to the ocean."

But now he wondered—about whether sidewalks *did* go under streets when you came to a corner and then just continued on. If you dug up the street, would you find concrete under the asphalt? Or, if you dug up the woods...?

He squinted. Was it really a sidewalk, or maybe just one or two flat rocks that had had the topsoil washed off them? He went to the shed again and got his shovel and started to dig from the concrete squares in front of his cabin to the first gleam of white.

Under the soil, there *was* a sidewalk.

He had a telephone. He rarely used it, but now he tried to call the city, wanting to talk to the real estate office he'd bought the land from. Apparently it hadn't always been woodland—at one time there must have been some kind of town there. He wanted to find out, but, after three tries, each time getting no answer, he realized that it was the weekend and no one would be there.

He stopped for lunch—it was time to eat anyway—and then he wondered if maybe he ought to follow the sidewalk, to see where it led to. He looked out the window and saw it had started to rain again and decided instead that first thing the next morning he'd pack a lunch. Maybe do more than that. Maybe pack canned food and extra clothes and camping gear and *really* follow it past the ridge to see where it led to. To see if it really led to the ocean.

<<>>

That night he remembered more than he wanted to. Things he had thought were safely forgotten. Eve had argued that Kathi was too young to have her own bike, but then had given in far too easily. And when Kathi asked him again where the sidewalk ended and he'd said the ocean, she paused as if she were thinking hard and then she asked him another question.

"Doesn't the ocean have bridges, Daddy?"

He didn't remember what he answered. Maybe nothing. And afterwards, how his wife didn't speak. After his daughter had ridden her bike by herself on a Saturday afternoon—he'd had to be in town at his office—and came to where the sidewalk "went under" a neighbor's driveway. And hadn't seen the car pulling out.

The police had called him. She'd just bumped her head, they'd told him. She *should* be okay. After all, it wasn't as though the car had been going fast.

But she died anyway in the hospital and, after that, his wife had refused to speak at all about the accident. She refused to go into Kathi's room, even to clean it. Then, later on, she moved her things into the extra bedroom, refusing to sleep with him.

"Why?" he asked. Only once.

"Because," she answered, "I don't want to take the chance that we might have another daughter."

<<>>

The morning was foggy, but he could still see when he looked out the window that the patches of yesterday's sidewalk were now connected into a shimmering, silver-white ribbon. He went to the closet and took out a knapsack and packed it with the things he had laid out the night before. Then he put on his jacket and slung the pack on his back, pausing at the closet again for a wide-brimmed hat, then stepped out on the porch. Closing the door behind him, he strode across his front yard to the strip of concrete where it stopped, then started again past the gravel trail that was *his* driveway. He looked down it both ways, then, flipping a mental coin, he followed it through the trees and up toward the ridge where the patches of concrete had seemed to lead the previous morning.

He walked and remembered as he topped the ridge. He saw it lead down the other side, a perfect sidewalk and all cleared off now, and he thought about how his daughter had stalemated him on the question of the ocean.

"Well, *aren't* there bridges?" she'd asked him again the Friday evening before she died.

"I don't know," he'd answered. He'd been preoccupied with problems at his office and how he would have to go in the next morning.

"Well, then, who does know?" she persisted. "I mean, someone *must* know."

He'd been preoccupied. He hadn't been thinking. He remembered how she'd been unconscious the next afternoon when he had come home. How she never awakened. But that night, without thinking, he'd been inspired.

"The Sidewalk Superintendent," he'd said. A term he remembered from his own childhood, though one that was used in a different context. "That's the one who would know. The man who's in charge of all the sidewalks."

She'd nodded, accepting. An old-time term for an idler who spent his time watching others work, but, as he used it, it had its own logic. The man who's in charge of all the world's sidewalks—even including ones found in the forest.

That's when he realized he might be dead himself. In his hermitage he had neglected seeing his doctor, even though, after the accident—the double accident, counting his wife's later—his heart had started to give him trouble. He'd taken it easy after he'd moved out here, making a point of not straining himself. But the morning before, and all that digging...

He shrugged the thought from him. He followed the sidewalk where it curved through the trees, sometimes lost in fog, sometimes rising clear. On either side, the forest pressed closer as if the trees resented the sidewalk's invading their domain. There *shouldn't* be sidewalks here, should there? he wondered. And yet as he strode on, two steps to each square, the pebbled concrete of its weathered surface stretched out undeniably under his feet.

He stopped and reached down and felt its roughness, then looked around him. He saw something yellow flash. Yellow, the color of caution, the color of Eve's coat the day his wife left him. "To take a drive," she'd said.

The yellow was in the woods—memories came back to him. How they had argued exactly one year after Kathi's death. How he had said she had to start living again for the present, living life for herself if not for him. How her eyes had spoken blame at him as she'd grabbed the car keys.

"When will you be back?" he'd asked as she left the house.

She hadn't answered.

He saw the flash again. Yellow between the trees. He tried to get up and leave the sidewalk to see what it was, but the underbrush pressed at him, tangled with thorns, not letting him push through.

And so, after resting a few minutes more, he continued forward.

<<>>

Four ridges later he first spotted Kathi riding her bicycle. He saw her jacket, her light red-brown hair far ahead on the sidewalk. He quickened his pace—three steps to each two squares—trying to catch her as her bike wobbled up over the next ridge. Winded, he topped it too, then stopped and called her name.

He heard the wind sigh far above his head while, in the valley below, the mist thickened.

<<>>

The next time he saw her it seemed like days later, but he couldn't be sure. The mist around him would lighten and darken, thicken and dissipate periodically, but on what seemed to be no set schedule. He knew he had rested at least three times, once lying at full length when he had found a small stretch of clear ground next to the sidewalk, but, as to whether he'd slept or not even then, he wasn't certain.

He hadn't eaten, despite his still full pack. He hadn't been hungry. Nor had he been bothered by the pack's weight or been tempted to take it off his shoulders except for that one time when, shucking it up beneath his head, he'd used it as a pillow. And yet, even though he rested at times—it seemed the thing to do—the thing he *should* do—he didn't seem tired either. Rather, between rests, he kept to his first pace, two steps per concrete square, whether the sidewalk led upward or downward.

That's how he finally *knew* he was dead. The dead didn't get tired either, did they? Kathi could go on riding her bike, if that's what she wanted, until she *did* come to the end of the sidewalk.

His wife Eve could keep driving, even if in life her car had spun on a wet patch of highway and slammed into a concrete bridge abutment, killing her instantly. Heaping the guilt of a second death on his head.

That's why he rested. The thoughts came back to him then. Thoughts that in life he had kept suppressed.

Buying the bicycle—one life lost with it.

Failing to stop Eve when, blaming him, she left. Failing to argue because he felt too weak.

That's when he looked up and saw his daughter, bending over him where he sat.

"Kathi?" he whispered.

He felt her hug him, then watched as she skipped a pace away.

"Kathi," he said again as he got to his feet. He reached to take her hand, but she skipped back again, just out of reach.

"Daddy," she said. "C'mon with me, Daddy. My bike's on the other side of the hill. I've got to get going."

"Wait," he called after her. He tried to think. "Kathi, tell me, are you in heaven?"

"I don't know, Daddy," she answered. "It's dark where I'm going." She paused a moment, then smiled. "But it's nice, too."

He tried to go after her, but she was backing away from him faster. "Is your mother there with you?" he asked.

He thrust his hand forward, straining to reach her, but something was forcing her down the sidewalk now, faster and faster, even as she stretched out her own hand to let him take it. He saw the mist that surrounded her thickening.

"She blamed *herself*, Daddy. Didn't you know that? Saturday, when you were at your office, I asked her if I could go out riding and—she was busy then, in the kitchen—she said 'Okay.' And later, she blamed herself."

"Kathi!" he shouted. He couldn't see her now. Then behind him, out of the corner of his eye, he thought he saw yellow. "Eve?" he called. But that disappeared too.

"Daddy?" he heard, again in front of him. Lost in the fog, his daughter's voice calling, choking slightly as if in a moment she might start crying.

"Kathi?" he whispered.

"Daddy," she called out, her voice receding. "If you see the Sidewalk Superintendent, *ask* him where I am."

<<>>

He cried himself now. He didn't know how long—perhaps days by "normal" time. He was alone, trapped in a dense fog, the only thing visible to him the sidewalk down at his feet. He followed its concrete path in the direction his daughter had gone, but knew at the same time that she was becoming more and more distant. And yet she had told him it wasn't his fault.

At least Eve had thought that. It wasn't his fault that his daughter had been killed, despite his wife's insisting at the time that she was too young to have a bicycle.

But then whose fault was it?

He topped another ridge, after the mist had again become thinner, and saw his wife again, off in the forest. But once again he was unable to leave the sidewalk to go to her.

"Eve," he called out. "It was not your fault either."

But she didn't answer. She pointed instead toward the trees behind her. Then suddenly some kind of animal crashed out, bear-like and slavering, ripping at her flesh with its curved claws. She started screaming.

"Eve!" he shouted. Her shrieks drowned his voice out.

Then the mist closed again and all was silent.

But then, whose fault was it? He remembered how, after Kathi's death, his wife had drawn within herself. Her health had begun to deteriorate in the months that followed but, even though he asked her again and again, she refused to see a doctor. And then, when she finally *did* leave the house, exactly one year after...

He remembered talking to the police at the crash site. How one had coughed, as if reluctant to say anything more.

How he had insisted. "What is it, officer?"

And the policeman told him then how his wife had been speeding—Eve, who had normally been a good driver—as if she'd intended for her car to hit the bridge.

"*But it wasn't her fault either!*" he shouted. He shouted the words out loud, hearing them echo off the nearest trees before they were lost in the fog. It wasn't his fault—and it wasn't hers either. Nor was it the neighbor's fault, who had hit Kathi. The driveway had been clear when she started backing out. It was an accident.

Only an accident.

But... wasn't there a President once who'd had a sign saying "The Buck Stops Here." That things weren't just random. That *someone* must be to blame.

Where did the sidewalk end?

And where was Kathi? Was that where he'd find her— and maybe find Eve too—at the sidewalk's ending?

<<>>

He finally decided. The buck stops *there*, with the one Kathi said he must ask to find out where he might find her. The one who knew where the sidewalk ended.

He found the Sidewalk Superintendent at a desk at the top of the highest hill he had climbed thus far. At a widening of sorts in the concrete surface, much like the stopping points one sometimes finds on a mountain trail to mark the location of some scenic view.

But there was no scenery here, only the fog and a hunched, gray figure—a man or a woman? he couldn't tell—in a sort of gray business suit, shuffling papers.

"Is this it?" he asked.

The figure looked up at him. It had no eyes.

"Is this it?" he asked again. "Where the sidewalk stops? Is this where I'll find my daughter safe? Where I'll find my wife? Where I'll find out who *is* to blame for all that's happened?"

The figure shook its head slowly, then bent back down to the papers it had been sightlessly reading.

"Dammit, answer me!" He grabbed the figure, intending to shake it, to hurt it if need be to make it say *something*. His hands went through it.

His hands went through mist—no more than a thickening in the pervading fog.

That's when he knew Hell.

It hadn't been his fault, nor Eve's, nor his daughter's. He understood now. Not the neighbor's fault or even the bicycle's or the sidewalk's. Not even the Sidewalk Superintendent's—there *was* no Sidewalk Superintendent. He had just proven it. No god or devil.

Only a thick mist of random happenings. Accidents. Flukes. Just simple happenstance.

And, understanding, he turned and climbed the last few yards to the highest hill's crest and saw the ocean stretched before him, the bridge whose approach ramp he had just mounted arced up and out until its vast span was lost in a dim, unending distance.

Spawn of War and Deathiness

Mr. Wetzel and His Wurlitzer

Bruce Taylor

He had been driving slowly a long, long time. Alone, he drove a 1953 Chevrolet truck, painted pale blue. In the open bed of the truck was a Mighty Wurlitzer jukebox.

Before the event, when he had breath, he was thin, lean, and inclined to smoke a pipe. His white hair was sparse, his skin tan, and he'd liked wearing a jean jacket and jean overalls. Now he drove his Chevrolet across the featureless plain, beneath the dark and starless sky, driving forever to the pale horizon.

"Get there someday," he frequently said as he drove. "Don't know what's there, but I'm gonna get there someday. Who knows when?"

He drove in a daze for long periods of time. He never looked at the dashboard because the gauges did not work and he never ran out of gas.

Finally, he slowed. "This is a good place," he mused. Automatically, the truck stopped, and the engine turned off as Mr. Wetzel got out of the truck. He slammed the door, climbed into the bed of the truck and sat in a rocking chair. The Mighty Wurlitzer jukebox lit up and on came "Sentimental Journey."

He liked the song; he liked all the songs—they were songs that he knew well and as he sat and listened to "Sentimental Journey"...

... Little Johnny Jenkins from down the street, wearing his usual white t-shirt and blue cut-offs and blond hair uncombed, came running into the store, "Mr. Wetzel! Mr. Wetzel! Can you fix my bike, Mr. Wetzel? Please?" His dark eyes had that imploring look as if saying that if anyone knew how important a bike was to a six-year-old, it had to be Mr. Wetzel.

"Sure can," said Mr. Wetzel, and he came out from behind the counter of Wetzel's Grocery.

In the humid afternoon, in the hot Florida sun, Mr. Wetzel fixed Johnny Jenkins' tire.

Johnny was eager to help; for a six-year-old, he was pretty strong. Deftly, he used a wrench to undo the nut on the front wheel. Once the wheel was off, Mr. Wetzel removed the tire and patched the inner tube.

In the background, his jukebox played *Sentimental Journey*.

After the tire was fixed, Johnny came in, went to the cooler, got a bottle of orange pop and plopped down ten cents for it. It was actually fifteen cents, but Mr. Wetzel said, "Perfect; right on the money."

And Johnny left, slamming the screen door with the diagonal "Hires Root Beer" sign across the bottom of it. He yelled back, "Thanks, Mr. Wetzel!" and he waved.

"Okay, Johnny!" yelled Mr. Wetzel and he began to write out his order.

Next, Bud Williamson came in. He wore a straw hat that he kept pushed back. He was Florida-tanned, wore his light blue shirt open and the long sleeves rolled up. Mr. Wetzel always wondered why, in this hot place, didn't he wear something cooler? Why the shirt? The heavy work jeans?

Bud's hair was black, his eyes were pale blue, and he chewed gum.

"Hi, Gus," he said, "how goes?"

"Pretty good, Bud," said Mr. Wetzel.

Bud went over to another cooler and got out a six pack of Hamm's. He sauntered over to the counter and easily reached back and pulled out a wallet. "Another hot one," he said.

"Yup," said Mr. Wetzel. "Sure feels like it." He rang up the beer. "Ninety cents."

"Good 'nuff," said Bud. He opened the coin compartment of the black wallet, counted out the change and let it slowly flow from his palm to Gus's.

"Ah," said Mr. Wetzel, looking at a new, 1955 dime, "first new dime I've seen this year."

"Hm," said Bud. "If I don't get some work, it may be the *last* dime you'll see from me for a while."

"If I hear of anything, I'll let you know," said Mr. Wetzel.

"Thanks. 'Preciate that." And swinging the beer like a slow pendulum, Bud sauntered out the door.

Sentimental Journey played all day long; Gus Wetzel dusted, arranged, put away stock.

Mary Jean Saxton, sixteen-year-old daughter of the sheriff of the small town of Whittonville, wandered in, wearing a dark red bathing suit. "Hi, Gus," she said; her dark hair was stringy from swimming and she had a dark blue beach towel draped around her brown shoulders. Her feet went *slap-slap-slap* against the green and white tile floor.

"Hello, Mary Jean. How you doing?"

"Pretty good." She went to the cooler and yanked back the top to peer into the depths of bottle and ice. "You got any Honey Dew?"

"Sure. Should be some in there."

"Oh, there it is." She pulled the bottle to the side and down the rails.

"Been swimming, eh?" said Mr. Wetzel.

"Yeah," and Mary Jean's smile was wonderful. "Great day for it."

She counted out fifteen cents from a small, plastic purse (even now he knew the details of it: the gold trim along the opening where two nubbins of metal, like stubby fingers, cross when the purse is closed, the yellow flowers on the outside of the purse and how bright they were against the white background). After she put the money on the counter, *snap*; she closed the purse.

"How's your dad?" asked Mr. Wetzel.

"He's better," she said. "Can you believe it?" She went over to the cooler and snapped off the lid. "Someone backs over his foot! Can you believe it?"

"Mr. Wetzel shook his head. "Can't say that I do."

She pulled long on the Honey Dew. "Wow! That's good." She then turned around and waved. "You take care."

"Thank you," said Mr. Wetzel. "You, too." He watched her leave, watched the shoulders, the tanned and strong legs and loved the red bathing suit.

Later on, he sat outside on the porch and watched the fireflies flicker on, flicker off. He sat out there, drank a beer, and sighed contentedly. He smiled at hearing the playful yells and shrieks of the Watson kids next door, delighted in the faint smell of fried chicken on a gentle breeze. Rex, the old German shepherd, loped along the sidewalk, favoring his left rear leg.

Across the street, Mr. and Mrs. Hawthorne walked slowly; a retired couple, they stayed rather distant from others, but superficially, they were friendly enough.

And Mr. Wetzel drank his beer and in the background, the tune of the day, "Sentimental Journey," played and played, never stopping, just going on and on.

About ten o'clock, Mr. Wetzel went inside the store, shut out the lights and just stared at the Mighty Wurlitzer jukebox. He stared at it, listened to it, became captured by it, carried by it and exactly at midnight—it stopped. The lights went out and...

Mr. Wetzel opened his eyes. He sighed, and patted the jukebox affectionately. "Mighty nice," he said, "mighty, *mighty* nice. It's nice to go back and visit." Then, getting up, he climbed out of the back of the truck, opened the front door; the truck started up immediately and he drove his Chevrolet across the featureless plain, beneath the dark and starless sky, driving forever to the pale horizon.

Wallflower

Tom Easton

Once Avril Montez had been able to hear the cries of children at play in the schoolyard not far beyond the tumble-down stone wall.

Once there had been the roar of traffic on the highway, the whine of aircraft overhead, footsteps and bouncing balls on the pathways.

Once there had even been visitors.

Now there was nothing. A thread of obsessively piping music. Sidney Mailloux's plaintive voice crying, "Is anyone on yet? Evan? Amelia?"

Nothing. Nothing real. Nothing but ghosts and memories.

She could see a pigeon pecking quietly in the bramble-narrowed path that entered through the gates, a crow sitting in the branches of the apple tree on the knoll, a seagull in the distance. They were all that was left, the opportunists, the scavengers. Pigeons and crows, seagulls and ravens, sparrows and starlings. Songbirds had been only memory even when she was alive.

"I'm bored," came Sidney's voice. But there was no other sign that anyone was present. The brambles and everlasting were still and quiet beneath the yellow sky. The only movement was a small red ground squirrel emerging from its burrow beneath a stone. Once in a while, there was a skunk, a raccoon, or a mangy cat.

"Where have all the people gone?"

Avril laughed out loud at the echo of the old, old song. "Gone to graveyards, every goddam one of them," she said. "Just like us."

Yes, she told herself. Graveyards. The rusty gates hung askew on their pillars, and the letters that said so were still there. "Eternal Rest" on one of them. "Cemetery" on the other.

"I mean us," said Sidney. "It's not as if the storms have been bad lately. There's been plenty of sunshine."

All charged up and nowhere to go. To either side of the gateway's pillars stretched a stone wall distorted by frost and roots and time, something growing in every cranny. Violets in the spring, their color magnified in the lilacs that billowed in one corner of the cemetery. Wild roses in the summer. Tiger lilies in August. Wild asters in the fall. She thought of Tennyson and smiled at the thought of him uprooting roses and lilies. What he once had craved to understand no longer existed, did it?

"Oh, shut up." That was Ricky Moi. Shrubbery obscured the lettering carved into the face of his stone, but she could see its encircling band of visual sensors. Since it sat a little down the slope of the land, she could also see the panel of solar cells on its top. "We don't have to chat-chat-chit-chat all the time, you know."

"Save your energy." Avril had never learned this one's name. She had never said, and bushes obscured her inscription too. But the stone was the same, as were almost all of the cemetery's occupants. Sarcophagi full of circuitry, solar cells and light sensors, microphones and speakers. Once they had thought it would pass for life. "Maybe someone'll finally show up, come walking through at midnight, and we can all yell 'BOO!!' and give the poor bastard a heart attack."

"The last man on Earth, and you'd do that to him?"

"Serve him right."

"Might be a woman."

"Serve *her* right."

"I'm laughing."

They were waking up, then. All the eternal residents of this eternal rest home, eternal witnesses of time, rank on rank of blocky stones, surrounded by weeds and brush and brambles.

Eternal rest? Not that, not really. They talked too much. But eternal loneliness, yes, and no way out, not so long as the sun still shone and earthquakes and volcanoes and the sea refused to cover them with mud or ash or deep, dark water.

A mad, mad giggle reminded her that not everyone could take it.

A dog barked. For a wild moment she thought her heart leaped within her chest, though she now had neither heart nor chest. It had been so long since she had seen a dog, and then it had been only a scrawny mongrel that snuffed along the ground as if searching for the master and the home it had never known.

Another bark, and, "Want bone. Want ball. Want run and chase and..."

"Shaddap, Rufus."

His dog had been no Rufus, cosseted all its life until at the end its simple mind was downloaded into a solar-powered gravestone just as if it were a sacred human being.

His dog had been a beagle named Wooftop, and he had left it to wander. To be adopted by another student if it were lucky. To be caught and butchered and eaten if it were not.

If only she had not been so shy. If she had had the nerve. If she had spoken to him more than that one time, petted the dog when he walked it in the quad, sat down beside him on the lawn, in the caf, even in the lecture hall where she had first seen him. If and if and if, then perhaps Wooftop would also have had a pampered life and been preserved forever after. It might even have wound up here, with her. With *them*.

If only...

"Allie, Allie, Allie..."

Avril made a sighing noise just as if she still had lungs. "What do you want, Kirby?" He spoke to her more often than to anyone else, calling across the intervening stones as if across a breakfast table. He seemed to like her voice.

"You weren't paying any attention, not any, none at all, and I called your name, I did, I did. I know I did."

"There isn't any rush," said a thin, patient voice. "We're not going anywhere."

"Well, of course, Chandra. Of course. Of course. We're dead. But dead is boring, just like Sidney said."

"I'd rather be dead," said Chandra. "I was a soldier, you know? And the things we had to do on the Mexican border... I'm shaking my head."

"Did you die in action?"

"I must have. They had to use a year-old download for this stone."

"It was one of those new viruses that got me," said Kirby. "I don't even remember what they called it. But I remember dying, yes I do. I was on a Coast Guard destroyer, intercepting supertankers filled with refugees, telling them to turn around and go home."

"Not that they had any hope of surviving there," said Ricky Moi.

"We had our orders. We didn't like them, but we knew that letting them in would destroy the economy and use up the resources *we* needed. Overload the lifeboat. So, well..."

"You sank them." Avril had heard rumors when she was alive.

"Yeah. We had to. They carried diseases too, you know. That's where I got... It was pretty nasty. Made me choke and wheeze. I was burning up inside, and then that helmet was sliding cold, cold, cold onto my head. And I woke up here."

Silence fell across the cemetery, broken only by the buzz of insects and the rustle of the ground squirrel in the dead leaves beneath a shrub. But it did not last. How they had died was a favorite topic of the dead, one many of them returned to again and again, chewing it over and over like a dog with an ancient bone, as if some nourishment remained in the weathered husk.

"That's what I wanted to ask you, Allie."

Many of them.

"How did you die? You've never said."

And she never would, no matter how many times Kirby or the others asked. It was embarrassing, a shame she could have lived down only if she had remained alive.

Several voices came to her defense: "Oh, leave her alone. Some of us like our privacy, even here. She's got a right to take her secrets to the grave even if she can still talk. Leave her be."

Avril said nothing herself, though she could not help but remember, just as she did every time the subject arose.

She had first seen Paul in biology class. At the front of the huge lecture hall, the instructor had been pointing at a chart with two lines projected on a screen. "There is only so much land suitable for agriculture," she was saying. "Only so much water. We can grow only so much food. Yet for centuries we have felt that there was no limit on human numbers. We have multiplied until now..."

Three rows in front of her. Dark, curling hair, a square angle of jaw, a muscular arm emerging from a short-sleeved shirt. Head turning to look toward someone else, Roman profile.

When he winked at the target of his gaze, Avril felt a flash of white-hot envy.

The instructor tapped the screen. "Erosion costs us topsoil, fertility, the ability to produce the food we eat. Irrigation has already drained most aquifers, until now we cannot irrigate. It has also poisoned millions of hectares with salt and toxic chemicals."

She didn't even know who he was. She had never spoken to him. And when he winked at someone else, she raged with jealousy.

"We have converted forests to farms. We have all the benefits of genetically engineered supercrops. But the best we have been able to do is to keep agricultural production from declining. We've been holding steady for years, while the population has continued to increase.

"The effect..." Her voice rose as she pointed toward a student, who answered: "Less food per capita. More famines."

"Until...?" Who *was* he?

"Nature brings us back into balance with the world."

The instructor nodded. The point was obvious, conventional wisdom in this age of the world, hardly something one needed to have read a textbook to grasp.

"If we fail, there is a strong possibility that the human species will die out. We will be extinct."

Yet people still bred as if they had some special dispensation from the laws of nature. Suddenly Avril understood how they could do so, for she wished to do the same. She had seen her perfect mate, and her body tingled in anticipation of what they might do with and to each other.

A different student raised her hand: "Could the world recover?"

The instructor nodded. "Just as it did after the cometary impact that ended the Cretaceous and extinguished the last dinosaurs, along with seventy percent of all the species then alive. A few million years later, there were as many species as ever. Though there weren't any dinosaurs."

When Avril left the lecture hall, she noticed the posters as if for the first time. They lined the corridor just as they did every corridor on campus, just as once upon a time had proliferated exhortations to use condoms or to protest the draft or to save tinfoil for the war. One showed a multihued sea of faces, with superimposed white letters that said: "If you are not part of the solution, you are part of the problem. Get out of the way." Another said, "If you cannot contribute, it is your duty to future generations to remove yourself." The legend on a third claimed it showed a refugee camp filled with starving children. A fourth pictured a hospital crammed with cholera and plague victims. A fifth needed no legend at all; it showed the mullions of a window, a tattered curtain, a glint of glass, and beyond a dessicated landscape littered with shriveled human bodies. There were more as well.

But her arms felt as heavy as if she already held a baby all her own. Hers and his, *his* though she had no idea of his name.

Now, looking back from the vantage point of death, she could see that her body had been telling her why all the lectures the world had ever heard on the dangers of overpopulation were useless. People were as subject to biological imperatives as any animals. Reproduction was part of the program, even when it threatened long-term survival.

She had learned his dog's name before his own. For a week she had looked for him, sat as near as she dared in the lecture hall and in the caf. She had watched him with his dog and heard him cry, "Wooftop!" more than once, a laugh in his voice every time he said the word. Eventually their instructor had called on him by name.

"Paul," she repeated to herself, then and now, forever. "Paul Trainor."

"What the hell are we doing here?" Sidney Mailloux's voice, angry and querulous, called her back to the present.

"We're dead," said Ricky Moi. "Where else would we be?"

"Heaven or Hell or Purgatory. Not here. Anywhere but here."

"That's what they used to think," said Kirby. "Plant 'em deep and figure the important part rose up like smoke forever."

"The soul," said Avril.

"Yeah. With angels and harps waiting on Cloud Nine. Or devils and pitchforks in the pit."

"Maybe that's where the real us really is? We're just copies here?"

"I feel real enough," said Ricky Moi. "A lot realer than if I were just a name on a rock."

"That's how it started," said Professor Calmari, who rarely spoke. His voice was formal, unctuous. "Our ancestors captured the souls of the dead by naming them. Perhaps they thought this would pin their shades to their graves and keep them from terrorizing the countryside. Later they carved portraits in the stone, and attached photographs. When small, cheap voice recorders became available, those were embedded in gravestones so the survivors could hear the dead speak once more. Then there were video recorders, and interactive personality simulators, and finally downloads. Us. Each step a little closer to preserving all of us, until now all that's missing is that putative soul. Which I don't believe exists in the first place, you know."

"Eternal life," said Sidney. "If you don't mind a bunch of dead old farts for company."

"If you call this living," someone muttered softly.

"Beats the alternative," said someone else, not quite as gently.

There had been no alternative, thought Avril Montez. Not even after she learned his name. She had been shy. He had not. He had had friends to wink at, male and female. Friends to play with in the quad, throwing balls and disks to each other and to Wooftop and other dogs. Even when she had seen him sitting still, on the grass, in the caf, at the library, he had had friends around him. She had not dared to intrude, and he had never noticed her watching him. Or if he had, if his friends had and had mentioned her to him, he had been too polite to confront her.

That had only made her want him even more.

"Allie, Allie, Allie..."

"Yes, Kirby?"

"You sound so young." It was true, they all sounded their ages, or the ages at which they had died, just as if their vocal cords had been downloaded with their minds. "Were you a soldier?"

"Leave her be!"

But Avril chose to answer. "A student."

Only silence answered her. They too had seen the posters. They knew what it had meant to be a student in an overcrowded world. They too remembered the small buildings on every campus, each one with its little fake-brass sign:

HARRISON MEMORIAL EUTHANASIA CLINIC

"Making Room"
Funded in part by the Kevorkian Foundation
Open 5-9 every evening
ADDITIONAL HOURS THE WEEK AFTER FINALS

Similar buildings could be found in cities and small towns and even highway rest-stops. Each one had had a human attendant, but it was the artificial intelligence in the walls that took one's name, asked one's choice of methods and disposals, and said, "Now just lie down, right here on this couch. Close your eyes, and..."

No questions, no attempts to talk one out of it or to relieve depression. The world needed fewer people, and if you did not need the world, that was fine. You would not be missed, not even if you had special talents. In a crowded world, special talents were not rare.

She had wondered, after the bio course's first exam. She had done well enough, but Paul seemed dejected and angry and afraid all at once. In the quad, Wooftop stayed close by his side, staring upward, whining just a little. His friends were quiet, as if they sensed something dreadful looming over them all.

Her heart ached for them, but she dared not say a word. Paul was still too beautiful, too unattainable, too unapproachable, and she was too shy, a nerveless mouse clinging to the wainscoting, burying her nose in a book or a screen every time he passed nearby.

And he passed nearby more often then. He spent more time in the library, more time studying, intent and serious and still oblivious to the pounding of her heart just a few feet away.

"Yes," she said to Kirby once more, to fill the engulfing silence. "A student."

She had spoken to Paul only once. On her way to class, she saw him in the corridor, staring at one of the many posters on the wall. "If you cannot contribute, it is your duty to future generations to remove yourself." Stark white letters, glossy black background, photo of a roomful of white-bloused people intent on the screens of their terminals. College grads, every one of them, of course.

The poster beside it bore the same words, but the photo was of peasants knee deep in a rice paddy.

There were tears in his eyes.

"Good luck," she said. But she ducked her head, and her voice squeaked, and she did not think he heard.

After the second exam, he did not return to class.

She did not see him in the hall, nor the caf, nor the quad, and his friends—Wooftop sitting lonely in their midst—were sober. She remembered that it had hurt to breathe. Tension had made her shoulders sore. Her heart had ached.

She thought she knew where he had gone, what he had done, where he was now. Yet she dared not ask: if she did not confirm her fears, they might prove false. Paul might return, saying there had been an illness in his family, he had been ill himself, he had enrolled in a special training program, he had joined the army and only had a day or two of leave but he had noticed her, really he had, and would she...

Tears came at her own foolishness. Angrily, she shook them away—imagining that they flew into the void in her life, her world, and would fill it up with salty water—and tried to study. When the words no longer made sense, she took long walks down roads crowded with houses small and large, stores, offices, and apartment blocks. She found every cemetery within miles of the campus, dozens of them, small ones, large ones, old ones, new ones. She realized how crowded her world had become with both the living and the dead.

Was he in this one? Or this one? Or none of them? She dared not pass their gates to look for new stones, or shout his name in hope of an answer, though she listened carefully to the incessant rattle of the stones' conversations. But she never heard a familiar voice.

Sitting in the library, trying to study, she sensed movement in the corner of her eye and jerked, looked around, searching, hoping, heart pounding. But no one was there. Or someone was, but it was not Paul. The void remained.

Wooftop vanished too. Paul's friends once more threw balls and disks and ran and shouted, and at last she could stand it no longer. As soon as they collapsed panting on the grass, she approached and stood over them and asked, "Where's Paul?"

They looked up at her and saw... what? A short girl, brown-skinned, dark-haired, too broad in the hips, not broad enough in the chest, her dark eyes hollow with pain and yearning.

They looked at each other, silent, surely knowing why she asked. They shifted their shoulders and their legs uneasily. And at last one of them said quite simply: "The clinic."

That simple confirmation of her fears broke all that was left of her heart. She managed to turn away before the tears came once more.

"You're awfully quiet, Allie."

"May lightning fry your circuits, Kirby. A nice black raven should die on top of your solar cells."

"I love you too, dear."

She thought he might, but before she could speak others joined the game: "A squirrel with diarrhea should perch on you for a week. A hailstone the size of a grapefruit should..."

"I get the point, I get the point. I'll leave her alone, I will."

"Pick on somebody else."

"Okay, okay, okay. Chandra?"

"Yeah?"

"You ever feel guilty?" asked Kirby.

"Do you?"

"Hell, yes. You think it was easy, sinking ten thousand walking skeletons at a pop?"

"Probably. We got pretty used to gassing Mexicans."

Silence, as the dead reflected on what horrors one could commit in the name of survival. Then Ricky Moi said, "Yeah. In Peru and Chile, too. The guilt comes later."

"I still have nightmares," said Kirby.

"I'm nodding," said Chandra.

"Me, too," said others. "Me, too."

Yes, thought Avril. So did she. Though not because of the deaths she had caused. Over the next few weeks, she had revisited the cemeteries. She dared not enter, for finding him at that point, speaking across such a barrier, would have been unbearable. But she had to look.

She had managed to keep up her studies. She had completed the term successfully. She had not been one of those whom the posters urged to get out of the way.

Yet... Talent was not rare. She would not be missed, she had told herself. Except by her parents, and she had been quite unable to tell them what had happened or what she now thought she would do. They would never understand.

Every day she walked past the one-story brick building that housed the clinic. Once she opened the door to study the foyer. It had three doors. The one straight ahead stood ajar to reveal a utilitarian array of metal cabinets and a long conveyor belt that entered a dark hatchway. Stark and real, reminder of finality and irrevocability. The door on the right had a glass window through which she could see three desks and a filing cabinet. Only one of the desks was occupied, by a young man who did not even look up from the screen he was studying. He was used to ambivalence, she thought. The door on the left was solid wood or wood-look steel, closed tight. Behind it...

She was listening to sociology lectures in the hall where she had first noticed him. Perhaps, in a better world, he would have been there too, but his seat was now occupied by a skinny fellow with boils on the back of his neck. Wooftop was gone. And his friends were as active as they had ever been before he vanished.

It had been only a matter of time before she let herself touch the clinic office's door and push it open. The attendant, no older than she, surely a student putting in hours for his tuition, looked up from his screen.

She felt as shy and hesitant as if she had finally forced herself to speak to Paul. "I've never done this before."

He sighed gently. "No one ever has." He pointed behind her. "Just step right in. There's no one else."

She turned and stared at the other door, solid and closed, a barrier.

"It won't open for you. *You* have to make the decision."

She took a deep breath. Paul was gone. She would never meet him again unless... And she would not be missed.

She hesitated when she thought of her parents. Would they understand if they knew? But *she* was the one who had to decide. The attendant was right. And she had no great unique talents—no one really did. The world did not need her. Nor did she need it, as empty as it had become.

She laid her hand on the knob, hesitated, and finally twisted. The door pivoted away from her. As soon as she was in, it swung shut once more.

She faced a pair of padded couches flanked by metal tables and racks built of metal rods and glass tubes. Glass-fronted cabinets held mysterious devices. Soft music and the scent of flowers filled the air. There were the usual posters on the walls, and two small windows let her glimpse the campus outside.

It felt macabre, a mad scientist's laboratory, a place of horror and monstrosity. She wanted to turn and flee and forget Paul and the world and life and love.

A silky voice said: "Your name?"

She gave it, though already she had begun to tremble. Was this really what she wanted? She had assignments to study, papers to write, an exam next week.

"You have three choices: Gas, pills, or intravenous drip."
As the voice named each item, a small spotlight illuminated
a mask attached by a corrugated hose to a metal tank, a
bottle of bright pink pills, a metal rack beside a couch, its
top supporting a clear glass bottle from which dangled
several feet of plastic tubing.

"No," she said, and her voice shook on that single little
word. "I want to leave. I've changed my mind."

"It was too late for that as soon as you let the door close
behind you. You can't. Not anymore. But don't worry. It's all
quite painless. We've made sure of that."

"No," she said, shaking worse. Perhaps, if the room had
said she could leave at any time, she would have stayed. But
it had said no, and she could feel her panic growing. "No!"
She turned and tried the door. When the knob would not
turn, she tried to shake it. "No!" She kicked at the door. Tears
flooded her eyes. "I want to go!" She began to scream.

"Sorry, lady." Something hissed gently, and a sweetish
odor added itself to the air. "Just a little tranquilizer."

As soon as she inhaled, she could feel it working.
Loosening, relaxing, robbing her of protest. Of course, she
had had her chance to say no before she ever entered this
room. And the whole idea of the clinic was to remove people.
It really wouldn't do to let them back out at the last minute.
Would it?

"There's only one way you can leave now," said the room.
"You made your decision, and a good one it was, too. To stop
using food and resources. To make room for others. But you
don't really have to die, you know. We can download you."

When the room's last words penetrated, she slumped
against the door. Yes. Turn her into a...

"You'll be a stone, a gravestone, needing only sunlight.
Watching the world go by, still making new friends, chatting
with them. Would you like that?"

She had known of the option. She had even avoided
entering the cemeteries she had stared at for fear of finding
a Paul who could still speak to her. But she had not thought
of it for herself. Not seen the possibility of...

"Isn't it expensive?"

"Oh, no. It's quite routine, really. Something we offer everyone. See that helmet hanging from the head of the couch?" It had a cable that burrowed into a wall socket. When she nodded, the room added, "You just put that on. Set your arm in the support, and we do the rest. Very simple."

She nodded again. She stiffened herself against the door, stood straight, and took the first hesitant step toward the couch. If she did not, well, the room had said it could use gas. Surely, it could replace the tranquilizer in the air with something deadlier. And then she would fall to the floor in a tangle of disordered limbs. If she obeyed, she could arrange herself more gracefully. For some reason, that seemed important.

A moment later, the helmet was on her head, chill against her brow and nape just as Kirby would describe it in the future.

"We're recording already," said the room. "Now your arm."

The support was positioned like the arm of a chair. As soon as she set her arm in its groove, curved bands snapped over her flesh, immobilizing her.

"There, there. Don't panic. Just have to hold you steady."

A needle stung her arm. She began to feel sleepy.

"Do you prefer some particular cemetery? A family plot perhaps?"

"Where'd... Where'd you put Paul?" The tranquilizer in the air was combining with whatever was in the needle. Her tongue felt thick, her thoughts slow. "Wanna be near him."

"Paul?"

"Paul..." She hesitated, groping for his last name in the fog that was already engulfing her mind. "Paul Trainor."

"Oh, him. Tsk. We just cremated him. He didn't want to be downloaded."

She tried to protest against the injustice of it all, to roll back time enough never to have entered this room of death, to cry out, "Let me live! Oh, please! Let me live!" But it was too late. The drug was claiming her. She could not even gasp for another breath, though she could still hear the room's fading words:

"He didn't even want an old-fashioned stone. He'd had enough, he said. Didn't want to see things get even worse. But you'll be around to see what happens. Your download's done, very nice."

"Allie, Allie, Allie."

"Yes, Kirby?"

"Were you a virgin when you died?"

"How can you...?"

"That's pretty crude," said Chandra. "We may be dead, but we can still show a few manners."

"I was just thinking," said Kirby.

"Didn't sound like it."

"That's one of the things I miss the most, you know?"

"Me, too," echoed several other voices.

Avril broke the ensuing silence herself. "There was a guy..."

"Did he make you scream?"

"Not that way." She hesitated, but she could not bring herself to explain. "He died."

"Ah."

As soon as she had awakened in her stone, she had wanted to let her scream burst forth at last. But she had refrained, contained herself. Her head had felt clearer than it had for months, and she had known immediately how futile that would have been. Perhaps she had even felt it would have been rude to disturb the peace of the cemetery, or to alarm her parents, who were standing, heads bowed, beside her grave.

They had visited her for years. They had talked a little, and she had learned of wars and plagues that could no longer touch her. She had watched them age, and she had thought that perhaps one day she would see them installed in stones beside her.

But they had just stopped coming.

All love then was dust and thinning memory, one with Verona and Shakespeare and the past world's greatest lovers.

In time the cemetery's other visitors had stopped as well, and the supply of news had ended. The weeds had grown.

The buildings visible beyond the cemetery wall had fallen into ruins.

The life of the stones continued:

"Allie?"

"Yes, Kirby?"

"Do you think you could talk dirty for me?"

"That's all that's left, isn't it?"

"Right out in public like this?" asked Chandra. "It'd be like an orgy. Don't do it."

"Please," said a voice, but it did not say whether it wanted them to do it or not to do it.

"They should have wired us together," said Ricky Moi. "A ghost-net. Private lines. Then we could..."

Witnesses to eternal time, eternal presence, eternal chat, as long as the sun kept shining.

Perhaps there was even something that could pass for eternal love.

But where *had* all the people gone?

Dream Chair

Melvin Charles

My name is Vernon.

That was the first thought that came to me. I was sleeping a good sleep, but it was time to wake. The mild warmth of an early spring sun touched me softly. The grass tickled the back of my neck. How long had it been since I'd felt the grass? I pushed my fingers deep into the cool roots, savoring the texture.

The air was fresh; no decay, no urine, just the sweet scent of the meadowlands. My eyes stayed shut as I let my senses wake, one after another. There were birds in the distance, their sound made fainter by the light brush of the wind on the trees.

I stretched. No twinges of pain. I felt good. I opened my eyes. The clarity of the sky, the blue! The honest-to-God blue. My eyes watered at the awareness of how beautiful the sky could be. The sun hung low in the West though, much of the day gone.

I climbed to my feet. Too much time wasting.

The meadow shimmered in the warm breeze, a sea of green waves. Ahead of me, a path followed a small brook into the trees, beyond that was home, home with its picket fence and red tile roof.

The brook was little more than a trickle flowing from between a pair of boulders. It poured gently out, slipping over the algae-covered rocks to a pool in a small rock basin.

I knelt beside the pooling water and looked at my wavering reflection. I looked just as I remembered. Laughing, I scooped a double handful of the cold water and washed the last vestiges of sleep away.

The blow came suddenly and knocked me into the water. I rolled with it and caught a glimpse of my attacker. He stood watching, contemptuous as I struggled to my feet. My back stung. I stood in the icy water and looked up at him. He and his two companions, he was never one to be found alone, watched with disdain as I staggered to the edge of the water.

The men were young and sallow. Yellowed teeth protruded past misshapen lips. My attacker leaned on a quarterstaff.

"What'd ya bring us, old man?" hooted the smaller one. His sharp-eyed glances shifted quickly between his fellows and the pouch tied to my waist. His hand darted and gestured as if he could bridge the distance and grasp the pouch by will.

My pouch. In it was all I possessed. To me, it was nothing. I had forgotten it. For them it was my purpose, the reason for their interest. It carried what I had and what they would take, if I let them.

They cast long shadows; the sun was now even lower in the sky. I should not choose to spend my time on this. With resolve I took a step to pass them by.

"You need more convincing old man?" growled the one with the staff. He shifted his staff until it crossed my path. Resting lightly on my chest.

"Leave me alone." I said with a silent hope they wouldn't. I could feel my muscles flex in preparation for what I knew was about to happen. What I wanted to happen. I felt a hunger, a lust at that moment for blood, for pain, their blood, their pain. I would hurt them. I needed to hurt them. They wouldn't be here if I hadn't called them forth.

I looked down the path to home. I could almost see the roof of the cottage. It would gleam as gold in the setting sun.

Suddenly, I didn't want them here. They were stealing more than my food; they were stealing my time, my life.

"Go away," I said flatly. "Leave me alone." I meant it this time, but it was too late for words.

I stepped boldly onto the path, the staffer made the first move. I blocked it easily, and trapped his staff, and using it as a hand-hold, I pulled him into my waiting elbow. I could feel the satisfying collapse of his cheekbone.

The second youth had no time to look up from his collapsed companion as a roundhouse kick twisted his head further than the neck would allow. The lifeless body crumbled in place.

"You still hungry boy?" I said to the third, the boy with the quick eyes and active hands. "I still got food," I held my pouch in my hand. My nostrils were open, I could feel the air coursing into my body. I was on fire with the urge to finish this. My mind's eye could feel his throat in my hands.

No. This was wasting time.

The youth looked at the pouch. His tongue darted out to wet his lips. He looked down at his companions. The ragged breath of the first was the only sound. The youth backed, one step at a time until, as his courage grew, he turned and ran.

I dropped the pouch on the ground. I didn't need it. If this one lived he would need food. More than likely his companion would take the food and leave the injured man for the crows, but that was not mine to resolve.

I let my stride stretch from walking to a run as I closed the distance between myself and home. Between the white slats of the fence the flickers of color took on the detail of flowers, slowly fading into shadows as the setting sun expanded on the horizon.

I looked back down the path. The beauty was endless. There was no sign of the boys. Only the fading satisfaction reminded me it had happened.

I touched the dark cottage door, the solid wood warmed by the sun. I lifted the latch and entered.

When I saw her, my breath froze in my chest. Any fear that she wouldn't be here faded into a mist. My eyes adjusted to the cool darkness and a picture developed. Her cheeks were the color of autumn leaves under her pale blue eyes. Her hair was wrapped loosely in a handkerchief, the reddish gold tresses falling down her back. Her lips held a half hidden smile. The simple smock, on her a gown, was crisp and clean, outlining the limber curves that were her body. She was as I remembered.

My blood roared in my ears.

"Vernon?" she spoke my name. The sound of her voice was like music. I could feel my knees weakening in anticipation of her touch. I thanked God I had gotten here in time.

She stood and reached to me, and I for her. Her hand was small in mine, cool and soft, so right. I pulled it to my lips and kissed her palm softly. She smiled as I reached my other hand around her waist to pull her closer.

She fell back from me with dizzying speed. Her hand, no longer soft in my palm, hardened to the worn smoothness of worn poly.

I could hear voices. Not hers. Not mine. The dim light of the cottage gave way to blinding fluorescence.

Before me the dull chipped walls materialized, a blue meant only to cover the raw cement.

I coughed as stale dry air hammered my lungs. The racking motion sent waves of pain through my body.

"Come on old-timer, outa there, your time's up." I felt the hands prying me to my feet.

My awareness returned. My wife was long dead. She would never again hold my hand, we would never walk along the path. My name was Vernon Bancroft and no future lay before me. No unexplored adventures. I looked down at my hands. The skin was loose and spotted. I was old.

The technician efficiently stowed the sensor lines that fed my illusions; that gave me back my wife. He wore thin gloves and was careful not to touch too much of what had touched me.

I looked at the clock on the wall. Twelve minutes had passed. I was allotted fifteen.

"I had more time, I know it, I do... just check," I pointed to the clock. I could hear myself. I was pleading.

"Yeah, right... we'll check," the attendant's voice softened, taking on a soothing tone. "If you do, we'll give it to you next week." Then, with a quick fluid motion, he pulled my card from the machine and placed it in my automatically extended hand and abruptly he turned his back, adjusting the settings on the sens-pac as a woman took my place in the chair.

I stood there. My eyes glued to the clock. I had more time.

"I had more time." I said it aloud.

"Just tell them at the desk." I was dismissed.

I knew they wouldn't care at the desk. They didn't live here; they only worked here. They didn't have to care. Why didn't they build more dream chairs? I paid my taxes all my life. Was it asking too damned much for me to have my fair share?

I turned again; the attendant caught my motion.

Already the woman was settling in place. A vague yearning look on her aging face, her tongue darted out, wetting the dried lips. I held the attendant's eyes as the client clumsily slid a food packet into his waiting hands. She wasn't old yet, but she looked it. She wouldn't last long. Not without food.

The attendant's visage faltered for a second, then a surly glare gained hold. The client tried to smile. She couldn't.

The vision of reddish gold hair and soft hands faded under the tension of the moment.

I turned towards the exit. My oversized coat no longer fit me. I wrapped myself in it as I pushed through the lobby, full of people, some standing in silent thought, others shouting and waving at the speaker grill mounted in front of the reception desk. They were like me. Old or otherwise of little use.

A pleasant looking young woman sat behind the panel working her screen. I suspected little of her work dealt with the shouting people. She probably got all the chair-time she wanted. Probably gave the attendants all the sack-time they wanted.

At the exit, I slid my citi-card in the slot and passed through the opening door.

The line for the entrance lobby stretched out. Sad silent people, some clutching their citi-cards in their hands as if having it ready would make sooner the experience. The blank dismal stares mirrored my own.

Unfiltered air burned my lungs. Another fit of coughing passed as I cleared my lungs of a gray gooey mass. I had taken to noticing the bright red flecks of blood. That told me it mattered little any more. No one else took notice.

I felt the urge to hurry again. The streets were darkening earlier as another winter came. How many had it been? Better to be indoors at night. Power was reserved for the streetlights and official buildings. The official buildings also included dormitories, but they were run by bureaucrats with thick rule books, and heavy guards with outstretched hands. I found that I could bear the less regulated, less safe, life in the multitude of abandoned buildings. Rent was cheap, only a few food packets, maybe nothing. Few cared.

I crossed the street in the center of the block. No one feared traffic any more. I remembered when you risked your life to cross this street. Now it was easy. The only cars were the rusted hulks not yet gathered for scrap. The buildings were dark.

Early on, when the power was cut back from "low-priority" services, whole blocks became rat holes where people who couldn't, or wouldn't, live in the dormitories found a place to sleep. They slept when not standing in line for food, water or Chair privileges.

The city wasn't what it used to be, there were few reasons to stay except there was no place to go and no way to get there. Exit permits were technically available, but the office that provided them opened its window for only an hour a day. The line never went away.

You were born in the city, you stayed in the city.

The trains sometimes brought in people. People from the train station usually went to the dorms. They often spoke of the family they had on the outside. The family that was building them a room to live in, that would be sending them credits. I remember a man I played chess with. To the day he died he believed his daughter would come for him. He was so proud of her. He knew she would come. He died knowing that she would come. They hauled his body off to the crematorium. He was my last friend. There were others to play chess with but I didn't care anymore. They were people like me. Worn out by a lifetime, shipped to "population centers" where they could be "cared" for when they couldn't care for themselves and their family wouldn't. Often times they were just criminals that didn't merit execution. Prisons were expensive.

Above me the city watched from the dark faces of the buildings. The broken glass was less as you looked higher, few ground floor windows remained. Sometimes a person who didn't know any better would try and move glass windows from the upper stories down. Someone always broke it. Misery loves company; no..., misery demands it.

The food and water lines were long, old men old women left over citizens. Their clothes, like mine, were castoff and found. The line time passed without effort, no one spoke. Standing in line was a learned talent I supposed, to completely pass from this existence while moving slowly in the shuffling procession that was the line. I remembered reading of mystics in the East who spent their lives learning to pass into that type of existence.

Somewhere above the smog the sun still shone. The diffuse yellow light lent itself well to this type of escape. It stressed neither form nor shadow. It merely made light. Light that was strained through the thick air from the factories that ringed the city. They were almost fully automated. That meant the stacks didn't need filters, only we, the city people, lived inside their ring of death.

When my time came at the food dispenser, I inserted my card, flashed my wrist chip, and was rewarded with the sound of the food dropping down the chute. I worried at times that the chip might cease to function. If it failed, I would face a death by starvation long before the bureaucracy would fix the chip.

When prompted, I placed my battered 5-liter bottle under the spigot and watched as 3 liters of brown water flooded it. They used to be filled full. A panel slid back and my allotment of food lay there in neat packs. I took it, retrieved my card, and turned for home.

The smiling youth sat on the steps when I arrived at the building I called home. He fooled no one with the smile. It had been years since a smile from his kind had been anything more than a prelude to predation. I dreaded in my gut what I knew was to come. He stood expectantly as I climbed the steps. No hand came out to steady my step. No door was opened for me. He simply watched and then followed me inside. Once inside he pushed me forward. I shrugged off his touch.

"What the fuck, old man. Feeling froggy?" He spun me in place, his face inches from my own. The leering face was the same I had felled in the meadow. But here, there was no power in my spirit. My muscles were weak. They barely held me erect.

I felt the pain as the youth placed a hand against my chest and pushed. I fell to the floor, white hot pain driving through me as my elbow struck the step. I felt myself beginning to sob. It hurt so much. I looked up at him through teared eyes.

"Please stop," I begged.

"Same old shit, huh old man," he sneered as he looked distastefully through my food. When he was satisfied that he had taken enough, he dropped the remaining packets to the floor and returned to the stoop.

I picked up my food and began to climb the stairs. My elbow throbbed.

I placed one foot ahead of the other as I pulled myself up the four flights of stairs. By the second flight my chest was a mass of pain as I strained to breathe. I sat for a time at each landing. Gasping for sustenance from the filthy air. By the time I reached my space, my breath was coming in quick ragged gasps, caught between coughing spasms.

I still had a door. That made my space rare. This was the fourth floor. It wasn't as filthy as below. I had once lived higher, but I couldn't make the climb.

I was alone on this floor except for the rats. They tended, like their human brethren, to congregate on the lower floors. My space had once been an office. It boasted little except for an executive chair. I had brought it from three floors up. I sat in it and watched out of a tall window that executives had once looked out of. It was now an empty frame, broken, an open doorway to the city.

Next to the open window hung her picture. We were young when I took it. I touched it gently as I sat down. I had touched it a thousand times, each time remembering the feel of her hair, the bells in her laugh. It was only in my memory that the picture still held the golden red color of her hair. I didn't need the chair to remember the feel of her skin, the flow of her hair in my hands.

"Next time," I said, and leaned back into the chair and looked out the open window frame.

When she came into his dreams she was just as beautiful as ever. She stood in the open window, it was now a doorway, and beckoned.

"It's time," she said. He followed, stepping through the doorway into her arms. She held his hand for the brief moment until the pain passed.

In front of the window his food packs sat alone by an empty chair until the rats came.

Spawn of War and Deathiness

The Schrödinger War

D. Thomas Minton

You'd think after seven tries, I could get the living part right, or at least be a pro at dying, but both are still messy and painful. At least dying doesn't scare me anymore.

I yank Olshevski back into our wrinkle of black basalt before the Eatees mist his head.

"Keep it down," I say, my voice tinny in the helium tri-mix of my armor's helmet. As if it matters; if the Eatees don't get him, something else will.

To either side of me, prone soldiers in combat armor bead the lava, like dewdrops on a burn victim. Overhead, sunlight reflects off an arch of orbiting debris, which in another fifty million years will coalesce into the Earth's moon, the same moon under which I will lie as a kid, fantasizing about fighting space aliens.

A streak of fire scratches the sky.

"A shooting star," Olshevski says. His chuckle crackles through the radio-link. "Make a wish."

He's a first incar, fresh down the well from 2075 or some such. Like most firsts, he's gung-ho and stupid and won't live through the day. I'd like to think I wasn't as stupid as Olshevski, but I suspect I was. Then I died. And died again. And again.

Voices buzz through the radio-link. The Eatees are forming up across the no-man's land for an assault on the prize: a steaming pool of long-chain proteins, RNA, and protobionts that may one day evolve into Earth's higher carbon-based life, provided we stop the Eatees.

"Cut the chatter," Tanner says. He mutes the squad's mics. The sudden silence presses on my ears.

I've known Tanner since we were first incars. He was a good soldier then; he's a good leader now.

Olshevski pops up again. Before I can pull him down, an Eatee sonic shears the top half of his body clean off, the atoms of his suit and every living cell vibrated apart by the high energy noise. The pink mist floats away on the methane wind, and Olshevski's legs tumble over like felled trees.

If he's lucky, his genetic algorithm never finished transmitting to H-Station, and he can find peace in the Big Dark.

The Big Dark sounds good. It doesn't matter if Christina is there or not anymore, either. I hope she is, but—

Fuck it.

I scramble over the basalt lip and charge the cluster of black lumps in the distance. If I hadn't known what I was looking at, I never would have recognized them as alive— featureless lumps of metalloborane, no head, no eyes, only a hole that periodically gapes open, presumably to breathe when it isn't emitting blasts of high frequency noise.

"Sam, what are you doing?" Tanner asks.

Behind me, soldiers scramble from the trench into the glassy no-man's land.

The Eatees rotate toward us. Their orifices open. A sonic blast glances off my armor hard enough to knock me down.

I struggle to my knees and launch an O_2 cluster-bomb. The skittering pellets explode, washing the Eatees in reactive oxygen. Their bodies fizz and glow, catch fire and burst.

Eatee sonics shimmer across the battlefield. The whine grates my ear drums.

My right arm vibrates, all the molecules shaking like ping pong balls in an earthquake. I'm lifted off the ground, spun around, and I lose all track of up and down. Then the glassy basalt crashes into my helmet plate and my feet flop over my head as I fold in half.

Red mist covers the right side of my visor. I struggle to recall who had been next to me.

Warnings flash across my HUD. Suit breach, and I realize my arm is gone. Whatever hasn't spray-painted my helmet has been splattered into the wind. But I'm still alive.

Dammit, I'm still alive.

I lie on my back, laughing at my misfortune through the haze of pain blockers.

Overhead, meteors etch fiery lines across the sky, like tiger claws opening up skin. They trace graceful arcs that anytime else would have been beautiful. I remember the time Christina and I made love in a Nebraska wheat field beneath the Perseids. They were beautiful. She more so.

Through the narcotic haze, I sense something wrong, but it takes me a full minute to realize what. One of the lines is shortening and growing brighter. Pressure sensors scream as the hammer of air pushed in front of the dropping meteor crushes—

<<>>

I sit up, clutching my right arm and gulping bites of air.

"It's okay, Sam, we made a full recovery." Kim's hand is soft and smooth and warm.

H-Station's recovery room is a morgue: antiseptic and harshly lit. Odd, because H-Station is a mathematical construct cycling through nano-cores lodged in Hilbert space. You'd think they could create something more friendly to wake up in.

Algorithms or not, the cold metal beneath me burns against my balls.

At the foot of the table are a folded flannel shirt and familiar denim jeans broken in by hard use.

Kim rips a sensor patch from my neck.

I grab her wrist, a lightning quick reflex that makes her gasp.

Kim's face is different again. Her narrow eyes have grown rounder, the sharpness of her nose has dulled, and her hair, once black and thick, has lightened to a sun-bleached tan. Today her hair is pulled back into a ponytail, revealing a morning-clean face with freckles splashed like the Milky Way over her cheeks and nose. The same as—

I release her and pull the shirt over my shoulders; focus on pushing buttons through their holes.

Kim rubs her wrist.

"I'm sorry," I say.

"I should have warned you." She turns away as I pull on the jeans.

When I look up, a desk and chair have appeared, and the morgue table is gone. The lights have softened to the gold of a Nebraska sunset. As a new recruit, I had found H-Station's sudden shifts disconcerting, like the architects had gone to great lengths to create the illusion of a real world, but had never finished the programming. Like living in a movie—the unimportant stuff had been cut away, leaving only the scenes necessary to move the story forward to its inexorable climax.

I've never taken a shit on H-Station.

The chair squeaks as I sit. The leather cools my back.

A window behind Kim opens onto a field of wheat and a curtain of blue sky. Sometimes that window has familiar Colorado mountains or a slice of Caribbean beach or a hillside of golden poppies. Tanner thinks we have subconscious control over what we see on H-Station, and that Kim uses this information in her work.

"Can you tell me what happened?"

"A meteor," I say. It isn't what she wants, but if I give her what she wants too quickly, I would have to leave.

Kim taps a yellow pencil against her cheek.

After every recovery, Kim is here. I sit in the same chair and answer the same questions. The only thing different is the view out the window. And the way Kim looks.

"I got hit by an Eatee."

Out the window, the wheat bends over in an afternoon breeze. I expect to see Christina in her jeans and floppy hat checking its ripeness by the angle of the heads.

The lump in my throat hurts.

"And how did that happen? You getting hit."

Each visit, I find it harder to concentrate on the interview. I get distracted by what lies beyond the window or by the changes to Kim's face or the clothes I'm wearing. I see ghosts of my past everywhere, but I know they're not here, except in my head. No matter how I try, I can't seem to get rid of them.

Every death seems to chip away a flake of my sanity. Eighths and ninths talk about not being whole anymore. As a third, I thought it would never happen to me. When I was a sixth, I fought it. Now I'm a ninth...

"I sighted the enemy, and I charged." I feel oddly disconnected from the room and the moment. When I blink, I see Olshevski's legs tumble over on the back of my eyelids.

Something that horrible should have crippled me, but it didn't faze me at all. "How many were recovered?" I ask.

"There was no order to advance. What were you thinking when you made the decision to charge?"

"I don't get paid to think."

"You don't get paid at all." A half-grin slides across her face, her lips parted to reveal perfect teeth.

Christina had perfect teeth.

My knuckles pop as I crack them. The noise surprises me, and I look down at my hands. The scars I remember having are gone, because they are not part of my genetic algorithm. The physical ones, that is.

"Why did you charge?"

I forget sometimes that Kim knows everything that happens on the battlefield. These post-recovery sessions allow her to learn why. Kim has been tasked with optimizing our fighting force.

H-station sits in Hilbert Space, just up-well of a white hole that opens into the solar system four and a half billion years in my past. H-Station is a haven of sorts, safe from the Eatees, but disconnected from space-time as we humans know it. It's also the critical junction point for down-well travel, because you can't send matter down-well, only information, in this case a soldier's genetic algorithm, a multidimensional information array that captures a person's genetic code and a neural map of the brain. The problem is, H-Station can hold only a limited amount of information, so Kim is searching for the optimal soldiers to fight this war. So we fight and die and learn and change, each time spawning new incars that Kim tosses back into her battfield experiment. At some point, one of our incars will reach the zenith of our martial skill, and Kim will delete the rest of us.

"Why did you charge?" Kim asks again.

"I saw an opportunity."

Kim doesn't say anything.

Does she know I'm lying?

Kim resumes tapping her pencil against her cheek. "How do you feel otherwise?"

"Like hell. I just died, for the eighth time."

"Fair enough." Kim's pencil scritches against the pad. With her head down, I see her scalp in the wide part of her hair. The skin is pale and smooth.

The familiarity unsettles me. "Is that all?" I ask, wanting to get away.

She doesn't look up from her writing. "Are you ready to go back?"

"No, but it's what I signed up for."

<<>>

H-station is a maze of memories half-remembered. Maybe it's the shared human condition, distilled by algorithms into surroundings that are both numbingly generic and achingly familiar. Like the wheat field outside Kim's window.

When I first came down-well, nothing about H-Station was familiar. Yet each time I come back, I see more places that remind me of my past. I suspect it has something to do with Kim's work.

This time, the processing room is a smoky bar with a low ceiling and barely enough space to breathe. It reminds me of the beaten-up honky-tonk on the outskirts of Omaha, where a fresh-faced girl from the wheat fields snookered me of forty bucks at eight ball. She was nice enough to share her garlic fries with me, confident enough to kiss me afterward, and stupid enough to spend the rest of her life with me.

Why do I remember this? There's no pool table here, and the air smells of anticipation, not garlic.

I recognize few faces; most are firsts and seconds I don't want to know.

Against the wall with his arms crossed, Tanner raises his chin to catch my eye. I slide through the crevices between conversations, but before I can reach him, a woman grabs my collar and kisses me on the lips. "Hey lover," she breaths across my cheek.

From the patch on her uniform, I see she's a fourth, but I've never met her before. "You've mistaken me for someone else," I say.

She frowns. "You don't recognize me, Sammy?"

Then she sees the patch on my shoulder and looses an expletive. "Sorry," she says, straightening my collar. "I knew a third—"

I raise my hand. She knows an earlier incar of me, a third, but not my third. I don't know how many different incars of Samuel Hohlman exist, but each one is spawning branches in the probability function that is me. Kim is betting that one of us is an optimal soldier.

Before I can say anything, the woman turns her back to me and pretends I don't exist.

I continue through the crowd until I get to Tanner. He shoves a glass tumbler in my hand. Vodka on the rocks.

I see from his patch that he's a sixth.

Tanner arches an eyebrow when he sees my own patch. "Lava?" he asks.

I've served with many of Tanner's incars, so there's always a good chance we can find common ground. Tanner and I decided long ago not to associate if we had more than a four incar difference—too much personal misery to overcome.

"Methane explosion?" he asks.

I nod, recognizing how I died as sixth. This incar knew me two or three lives ago.

The lines pinched into Tanner's forehead relax. "So a ninth," he says. "Still no command?"

My patch has the crossed swords of a G. I. grunt. "I'm not leadership material, but it looks like you are."

Tanner flushes. As a sixth, this is his first command.

"Who's the fourth?" he asks, motioning with his glass. "She's hot."

I shrug. "Never met her, but that doesn't mean I didn't..."

Tanner makes a noncommittal sound. He's died enough to understand.

As a second and third, I screwed everything and anything willing. There are probably three dozen incars making it in the bar's backroom right now. Dying is still scary to them, and they don't fully appreciate that they'll be back again and again. To cope with the fear, they seek solace in the most base and carnal of human actions. It's a way to forget, at least for a little while.

Tanner searches the bottom of his glass and asks, "Is it still worth it?"

He knows he isn't supposed to ask questions like that; it violates our agreement. Even so, I find myself answering. "I don't know," I say softly.

Tanner frowns. I've said too much. I remember being a sixth, when I started to realize the senselessness of the dying.

"But we're still here, so we must win." The uncertainty in his eyes is gut-wrenching.

That isn't how it works. Our lives are an arrow, always moving forward, and we can never know the future until we get there. The future has no bearing on my past. If we fail to save humanity, I won't simply poof out of existence. I'm fighting the Eatees for some other humanity. I'm not fighting for Christina, because she's lost three years in my past, and while one day there may be another Christina, she will not be my Christina.

That thought drains the noise from the room, and all I hear is the roar of silence in my ears.

My drink tumbles from my shaking hand and shatters on the floor.

What the hell am I doing here?

The conversations crash in around me, like a cave collapsing. I can't make out any voices or words. It's all just noise.

I leave Tanner standing alone, staring into his glass.

The noise dies around me as new deployment orders flash across my visual cortex.

It's time to die again.

<<>>

I inch to the top of the trench and peer through the heat ripples distorting the no-man's land. I can't be certain that I've been here before, but I get an unsettling sense of déjà vu.

I've heard ninths and tenths talk about rejoining battles they've already died in and sometimes even meeting earlier incars of themselves. It's never happened to me before, but if it did, I think I would tell myself to find a way to put an end to the circle, to join the Big Dark.

My HUD picks up movement and zeroes in on a line of Eatees half a kilometer away. Like a train of charcoal briquettes, they move in formation across the jumbled basalt, venting trails of pinkish gas from their orifices.

I slide down the trench wall and check my weapon. Working on military muscle memory, I chamber an O_2 grenade without thinking.

By now, others have seen the Eatees. Chatter pollutes the coms.

"Keep it down," Tanner says.

The second incar on my left stares at me with saucer-big eyes. For a moment I see Christina's face through the helmet shield. Not her face as the cancers ate her body, but her face on our wedding day. Even though her hair had already fallen out, she never looked more beautiful.

I squeeze my eyes shut. I have done everything I can to forget her and make the pain go away, but she never seems to leave me.

The recruit with big eyes touches my shoulder. "You okay?" she asks through the private touch-link.

I recognize her now. I know her, or at least who she will be. Her sixth saved my life, back when I was a fourth, and paid for it with her own. I died a few seconds later, but I've never forgotten her. A few more deaths, and she'll be a good soldier.

I brush her hand away.

I'm not okay. I came down-well to get away from everything that reminded me of what I have lost. I needed to kill something, to become less human, so I could stop feeling. What Christina and I had is too strong, however, and now it eats at me like her cancer ate her bones.

My only way out is the Big Dark, but I can't have that.

My teeth vibrate painfully as Eatee sonics discharge nearby. The chatter in my helmet ends as Tanner kills the coms so his orders can be heard. We're to lay down a wall of O_2, and make sure the Eatees don't flank us. It all strikes me as pointless.

"Get down, Sam!"

Tanner's words jar me, and I realize I'm standing and firing my weapon over and over. My HUD tells me I've launched a half-dozen O_2 grenades as a seventh whumps from my launcher.

Across the smoldering cinder, an Eatee swivels. Its orifice opens and the world ripples. I close my eyes and see Christina.

My heart starts to vibrate and come apart.

<<>>

"You're safe, Sam."

It takes a moment to put a name to the voice... not Christina... Kim.

"It hurts," I say. It's not supposed to hurt—because I am no longer that person—but it does.

"It'll pass. Your brain is still reconciling what happened."

The cold metal gurney presses against me. Shivers wrack my flesh.

"Try to calm down," she says.

I raise my head from where it's tucked against my chest. This time, her eyes are amber, flecked with gold. They aren't Kim's eyes; that isn't Kim's face.

"We made a full recovery," she says.

"No," I say.

Her brows pinch together. I know she is checking H-Station's data-core, confirming a full recovery of Samuel Holman, tenth incar.

But I'm no longer complete, no matter what the genetic algorithm says.

Kim helps me to a sitting position, and I pull on the clothes at the foot of the table. When I look up, Kim is sitting at her desk. Outside the window, aspens quiver at the edge of a lake, glassy smooth and filled with clouds. I recognize the place immediately: the Montana cabin where Christina and I spent a week every summer, and where—

"Tell me about this place," Kim says.

I am surprised for a moment by the change in script. "No."

I expect her to pry, but she doesn't.

Backlit, Kim's ponytail is pulled so tight she looks bald.

The silence picks at my resolve. I exhale, and my body deflates like a punctured bladder.

"Every summer, we'd come to this place."

"This is a special place then."

"I hate this place." The lump in my stomach threatens to come up my throat. "Christina died here, the day after we were married." I have never talked about Christina with Kim. I'm sure she knows about her; she knows everything about me.

Kim's pencil stops, frozen mid-tap. Everything seems to stop—the shimmering trees, the clouds on the surface of the lake—like the program that is H-Station has crashed.

"She had been diagnosed with an inoperable brain tumor. They tried chemo and radiation, but it didn't work. The cancer spread into her lungs and bones. When the doctors gave her a week to live, she asked me to bring her to the cabin. We were supposed to have a life together."

Christina is motionless behind the desk, the pencil frozen near her perfect lips. It's not her, I tell myself.

"I want to forget because it hurts."

I hear a pounding sound that starts in time with my heartbeat, but slowly slides out of synchronization. When I blink, Kim's pencil is tapping again.

"Is that why you volunteered?"

There are as many reasons for joining up as there are soldiers. What does it matter if I came here to lose my past? It's not like I volunteered as a way to commit suicide.

My fingernails are square and perfect, not chewed to the quick like when I enlisted. Every time I'm recovered, the scars of living are polished from my surface.

"Everything back there reminded me of Christina. The way the wheat bent was her smile. The smell of sunshine was the fragrance of her hair. Now, everywhere I look here... I don't want to go on."

Kim studies me quietly. After a moment, she says, "That's not up to you."

"You have nine incars of me, and probably dozens more I don't know about. Why can't I retire?"

"There is no retirement here, Sam." Kim's lips continue to move, but I don't hear her through the pounding of blood in my ears and the rasps of breath through my lungs. Those are the sounds of life, but I'm not alive anymore, so how can I make them?

Kim scribbles on her pad with her pencil; then she looks up at me. "I need you to go back."

The words stab me like a cruelly-curved knife. I can't go back there. Why can't Kim see that? "I'm finding it hard to be a good soldier," I say. "I don't know what I'm fighting for anymore."

"Maybe you didn't come here to forget. Maybe you came here to remember."

It sounds like something Christina would have said when I was belly-aching about something ridiculous.

"You need to go back one more time, Sam."

My HUD flashes to life with new deployment orders. I squeeze my eyes shut, but I still see them on the inside of my eyelids.

It's time to die again.

<<>>

The basalt crunches like broken glass as I step off the drop-ship. More ships streak in low across the crimson sky, their engines sun-flaring as they pivot and drop. The clouds glow as the orbital battle continues; each flash is one of our ships bursting and burning.

A concussion wave from a distant explosion vibrates my faceplate. Even though the surface battle is a kilometer away, first and second incars dive into a laser cut trench at the edge of the drop circle. Their chatter is loud and fast in the coms.

A ship booms overhead and skims the battlefield, stirring up dust and sulfur steam. From its bottom, cluster bombs whiz toward the ground. They explode, killing Eatees and humans alike.

My third incar died from friendly fire. It had been painless—a bright flash, intense heat, like I had been dropped into the middle of a supernova—and then I awoke on H-station with baby-new skin and another hole in my psyche.

My visor lightens as the flash fades and the glowing battlefield cools from white hot to red to glassy black basalt.

Tanner taps my helmet, opening a touch-link. "Orbital's picked up an Eatee incoming; we got ten minutes 'til this place gets hot." He dashes off toward the rally point.

The last drop-ship lifts into the red sky, vanishing slowly into the methane clouds, like a fleck of copper sinking into blood. For the moment, the world is quiet.

The edge of the landing zone drops off into a steaming pool of scummy organics and proto-life. In a hundred million years, this pool will be teaming with the first anaerobic lifeforms, which will produce oxygen as a waste product of their metabolism. It's that oxygen that will make this world uninhabitable to the Eatees, and will make it my...

No, it will never be my home.

I close my eyes and see Christina's face, beautiful and smiling. Every minute I had with her is something to cherish, not forget. Maybe Kim is right.

Damn her.

Movement to my right catches my attention. A third has stepped up to the edge and is looking down into the steaming pool. Maybe he's thinking about throwing himself in. It's hard to say with a third; they're a critical transition incar, from the wide-eyed newbie to either a well-adjusted soldier or to someone who will eventually be like me.

I'm not sure why, but I place my hand on his shoulder, opening a touch-link. "It's not high enough to even damage the suit," I say.

When he turns toward me, I stumble back. He grabs my elbow and saves me from tumbling over the edge.

His face has the same lines as my own, only fresher, and the same eyes, only more alive. He shows no recognition of who I am, even though he looks into his own face, half a dozen deaths later. I am no longer the same person, but am I so damaged he does not recognize himself?

But he is also not the same person I was as a third. He has been shaped by different experiences and today he will likely die a different death, which will make him a different fourth, and a different fifth, and so on. Yet, in his eyes is the shadow of our common bond, and I know this grief will force him down a path parallel to my own.

His eyes narrow, but they do not yet glimmer with recognition. "You okay?"

Afraid he will release my arm, I seize his wrist to keep the touch-link open. "I've learned something recently," I say softly. "Our past makes us who we are today. If we forget what happened before we came down-well, then our past is only this: war, dying, and more dying. How can that be any good for anyone?"

"I..." His eyes widen then, and he sees what could be his future, but I also know he's smart enough to realize the future holds infinite possibilities, and that I am not necessarily his fate.

It's too late for me—my scars are all below this perfect skin—but I am only one possible future for Samuel Hohlman. How many of my thirds are out there, forging new futures and trying to get it right. Maybe, because of me, this is the one that will get it right.

"Wait..."

I release his wrist, breaking the touch-link. I move toward the rally point. He follows me at a short distance, but stops when our HUDs come alive. The Eatees are here.

Time for me to die.

The Last Death

Sahara Frost

I stare into the endless dark, watching, waiting. It's like all those years ago, when I was a kid on Christmas Eve. Me, lying in bed, wide-eyed with anticipation, listening for the clatter of eight tiny reindeer landing overhead. Only this time, it's not jolly old Saint Nick I'm expecting. Nor is it sugar plums that dance inside my head, keeping sleep at bay.

The silent night drags on, one moment melding seamlessly into the next until I think the world must have stopped. Only the stars show me different, each glance out my window revealing their gradual progress across the sky. Then, at long last, it's over. The dull gleam of first light crests the horizon, and once more, the world begins to move.

"Well," I say to myself, "Suppose I might as well get ready."

Heart fluttering with a giddy tingle, I throw back the covers and sit up. Immediately, my poor old bones creak in protest, reminding me to slow down. "Easy, girl. Easy!" I chide, quelling the urge to spring from my bed like some youngster, "No sense in falling and breaking a hip. 'Specially not today of all days." I release my impatience with a huff and bob my head in a reluctant nod. Then I plant my feet firmly on the floor, reach for my cane, and carefully hoist myself up.

Once my balance is sure, I begin to move about my home, preparing for the day. There isn't much to be done. There never is, these days. Still, I want everything to be absolutely perfect. So I throw open all the doors and windows to let in light and fresh air. Then I busy myself with one last tidying-up, straightening the bed, sweeping the floor, and wiping a rag over any surface that might have collected dust overnight.

The next time I look up, my heart skips a beat. Slashes of crimson and gold have already begun to streak the sky. It won't be long now. Going to the front door, I search the skeletal remains of what had once been a thriving subdivision with bated breath. "Today is the day," I insist, the words hissing through my teeth like a prayer, "Surely, today is the day."

I sweep my eyes back and forth for only a moment longer before spying what I seek. There, where the empty street curves out of sight behind a thinning copse of bone white trees, is the stark outline of a shadow. A shadow with which I am now quite familiar. Every morning, it appears on my horizon and, throughout the day, makes its slow approach. When the sun sets, it runs away, but by the next morning, it's back again, a little closer than the day before. Yesterday, it nearly reached my doorstep before it turned and fled. "It has to be today. It has to!"

Knowing there's not much time left, I go to my bookcase and take down the lone photo album occupying its shelves. I turn it over and over in my hands, slowly tracing my fingers over the familiar creases in its soft, worn cover. When at last I crack it open, I do so with my eyes closed, breathing deep the sweet, musty tang wafting up from its yellowed pages. Then I open my eyes again and finally allow myself to look at the smiling ghosts trapped within.

An old pain twinges deep within my chest at the same time that a smile tugs at my lips. "Hello, loves," I say, "It's been too long, hasn't it?" I gently turn the album's pages, pausing to touch the faces captured in each photograph. "Yes, far too long indeed." When I finish going through and greeting them all, I shut the photo album and clutch it tight to my chest. "But it won't be much longer now," I promise, "I'll be seeing you soon."

As the words leave my mouth, I am again seized by a giddy feeling. "Soon," I say to myself, as though repeating the word will make it that much more real to me, "Soon!" Bolstered by my own words, I stand a little straighter and even allow myself a small, excited grin. Returning the photo album to its shelf, I let go my last earthly treasure. There's only one thing left to do now. Just one last thing. Filled with a sense of renewed determination, I turn to go outside.

"Good heavens!" I cry, heart leaping into my throat when I see the pintsized, hooded figure now standing in my doorway. Thinking I've lost track of time again, I ask, "Is it that late, already?" and glance over its head. The sun's bright eye meets my gaze through the open door. "Oh," I say, understanding dawning with a bittersweet twinge of disappointment, "You're early."

"No, not early," the figure sighs with a soft, mournful wisp of a voice, "Quite late, actually."

"Ah," I say, not entirely sure how to respond, "Well I'm sure you had your reasons."

"Reasons," replies the figure, a tremor now audible in its voice, "Excuses."

"You're here now," I try, "That's what's really important, right?"

In a gesture reminiscent of a sullen child, the figure twitches its slumped shoulders in an indifferent shrug. I wait for it to say something, but no word comes, and soon, the silence grows awkward. I'm not really sure what it is I envisaged for this moment. A word or a beckoning hand. I just know I'm waiting for something. Anything. But the figure says nothing, does nothing, and we just stand there facing each other, a chasm of silent expectation growing ever wider between us.

Keen to go, my impatience starts to get the better of me. I begin to wonder if I shouldn't say something. After all, maybe it's not just me that's waiting. Perhaps I need to give some sort of sign to show that I'm ready. "Or," my second-guessing mind whispers. Or maybe I was wrong about today. Maybe my time hasn't come after all. Maybe it never will. "Or," it whispers again. Or maybe it already has. Maybe my time came and went long ago. Maybe I'll wait here forever, suffering in this lonely hell. "Or."

Panic twists my stomach into a knot and tightens its claws around my throat. I struggle to catch my breath, my lungs dragging painfully, desperate for air. My mind whirls, and I feel myself slipping into a tailspin. As the room seems to tilt around me, I squeeze my eyes shut and hold onto my cane for dear life. It is then, just as I think the chaos will devour me whole, that a sound cuts through the silent screaming in my mind, the soft sobbing of a weeping child.

Opening my eyes, I cast about for the source of the sound. But my home is empty. Nobody else is here. Nobody but me and my strange, small companion. A closer look shows me that it is, indeed, my visitor who weeps. Its shaking form is evident, even beneath the concealing folds of its several-sizes-too-large robe.

As I look at the pitiable creature trembling in my doorway, my panic loosens its grip upon me, giving way to another emotion. One I have not felt in far too long. Compassion. "Oh, come now!" I say, "No need for that! Here, why don't you come in and sit awhile with me. It's been a long time since I've had anyone to talk to." Moving to my kitchen table, I slowly lower myself into one of the two chairs I had already pulled out in preparation for today. When I look up to see that my visitor has made no move to join me, I gently add, "Besides, you're already late. I'm sure it won't matter if you're a little later."

My words apparently afford some small measure of comfort. Though my visitor still hesitates in the doorway, its sobbing subsides into a quieter snuffling. "I suppose that's true," I hear it say, pinpricks of hope stippling its muffled words, "Maybe if it's only for a moment or two." Then, as though expecting to be struck by a divine bolt of lightning, the figure ducks its head, hunches its shoulders, and takes one tentative step forward. Then another. Then another. When it at last climbs into the empty seat next to me and still nothing happens, it allows itself to relax once more.

"So," I start, only to discover I haven't actually thought of what to say, and thus petering out with a lamely trailing, "so..." A moment later, I open my mouth to try again, but having failed to solve the initial problem, am forced to shut it once more. Again and again, this cycle repeats itself, resulting in a long silence that my visitor shows no intention of helping to break. Until, at last tiring of my tongue-tying indecision, I throw all caution to the wind and begin spitting out my every thought as it comes to mind.

"Huh. Well what do you know. Here I am with someone to finally talk to, and I can't seem to find a single thing to say. It's not like I don't have anything to say. I've got loads to say! I just can't seem to decide where to begin. After all this time to think about it—and believe you me, I've had plenty of time—you'd think I'd have that part figured out. And maybe I did, once. But now that it's come to it, I just don't know. I just don't know!"

Laughing softly to myself, I shake my head and give my silent companion a wry smile. "Sorry, kiddo. Guess I'm a little out of practice with this whole conversation thing. What about you? What's your excuse?"

A beat passes in silence. Two beats. Three. Just as I am ready to give up waiting for a response, my companion shrugs and says, "You humans don't usually want to talk to me."

"Really?" I ask, genuinely surprised, "Why not? I'd think they'd have all sorts of questions for you. I know I do."

Another stretch of silence, then, "Some have questions. But they're usually the kind I can't answer."

"And the ones you can?"

"They still don't often lead to a conversation. Demanding. Cursing. Pleading. But not a conversation."

"O-Oh. I... I see." I falter, unsure of where to go from there, but I'm saved the trouble.

"But most people," my companion continues without prodding, "don't say anything at all. They can't. They're too shocked or sad or scared. And besides, I don't get to be with any of them that long. So by the time they realize there's nothing to be afraid of, it's too late to talk. They've already moved on."

As I listen to all of this with rapt interest, I become aware of a sensation like a knot being loosened within myself. It starts in my chest, works its way up the muscles of my neck, then spreads into my shoulders and down my back. I'm free, I realize. Free of a weight I hadn't even realized I was carrying. Free of a fear that I'd long ago buried and forgotten. The very same fear that I now recognize being reflected in the figure sitting next to me.

"Sounds like lonely work," I say, "Must be tough."

"Yes, sometimes, but I don't mind," it replies, a new vitality entering its voice so that it practically gushes, "After all, I was made for this work, and it for me. Only I can do this. No one else was made to endure the responsibility. And besides, the reward more than makes up for the hardship. I know it might be difficult for you to understand, but there's nothing quite like the sight of a soul when it realizes it's been brought home. Nothing quite like it at all."

"I can only imagine," I say, wondering what sort of expression now hides behind the cowl, "It sounds like you really love your work."

"I do," enthuses my companion, then more subdued, "I did."

"You did?" I question, a touch incredulous, "You mean to tell me you don't love it anymore? I find that hard to believe."

"Oh, no. Never that," assures my companion, "Never that."

"Then...?"

For a long moment, my companion doesn't answer, picking at its robes in silence. Then, in a voice so quiet I almost don't hear it, it slowly whispers, "I always knew, even from the very beginning, that it wouldn't last forever. That my work...my role...my purpose...would eventually end."

"End?" I repeat, slow to understand, "But wait...then wouldn't that mean—?"

"Yes," interjects my companion, anticipating my question before I even fully realize what it is I'm asking, "It is exactly as you suspect." Then, without warning, it begins to speak in a foreign tongue. "KAÌ 'O THÁNATOS KAÌ 'O HAÍDĒS," it says, its tone deepening and expanding, "EBLĒTHĒSAN EIS TÉN LIMNÉ TOÛ PYRÓS." Its voice continues to grow, reaching a powerful timbre of such magnitude that the walls around me begin to shake. "O'YTOS ESTIN." And though I cannot understand the words, "O DEÚTERÓS THÁNATOS," they reverberate through me, speaking to my very core.

In the silence that follows, my ears ache with a painful ringing. For a moment, I fear that I have gone deaf. But then I hear my companion, in a low voice, say, "Then Death and the Grave were cast into the lake of fire. This is the second death." Almost as an afterthought, it adds, "The last death."

"The death of Death," I murmur, at last understanding. I pause, contemplating this new development, then ask, "So I really am the last?"

"Yes."

"I see," I reply, inwardly marveling at how calmly I accept this confirmation of my long-held suspicions, "I had thought so, but there was no real way for me to know for sure." I pause again, longer this time, reluctant to ask my next question. Finally, though, I manage, "So if I am the last, then that must mean when I..." Here I stumble, unable to bring myself to say the word. "...you also...?"

"Yes."

This time, the confirmation hits hard, and I am unable to say anymore for a long while. When I finally do find my voice again, it comes out weak and fearful as I ask, "Is that why it took you so long to come for me?"

The silence that follows is all the answer I need. All at once, I am overwhelmed by the powerful sense of relief that washes over me. Dropping my face into my hands, I cry, "Thank God! Thank you, thank you, God! I had thought that maybe... but no. Thank you, Lord. Oh thank you, thank you, thank you!"

I continue like that for a time, letting out all my years of built-up feelings in a catharsis of tears. When I at last finish crying out all my fear, doubt, frustration, and despair, I dry my eyes and start, "I'm sorry, I..."

"No," interrupts my companion, its tone heavy with shame, "It is I who should be s-sorry." Voice breaking on this last word, it sobs, "I've been so afraid. I let my fear get in the way of my duty and have caused you such suffering. I'm so sorry. So, so sorry for what I have done to you."

I listen to these profuse apologies in solemn silence, unsure how to accept them. Part of me is tempted to wave them away with a blithely assuring, "It's okay," but that would ring false. Because the truth is it isn't okay. It hasn't been okay for a very long time. So rather than try to bandage over my pain with comforting lies, I instead reach out in the spirit of solidarity and say, "I think we all do sometimes. I know I've said and done things I'm not exactly proud of, all because I was afraid."

"But you're human!"

"And you're... well, I guess I don't really know what you are... but you're not God, are you?"

"No."

"Then I think it's probably fair to assume that you're forgiven a mistake from time to time too."

"Maybe," my companion relents, though still sounding unconvinced, "I don't know."

"Well why not? You're sorry aren't you?"

It nods.

"And you're here to repair your mistake, aren't you?"

It starts to nod again, then hesitates.

"You are here to repair your mistake," I repeat with a jolt of panic, "Right?"

It hesitates another moment, then finally dips its head, finishing its nod.

Releasing my held breath in a nervous laugh of relief, I say, "Well that's all anyone can really ask for. Just gotta give it our best shot and trust God to take care of the rest."

Speaking slowly, painfully, as though each word is a struggle to say, my companion admits, "What you say is true, but..." Its voice lowers to a whisper. "...but I am still afraid."

Leaning forward, I reach out my hand and, with a small smile, whisper, "Me too."

For a long moment, my companion sits there, staring at my outstretched hand. Then slowly, ever so slowly, it reaches out and takes my hand in its own. The moment our hands meet, my companion finds its courage. Before my very eyes, it undergoes a sort of transformation, straightening its back, squaring its shoulders, and lifting its head. Then, taking a deep breath, it looks me in the eye and bravely quavers, "Y-You have nothing to be afraid of. I-I'll stay with you every step of the way."

"And I with you," I promise, giving its hand a gentle squeeze, "I'll stay with you too. Every step of the way."

"O-Okay," it stammers, with a small frantic nod, "I-I'm ready."

"Okay," I say.

Getting to my feet, I help my companion down from its chair. Then, hand in trembling hand, we walk to the front door. When we step up to the threshold, we are met by a vision so breathtakingly glorious that I am momentarily stunned to stillness. As I look upon this final sunset, I am filled to overflowing with a profound sense of peace. I am ready.

We look at each other then, my companion and I.

"Together?" I ask.

"Together," it agrees.

Then, holding fast to each other's hands, we cross the threshold and step into bright, burning light.

Spawn of War and Deathiness

About the Authors

Alma Alexander's life so far has prepared her very well for her chosen career. She was born in a country which no longer exists on the maps, has lived and worked in seven countries on four continents (and in cyberspace!), has climbed mountains, dived in coral reefs, flown small planes, swum with dolphins, touched two-thousand-year-old tiles in a gate out of Babylon. She is a novelist, anthologist, and short story writer who currently shares her life between the Pacific Northwest of the USA (where she lives with the obligatory two writer's cats) and the wonderful fantasy worlds of her own imagination. You can find out more about Alma and her books on her website (www.AlmaAlexander.org), at her Amazon author page (https://amzn.to/2N6xE9u), on Twitter (https://twitter.com/AlmaAlexander), at her Facebook page (https://www.facebook.com/ AuthorAlmaAlexander/), or at her Patreon page (https://www.patreon.com/AlmaAlexander).

Rob Butler lives in Reading in the UK and has had around 40 pieces of short fiction published in a number of print and online magazines, including *Perihelion, Shoreline of Infinity*, and *Daily Science Fiction*.

Melvin Charles lives in a third floor walkup with 'Jiggers' his dog. He doesn't know what kind of dog Jiggers is, but he knows he is a dog. He's been writing for 40 years with little to show for it except the ability excoriate ass hats on face book and a small shelf of his 'paid in copy' anthology sales. He will occasionally turn them face out to let the garish covers light up the room while he eats canned sourcrout and dollar store hot dog packs. He feeds Jiggers Old Roy from Walmart.

Ian Creasey lives in Yorkshire, England. He began writing when rock & roll stardom failed to return his calls. So far he has sold seventy-odd short stories to various magazines and anthologies. A collection of his short fiction,

The Shapes of Strangers, was published by NewCon Press in 2019. For more information visit his website at iancreasey.com.

Jennifer R. Donohue is a Codexian and an Associate member of the SFWA. Her work has most recently appeared in *The Future Faire, Daikaijuzine*, and *Fusion Fragment.*

Indiana writer **James Dorr's** *The Tears of Isis* was a 2013 Bram Stoker Award® finalist for Superior Achievement in a Fiction Collection. His latest book is *Tombs: A Chronicle of Latter-Day Times of Earth*, a novel-in-stories from Elder Signs Press. Dorr has been a technical writer, an editor on a regional magazine, a full time non-fiction freelancer, and a semi-professional musician. He currently harbors a Goth cat named Triana.

Retired theoretical biologist **Tom Easton** has been publishing SFF since the 1970s and spent 30 years as *Analog*'s book columnist. His latest books are *Destinies: Issues to Shape Our Future* (B Cubed Press, 2020) and *Horror for the Throne: One-Sitting Reads*, coedited with James D. MacDonald and Judith K. Dial (Fantastic Books, 2021).

Louis Evans is the child of lawyers. He hasn't had his phone installed in his skull yet, but it's probably just a matter of time. He wishes everybody a good death.

His work has appeared in *Nature: Futures, Interzone, Analog*, and more, and has been long-listed for the BSFA Awards. He is a member of the Clarion West ghost class of the plague year. He's online at evanslouis.com and tweets @louisevanswrite.

Sahara Frost is a member of Codex, a group of pro-level speculative fiction writers. Her other short fiction has appeared in *The Arcanist* and Flame Tree Publishing's *Bodies in the Library* anthology.

Christopher M. Geeson has had work published by *Fantasy and Science Fiction*, The British Fantasy Society, Chaosium and others, the most recent being in the Flame Tree Press *Robots and Artificial Intelligence* anthology. He has a story in the forthcoming anthology by The North American Jules Verne Society.

Alicia Hilton is an author, law professor, arbitrator, actor, and former FBI Special Agent. She believes in angels and demons, magic, and monsters. She writes hopepunk—speculative fiction, neo-noir, and poetry about bravery and resistance. Her work has appeared in *Akashic Books, Cemetery Gates Media, Daily Science Fiction, Demain Publishing UK, DreamForge, Litro, Neon, Sci Phi Journal, Space and Time, Vastarien, Year's Best Hardcore Horror, Volumes 4, 5, & 6*, and elsewhere. She is a member of the Horror Writers Association and the Science Fiction and Fantasy Writers of America. Her website is https://www.aliciahilton.com.

Dan Koboldt is a genetics researcher at a major children's hospital and an avid bowhunter. He is also the author of *Domesticating Dragons* (Baen Books) and the *Gateways to Alissia* series (Harper Voyager), as well as the editor of *Putting the Science in Science Fiction* (Writer's Digest).

Gordon Linzner is founder and former editor of *Space and Time Magazine*, and author of three published novels and dozens of short stories in *F&SF, Twilight Zone, Sherlock Holmes Mystery Magazine*, and numerous other magazines and anthologies, including *The Mountains of Madness Revealed, Across the Universe, Humans Are the Problem*, and *After the East Wind Blows*. He is a member of HWA and a lifetime member of SFWA.

D. Thomas Minton's short fiction has appeared in *Lightspeed Magazine, Asimov's Science Fiction Magazine, Daily Science Fiction*, and numerous other anthologies and publications.

Patrick G. Moloney lives in the beautiful town of Killaloe on the banks of the mighty River Shannon in Ireland. Ever since his childhood obsession with the works of the Brothers Grimm, he has been fascinated with tales of otherworldly events. Inspired by the sometimes dark fairy tales of the Brothers Grimm, Patrick went on to write many short stories of dark fiction. Patrick's short stories can be found on his blog page at Booksie.com.

Mike Murphy has had over 150 audio plays produced in the U.S. and overseas, many for Audible. He has won The

Columbine Award and a dozen Moondance International Film Festival awards in their TV pilot, audio play, short screenplay, and short story categories. His prose work has appeared in, among other publications, *Hypnos, Dime Show Review* (including in three of their "Best Of" anthologies), *Gathering Storm Magazine, Inwood Indiana Press, Theme of Absence, Fabula Argentea, Fantasia Divinity, Mystery Weekly Magazine,* and *Crimson Streets.* He is the writer of two short films, *Dark Chocolate* and *Hotline.*

Anthony Panegyres has had stories published in numerous anthologies and journals, some of which include: *The Best Australian Stories, The Year's Best Australian Fantasy & Horror Volumes 2 & 6,* the leading Australian literary journals *Overland 204 & 214* and *Meanjin Quarterly.* In the speculative field, he has also had stories in the award-winning anthologies *At the Edge,* Lee Murray & Dan Rabarts, eds., *Bloodlines,* Amanda Pillar, ed., and *Dreaming of Djinn & Kisses by Clockwork,* both Liz Grzyb, ed. His next story will be in *Bourbon Penn* Issue 25. Although primarily a fiction writer, he has also had nonfiction published in *Meanjin* and *Overland* online and *The Guardian.* "Reading Coffee" was shortlisted for an Aurealis Award in The Best Fantasy Short Story category.

Irene Radford is a founding member of Book View Café, where you can find a number of her books. She has been writing stories ever since she figured out what a pencil was for. Editing, as Phyllis Irene Radford, grew out of her love of the craft of writing. History has been a part of her life from earliest childhood and led to her BA from Lewis and Clark College.

Mostly she writes fantasy and historical fantasy including the best-selling *Dragon Nimbus* Series and the masterwork *Merlin's Descendants* series. Look for her writing new historical fantasy tales as Rachel Atwood. In other lifetimes she writes urban fantasy as P. R. Frost or Phyllis Ames, and space opera as C. F. Bentley. Lately she ventured into Steampunk as Julia Verne St. John.

If you wish information on the latest releases from Ms. Radford, under any of her pen names, you can subscribe to her newsletter: www.ireneradford.net. Or you can follow her on Facebook as Phyllis Irene Radford, or on twitter @radford_irene25

Widely published poet **Gerard Sarnat** won San Francisco Poetry's 2020 Contest, the Poetry in the Arts First Place Award plus the Dorfman Prize, and has been nominated for handsful of 2021 and previous Pushcarts plus Best of the Net Awards. Gerry is a physician who's built and staffed clinics for the marginalized as well as a Stanford professor and healthcare CEO. Currently he is devoting energy/resources to deal with climate justice, and serves on Climate Action Now's board. Gerry's been married since 1969 with three kids plus six grandsons, and is looking forward to future granddaughters. gerardsarnat.com

David F. Shultz writes from Toronto, Canada, where he is Lead Editor at *Speculative North* magazine, and organizes the 800-member Toronto Science Fiction and Fantasy Writers. His 80+ publications are featured through publishers such as Augur, Diabolical Plots, and Third Flatiron. Author webpage: davidfshultz.com.

Alex Shvartsman is the author of over 120 short stories, published in *Analog, Nature, Strange Horizons*, and elsewhere. He won the WSFA Small Press Award for Short Fiction in 2014 and was a two-time finalist (2015 & 2017) for the Canopus Award for Excellence in Interstellar Fiction. His political fantasy novel *Eridani's Crown* was published in 2019. His translations from Russian have appeared in *F&SF, Clarkesworld, Asimov's, Apex,* etc. Alex has edited over a dozen anthologies, including the long-running Unidentified Funny Objects series, and he is the editor-in-chief of *Future Science Fiction Digest*. He resides in Brooklyn, NY. His website is www.alexshvartsman.com.

Canadian fiction writer, poet, and playwright **J. J. Steinfeld** lives on Prince Edward Island. His short stories and poems have appeared in numerous periodicals and anthologies internationally, and over sixty of his one-act plays and a handful of full-length plays have been performed in Canada and the United States. The most recent of his twenty-two books include *Madhouses in Heaven, Castles in Hell* (Stories, Ekstasis Editions, 2015), *An Unauthorized Biography of Being* (Stories, Ekstasis Editions, 2016),

Absurdity, Woe Is Me, Glory Be (Poetry, Guernica Editions, 2017), *A Visit to the Kafka Café* (Poetry, Ekstasis Editions, 2018), *Gregor Samsa Was Never in The Beatles* (Stories, Ekstasis Editions, 2019), *Morning Bafflement and Timeless Puzzlement* (Poetry, Ekstasis Editions, 2020), and *Somewhat Absurd, Somehow Existential* (Poetry, Guernica Editions, 2021).

David Tallerman is the author of the novels *To End All Wars, A Savage Generation,* and *The Bad Neighbor,* and the ongoing fantasy series *The Black River Chronicles,* among other works. His short fiction has appeared in markets such as *Clarkesworld, Lightspeed, Beneath Ceaseless Skies,* and *Alfred Hitchcock's Mystery Magazine,* as well as his debut collection, *The Sign in the Moonlight and Other Stories.*

Bruce Taylor, also known as "Mr. Magic Realism," lives in Seattle, Washington. He was a student at the Clarion West Science Fiction/Fantasy writing program at the University of Washington, with such writers as Robert Silverberg, Avram Davidson, Ursula K. LeGuin, Frank Herbert, Harlan Ellison, and Terry Carr. Bruce was writer in residence at Shakespeare & Company, Paris, and is known for blending magic realist writing perspective and techniques with science fiction, horror and fantasy. You can view his recent work at ReAnimus.com/brucetaylor.